P9-CBE-402

Santa Clara

Rio · Santa Fe

· Bajada

· Bernalillo

JICARILLA
APACHE

▲ Albuquerque

· Pecos

PECOS RIVER

Los Lunas
Valencia

Belen
El Bosque ·

· Sabinal

· Polvadera

· Socorro

San Antonio
Valverde

San Marcial ·

SIERRA NEGRO

FRA CRISTOBAL

JORNADA DEL MUERTO

SAN ANDRES MTS.

SIERRA SACRAMENTO

Warm Springs
×

SIERRA MIMBRES

A

P

SIERRA GUADALUPE

MIMBREÑOS    Las Palomas ·

SIERRA
DE LOS
CABALLOS

A

C

Santa Rita ·

× COPPER
MINES

Rincon ·

San Augustine Pass

H

E

APACHE

Dona Ana ·

· Las Cruces

La Mesa ·

SIERRA PORTILLA

Sierra Madre Plateau

PRESENT BOUNDARY — U.S. AND MEXICO

· El Paso del Norte

Rio Grande

Hatchet Mts.

Guadalupe ·

CHIHUAHUA

Diana Sweeney

*Books by John Jennings*

OUR AMERICAN TROPICS
NEXT TO VALOUR
CALL THE NEW WORLD
GENTLEMAN RANKER
THE SHADOW AND THE GLORY
THE SALEM FRIGATE
BOSTON, CRADLE OF LIBERTY, 1630–1776
RIVER TO THE WEST
THE SEA EAGLES
THE PEPPER TREE
THE STRANGE BRIGADE
CLIPPER SHIP DAYS
ROGUE'S YARN
BANNERS AGAINST THE WIND
SHADOWS IN THE DUSK

# Shadows *in the* Dusk

*Diana J Sweeney*

# SHADOWS
## *IN THE*
# DUSK

by
*John Jennings*

Boston   Toronto

*Little, Brown and Company*

COPYRIGHT 1955, BY JOHN E. JENNINGS, JR.

ALL RIGHTS RESERVED. NO PART OF THIS BOOK IN EXCESS OF FIVE
HUNDRED WORDS MAY BE REPRODUCED IN ANY FORM WITHOUT
PERMISSION IN WRITING FROM THE PUBLISHER

LIBRARY OF CONGRESS CATALOG CARD NO. 55–5530

FIRST EDITION

*Published simultaneously in Canada
by Little, Brown & Company (Canada) Limited*

PRINTED IN THE UNITED STATES OF AMERICA

*For my sister,*
*S. J. C.*
*With love.*

When the sun sets, shadows, that showed at noon
But small, appear most long and terrible.

— NATHANIEL LEE: *Oedipus*

# Shadows *in the* Dusk

# *Foreword*

*W*HO AM I, señores y señoras, that *I* should be telling this? It is the truth that there are others who could do as well, and, I do not doubt, even better; a few remaining who passed through the same experiences. Some of these could assuredly put pen to paper better than I. But when I speak of it to them, and say that it should be done, and beg them — if only to warn some future travelers of the dangers that may await — they only laugh at me and say to me that I make too much of nothing!

Of nothing, indeed! Por Dios! It was not nothing when it happened to us. If the slow death of nearly six hundred people, which includes many whole families, is nothing, then it may be that I *am* foolish. I, myself, I do not think so!

At the least, I am not foolish in the head, as is sometimes suggested.

It is, perhaps, that I am a little haunted by a sense of guilt. Again I do not think so. What happened — and what came after — was hardly of my doing. I speak truly! When Pontius Pilate washed his hands, so it is taught to us, he condemned Jesus in fact, and sought in this way to escape the responsibility. I do not seek to escape. But neither, gentes, did I wash my hands! I say only that what happened was

3

without my knowledge — and without any means by which I might have prevented, had I known of it. And, most assuredly, it was without approval from me. That I regret much of it, acknowledging a certain fault through ignorance, I hope will be understood.

If, by your favor, gentes, I may be permitted a moment of reflection, allow me to say that the Book by which so many of us live, now — thirty years after — has been amply attested: the evil that men have done has lived after them. Sí, and the sins of the fathers have been visited unto the children — of how many generations is it to be? Those who sowed the wind reap now the whirlwind, for if it had not happened, as I am about to tell, with your gracious consent, Mangas Colorado would not have led his Apache hordes against the intruders — Mexicans and Yanquis alike. And if Mangas had not taken the warpath at the time of which I am about to tell, he would not have been made prisoner many years afterward. If he had not been thus taken, how could he have been shot for "attempting escape"?

Do you know the story of that, señores y señoras?

Do you know that it was suggested by an officer that Mangas Colorado would be more valuable dead than alive?

Do you know that a guard heated his bayonet to the white hot point and thrust it into the Indian's leg, and that when Mangas leaped to his feet and sought to withdraw from the torture he was shot, out of hand, for "attempting escape"?

You do know, of a truth, gentes — for this has been told in the public prints — that it was a surgeon of the army who severed Mangas Colorado's head and extracted the brain and put it upon a scales, announcing afterward that

4

its weight exactly equalled that of Señor Don Daniel Webster!

Ay, caray! And it is we who say that the Apaches are savages!

To say to you further what we know — that where there was but one Mangas and one band there are now thirty chiefs of the first class — Victorio, Cochise, Gian-na-tah, Eskimotzin, Nana, Concepcion, Del-she, Nata-totel, Geronimo — to name but a few; and a hundred bands of Mescaleros and Chiricahuas and Aravaipas and Jicarillas and Mogollones and Coyoteros and Tontos, and others of the Apache nation — is but to whip the dog that sleeps! Can you blame them, gentes? Is it astounding that they rise against us and give terror to the land?

But enough of such! It suffices that I saw the beginning, and that perhaps my story will serve to warn others that it is better to live at peace with your neighbors than to covet his ox or his ass or anything that is his!

Bueno!

But I see that the first question is not yet answered!

Who *am* I that I should presume to be telling you this? Let it be told — for it will not take much time.

My name is José Herrero Alfonso Francisco Pereda Galindo y Ruiz, and by confession this is a great lump of much in the mouth. My friends call me Currito, and I like it much more. I have nearly fifty years of age, and my hair is yet a long way from gray. My eyes, my skin, my mouth, my nose — what would you? There is not time for such nonsense! For my ancestry, as the curious will ask, and to have it done with, once and for all, I am French of the French, Spanish of the Spanish, Mexican of the Mexican, and Indian of the Indios. It is possible that somewhere, back in all that, I am also English of the English! I would not know.

The whole truth is that today I am a Yanqui of the Yanquis. Such are we all a little of each, so are we told and so always have I believed. To follow all that in detail would be more than we need. Let it, then, simply suffice to say that my great-grandfather was French; my grandmother was Indian — a Lipan. My father was Mexican. My mother was Spanish. And where the English enters, I cannot tell! My father and my mother died when I was a child — not romantically, as members of a wagon train attacked — but of thirst and starvation as they crossed the Llano Estacado, from what we now call Texas. I suppose that I, but for God's blessing, might have done the same had not I been found by a party of priests bound for the mission at Taos.

These kindly men rescued me and took me with them and allowed me to grow in my own way, although they would have been pleased had I been inclined to the ways of God. But it is true that only those who have heard His voice can of an honesty follow where He leads, and my benefactors were wise enough to see that this was so. Because of this, when I came of age — or as nearly to it as anyone could tell — they let me go. And because I was so inclined, and did not want to be a churchman, I left Taos and went to Santa Fe.

I made my headquarters there, and for the several years that followed I ranged up and down and across the New Mexican Province, guiding parties of traders and trappers and immigrants. In a truth, I even went thrice so far as Saint Louis with Mexican wagon trains to trade silver for Yan-

## FOREWORD

qui products, and in time I came to have something of a reputation as a guide and a scout.

In Santa Fe, too, I had another kind of a reputation — which was not altogether unearned. Today, I am a staid old man, sitting in the territorial legislature, and, I may hope, behaving myself better than my wife tells to me that I do!

I think that is enough. Let us be on with it!

Su servidor que besa sus pies,
José Herrero Alfonso
Francisco Pereda Galindo y Ruiz
(Currito)

*Santa Fe,*
*3 August, 1870*

# I

## SANTA RITA DEL COBRE

# *Chapter 1*

OFTENTIMES it is not easy to remember exactly when
it was that something happened — especially if the event occurred some thirty years ago. But this thing I recall to the
very year, for it was at the time of the Chimayo Rebellion,
in Northern New Mexico, and that was in 1837; in August
of 1837, to be precise.

I cannot, however, be so certain of the month when all
of this began, although I believe that it could not have
been later than the middle of June. This much I can say
with confidence, for not yet had the rebels begun to fore-
gather at Santa Cruz de la Cañada, which was to become
their earliest base of operations.

Ay, yes indeed! Seguro! There was already hot talk and
bitter anger. Claro! For instead of appointing one from
among ourselves to be our gobernador, as had always before been the custom, the most recent gobierno at Mexico
City had seen fit to single out one of their own number to
serve in that post, and had sent him to us forthwith and
without por favor. It is scarcely of a necessity to say that
this "Coronel" Albino Perez, as he was called, brought with
him a pack of worthless bootlickers and flunkeys and hangers-on. In addition he seemed to flaunt his authority in our

faces, for one of his first acts was to announce the adoption of a new system of federal taxation, which was of a surety not popular.

It may be that the recent loss of Texas Province made them try to bind New Mexico the more closely by means of this governor and set of laws of their own choosing. But, if this was their thought, then it is sadly that they were mistaken. Any fool should have been able to see that it was hardly the good way to go about winning the loyalty and affection of any people, let alone one so proud and stiff-necked as ourselves. We do not like change in any case. But we like it less when outsiders seek to stuff it down our throats!

But little of this is much to our point. It is only that I wish to place definitely the time when those things that I am about to tell happened; and this I believe I have succeeded in doing. It was in the late spring, then — but not later than mid-June — that I came up through the Jornada del Muerto with a group of those same bootlickers and hangers-on that I have already mentioned, from El Paso del Norte to our own small provincial capital at Santa Fe.

Now, then, señores, it should perhaps be explained here that my way of contracting went simply according to the custom. Upon agreeing to take a party to thus and such a place, it was the rule for the contractor — who was usually the guide and scout, packer, wrangler, and chief defender — to accept half the charge; the balance to be payable upon the safe delivery of the party at their contracted destination. As I say, this was the usual agreement, and I do not think that ever have I seen any formal, written statement of the terms. It was understood, but surely, that there were certain hazards of the trail, which the principals must risk, and which would be no responsibility of the guide — or contractor. It was further usually recognized that the more hazardous the journey, the more of such risk must be assumed by the voyagers themselves. It is not surprising, hence, that I did not commit all such stipulating to documents at El Paso del Norte before I accepted their hire. Of a natural thing I assumed that they were aware of all of this. Otherwise I would have found their potato too hot for my mouth!

The outcome of this I shall presently show, with your permission — although, I make bold to say, you have probably already guessed at it! At least, gentes, I fulfilled my portion of the bargain as I saw it. The party which I agreed to escort — it seems to me this is a better way to put it — consisted of ten or a dozen of such as I have already described. Only one among them was of official status, and he was no more than a junior secretary of the clerical grade — and a most junior one at that. Indeed, he was not even the leader of the party, as he should have been, but of a truth had hardly the cojónes — how shall we say? the gumption, that will do — to speak his name in the roll call.

The rest were caballeros who were, I will dare to say it, too well known in Mexico City to have hopes of a lucrative post. In the provinces, however, and most particularly in New Mexico, they had friends who would see to the lining of their pockets — or, so they fondly hoped. And it happened that at El Paso del Norte they found me — or perhaps it would be more accurate to say that I found them, for even a conductor — a guide — señores y señoras, must eat.

Their leader, and the one with whom I concluded the business, was a great, black fellow. I do not mean black of skin, though he was almost as dark as an Indian in that way. I mean that he was black of brow and hair and eye — and of soul, too, as he gave ample proof. His name was Coronel — so he, too, called himself, though I found later that it was no official title — Raoul Hermoso y Maravilla; which in itself was for laughter, for in English it is translated "Ralph the handsome and marvelous"!

Of a truth, it was not his fault that he was born with such a name. But ciertamente, nothing could be further from the fact! He was a tall man, well set up as to physique; broad of shoulder and deep of chest, narrow of hip and strong of leg. But his great mop of black, stringy hair dripped down over his low forehead, almost to meet the black, bushy eyebrows that formed a thick, straight line across the bridge of his nose. The nose, itself, was thin and aristocratic, and it would have been handsome but for the fact that somewhere, at some time it had been knocked somewhat askew, I have no doubt in a barroom brawl. As for his mouth, it was full and fatuous; a Cupid's bow, in blue and purple, astretch for malicious laughter and full of sexual evil, sensuous and licentious and hateful.

This, I believe, is enough to say that I did not care much for him. There was also a woman of the party. Chucha, she was called. And she was supposed to be the wife of the little one — of the minor official, I believe, although I sometimes wondered, for it seemed to me that she slept in a different set of blankets every night. She was short and gay and buxom; ripe of lip and breast and thigh, and strong and hungry in every way that a woman should be. Throughout

14

the journey, I was aware, she had her eye upon me — and why should she not, for I do not boast when I say that I was the handsomest of the party. And, of a surety, it is a matter of record that I was by at least a dozen years the youngest of them all. Nor should I claim any hypocritical holier-than-thou attitude. I was young and I was virile, and I was as willing as the next. But I had no stomach to share the partner of my bed with so many others. If a woman gave herself to lie with me, I preferred to think that I was the sole object of her ardor. With Chucha this was impossible, so I put on the hat of contemptuous outrage, which, I daresay, simply made matters the worse.

At any rate, since this is such a small part of the story I will not delay matters by dwelling upon it. I brought them all through safely, over that twisted trail of death, although we had one brief skirmish with a returning war party of Lipans, licking their wounds and therefore ugly, after a brush with the Comanches to the north. We met them at the Ojo del Muerto — one of the only two water holes along the way — and beat them off easily, although three or four of our number received superficial wounds: a crease at the edge of one man's scalp, for instance, an arrow through one of another's backsides, a clean shot through the fleshy part of a third man's arm, while Chucha received an arrow wound high up on the inside of her thigh, narrowly missing her groin, which at least had the beneficial effect of making her forget her amorous propensities for the rest of the way.

I thought little enough of the event, however, since at least one brush with the Indians was considered almost a foregone conclusion, especially on that trail. Apparently, though, the "Coronel" and his comrades took a more serious view of it. At Santa Fe I delivered them intact at the Palacio del Gobernador, which was their destination, and, as I believe was no more than natural, asked for the balance of my pay.

The great, black "Coronel" turned upon me with a snarl.

"Bandido!" he shouted. "You will get nothing more from this party! Begone, before I turn you over to the soldados."

I could scarcely believe my ears.

"But," I protested. "But, Señor Coronel, you contracted — "

"So I did, pilcate!" he retorted. "But so did you. If you recall, it was your agreement to deliver us safely, and this you have not done."

"What do you say?" I cried. "You are all here — and alive!"

"Alive — sí" he replied. "But no thanks to you for that. But for our own courage and skill at arms we would all be lying dead and scalped back there in the desert at this moment. As it is there are four of us wounded. I do not call that safe delivery!"

In my astonishment I was so rude as to burst out laughing in his face, which was a foolish thing for me to do, for it only made him the angrier. Yet I could not help myself, for it was assuredly the wildest flight of fancy to consider any of them either valorous or heroic. Indeed, had they put forth a bolder front when we first encountered the Indians, we might have avoided the battle entirely. As it was the Lipans were encouraged to attack by their obvious apprehension and cowardice, and I fear I said as much.

I can only offer by way of excuse that I was young at

16

the time, and filled with the brash impetuousness of my age. My sneering statement served only to put him into an even more towering rage. He signaled to some nearby guards, and apparently he did have some sort of authority, for they moved swiftly to do his bidding. Since it was obvious that he had no intention of paying me, and since it was further evident that to stand and argue with him would only result in my spending the night at least in the calabozo, I could see no point in remaining. Accordingly I took myself away from there, beating a hasty and disgruntled, if altogether quite strategic retreat.

But I was by no means finished with the "Coronel" Hermoso y Maravilla. I did not see him again that day or the next. But on the third evening after my arrival I was sitting in the shadowed corner of the Cantina Águila when he entered with two of his recent companions and elbowed his way to the bar, where he banged and bellowed for aguardiente.

It happened that the Cantina Águila — The Eagle Bar, to translate the name — was unusually well patronized that night. In addition to its regular patrons there were many lusty, brawling, thirsty Yanquis — great, strapping fellows, mostly, in leather shirts and fringed leggings, Indian moccasins and fur caps — for a great, long wagon train had rolled in that day from Missouri, and a good many traders and trappers accompanied it.

These, for the most part, had usurped the bar for themselves and were busily sluicing the dust from their throats with great draughts of fiery mescal and aguardiente and quickly and methodically becoming drunk. Most of the rest of us regular customers, wishing no trouble, were drawn off to the side, to the tables along the walls and in the corners, whence we watched with either amusement or irritation, according to our own tempers.

Not so the "Coronel" and his companions, however. They squeezed in against the bar, as I have said, and from the looks that went their way, I half suspected that there might be trouble brewing for them before the night was done.

Far was it from my mind, however, to warn them. Whatever they might receive at the Yanquis' hands was quite all right with me! Still, I decided to myself, I might as well try just once more to collect my due. It was quite probable that the "Coronel" would again refuse, but at least I would have the pleasure and satisfaction of exposing him publicly for the cheap cheat he was.

I do not recall the names of the "Coronel's" companions. Nor is it important that I should. One was a handsome young fop from Mexico City. The other was middle-aged, bald-headed and paunchy. And as they stood at the bar they lined up in that order at the "Coronel's" left. On the "Coronel's" right were two of the tallest and brawniest Yanquis I had ever seen. Indeed, I believe I should say that they were the tallest and brawniest *men* that I had ever seen! Both were young — not more than twenty-one or two. Both stood close to six feet eight or nine inches in their moccasins, and I doubt if there was the difference of the weight of a peso between them. Both must have tipped the beam of the scales at well over two hundred pounds.

But there the resemblance seemed to end. The one nearest the "Coronel" was the dark one. His hair was black and his eyes dark, dark brown and brooding. His face was lean, his nose thin and sharp, his mouth wide, with thin lips. Yet he was not unhandsome, and when he smiled or laughed, as he was now, warmed by the liquor he had taken, his teeth flashed bright white in his dark face and his eyes shone with glee. His shoulders were broad and his torso tapered sharply to a waist that was almost as thin as a girl's. His hips were small and narrow, and though they were hidden now beneath his shapeless buckskin leggings, I guessed that his legs were equally well tapered and straight as those of a thoroughbred horse.

His companion, who stood on his right, on the other hand, was all made up of squares. His face was square, with a flat slash of a mouth that cut straight across it. His hair, what I could see of it under his shaggy cap, was of a tawny, sandy color and evidently curly. His eyes were light — almost a pale blue, and very direct. Still you could see the little wrinkles of humor at their corners. His shoulders were as broad as those of his comrade, but there was no taper to his waist. His body ran straight down to his buttocks and there seemed to be chopped off square, and it was quite evident from the way he stood, planted solidly before the bar, that his legs were as stout and sturdy and straight as young trees. Yet there was not an ounce of fat on him anywhere.

It was clear that these two, at least, were enjoying themselves mightily; and it was equally clear that they were close companions — inseparable, I dared guess, as a pair of peas in a pod.

On the other side of the "Coronel" and his friends I was not so observing, though I call to mind there was a short, blocky man with iron-gray hair and somber, bright blue eyes, and next to him a taller, lean and angular, middle-aged man with a long droopy face and a sad, watery eye.

However all this might be, it is to be admitted that I noted it only idly, not conceiving at that moment that the way these Yanquis were placed could have any bearing upon my own future. I rose and left my pulque at the table and walked across to where the "Coronel" stood and tapped him on the shoulder. He turned, and at sight of me began to glower.

I saw that he was about to begin to bluster, so I spoke first and quickly.

"Señor Coronel," I said flatly, "you owe me two hundred and fifty pesos for escorting you and your party to this place, and I will thank you to pay me!"

"Ladrón!" he roared. "I owe you nothing. You did not keep your end of the bargain — "

"Señor Coronel," I interrupted him. "If you refer to the fact that we were attacked by Indians, and four of your people were wounded, I say to you that I did carry out my contract nevertheless! I challenge you to ask any man in this room. He will tell you that the risk of such an attack is one of the hazards of the country and in no way affects the guide's contract."

"Cocky little bastard, ain't he?" the tall, dark young man at the "Coronel's" elbow chuckled.

I glanced at him coldly.

"I am no bastard, señor," I assured him in English, for this I had been taught by the good padres so well that I was often called upon to act as interpreter for the Yanquis. "My father and my mother were married in the church."

"No offense, banty!" the tall young man grinned. "Just

20

a figger o' speech, you might say. Go to it! Tie inta him!"

I turned back to the "Coronel" and held out my hand.

"Pay me!" I demanded.

I thought he would burst a blood vessel in his rage.

"Pay you?" he half screamed. "Pay *you*, you thieving, beggarly son of a ram and a she goat! I have told you that I have no money for you . . . !"

And he struck my hand aside roughly.

Whether it was the blow or the insulting names he called me does not much matter. The thing that is to the point is that I in my turn became angry.

"Señor," I stormed. "What you call me in this place makes little difference to me, for I am among friends who know me. What does matter, and I glory in it, is that out of your own mouth these good people have learned what kind of a lying, thieving cheat you are! As for you — and your money — Pah! I spit upon you!"

And I did — full in the face.

He lunged toward me as he wiped at the spittle, and I fell back into a position of defense, ready to make the best of a bad situation, for I am slight and he was more than a match for me. But to my surprise — and obviously to the "Coronel's" as well — the tall young man with the dark face reached out effortlessly and caught him by the back of the neck, jerking him back to the bar with a jar that shook the entire cantina.

"Hold on thar!" the young man growled. "Not so fast, mister! Pick on someone yer own size, why doncha?"

"Looks to me like th' young feller has a point, Jode." The sandy-haired young giant spoke for the first time.

The dark young man glanced at him.

"Think so, Yance?" he said, then looked back at the "Coronel." "Reckon as how he's right, at that! Supposin' you pay him, stranger?"

The "Coronel" choked, sputtered and refused violently, until the young giant picked him up in one hand and shook him till his head rolled.

"Now, lookee hyar, mister!" he said in a slow, soft-slurring drawl. "I'm loaded for b'ar, an' right now I'd like nothin' better'n an excuse t' bust off! I say ye'd better pay th' lad!"

Apparently the "Coronel" was himself convinced of that, for he dug down into his pocket and with surly grace counted out the balance of my fee, in golden reales, into my outstretched hand. When he had done so I pocketed the coins and turned to the two young men.

"Mil gracias, señores!" I said. "I am deeply in your debt. I would be honored . . ."

In so turning I had taken my eyes from the "Coronel," and it did not occur to me that his fury would drive him to further lengths. As a consequence I was amazed, I was startled, when my new-found friends did not even seem inclined to let me finish what I was saying.

Without warning the sandy giant lunged toward me, slamming against me and thrusting me halfway across the room. At the same time, out of the corner of my eye, I saw his companion's fist start to swing upward in a mighty arc. Before I stopped spinning in the middle of the room I heard the crack of fist on flesh and a yell and a grunt and a clatter, as a wicked, razor-sharp knife went spinning across the floor.

In that place and among those men, who seemed to love

22

a brawl above everything else, an outburst of fisticuffs was no more than a signal for a general battle. At the end of the bar someone howled joyously. A bottle went sailing through the air and shattered against the wall back of the bar. Somewhere a pistol cracked, and the single lamp by which the cantina was lighted came crashing down. All at once the place was plunged in pitch darkness and howling turmoil.

At that point, I will confess it freely, I would have fled if I could. It was one thing to stand up and fight a man openly in the lamplight. But it was quite another to punch blindly in the pitch dark in the midst of a good four score of brawling strangers.

Unfortunately, however, the young giant's shove had turned me all around, and I scarcely knew in which direction lay the door. For a moment I stood where I was, wondering and bewildered, trying to orient myself. But as I did so something hard caromed off my head, leaving it ringing, and at the same time a knotted fist grazed my cheek. I decided that whether I would or no I must fight back in self-defense, and so I lashed out and felt my own fist sink to the wrist in a flabby paunch. At the same instant I had the strangely satisfying experience of hearing the "Coronel's" stout friend gasp in pain.

But that was as much of fighting as I had time to do. In the next instant strong hands grasped me on either side, by arm and elbow, and literally lifted me from my feet and whisked me across the darkened room, out through the wide swinging door, into the moonlit street and the night outside.

# Chapter 2

*S*ENORES y señoras, it is a truth that these, my mysterious rescuers, actually carried me across the wide, dusty street and around the corner before they set me down upon my feet once more and released their grip upon me. They, themselves, leaned over against the adobe wall of the nearest building and fell to laughing as if their sides would burst.

For my part, however, I must say that I saw nothing to laugh at. There had been no time until this moment to pause and take stock of my own feelings, but now I began to realize that I was more than a little ruffled. In the first place I felt that my dignity had been rather roughly disregarded by these young ruffians. In the second place, I found myself almost resenting their interference in what seemed to me a purely private quarrel. The argument involved my honor, and my honor alone, and should have been fought out on my own terms — or at least on such terms as I was able to meet the "Coronel" with. But they had stepped in and made my private affair an excuse for starting a public brawl, pure and simple. They might lie against the wall in the moonlight and laugh until they died, but I, as soon as my heels struck the ground, drew myself up indignantly.

24

"Señores," I sputtered, "may I remind you that this was my quarrel? By what right did you interfere?"

The lean, dark one roared.

"Hark to th' banty cock!" he gasped. "Ye'd think we'd a done him wrong, hey?"

The big Yanqui with the curly hair and light blue eyes was more kindly — and more courteous. He studied me and smiled in the moonlight.

"Sorry we roughed ye up a bit, friend," he said. "But Jode an' me, we've got a kind of a peculiar objection to standin' by an' watchin' a feller — specially a right one — get knifed in th' back. They asked for it, an' they got it. Shore, you don't mind that, do ye?"

I must have frowned, for I was puzzled.

"Knifed, señor . . .?" I asked.

"Yup!" he chuckled. "That's what I said. You didn't see it because you were a-lookin' at us, but just as soon as you turned your back on him that black-browed bugger, in there, come out with his knife and was goin' t' let you have it where you'd never know!"

That certainly put a different light on the matter. I felt my temper sink to a simmer and then fade away altogether as gratitude took its place.

"Then, señores," I said earnestly, "I must beg you to forgive me for my rudeness! I am now doubly in your debt."

"Think nothin' of it!" The blond young giant seemed slightly embarrassed. The other was still laughing riotously.

"But I don't even —" I began, and then broke off abruptly. From around the corner came the sound of run-

**25**

ning feet, the grunting bark of quick commands, the creak of leather, the rattle of equipment.

"The guardia!" I exclaimed. "Come, señores! We must make ourselves scarce of this place, for our friends back yonder are not without influence, and if we are caught we may spend a most uncomfortable night in the calabozo! Come! There is another cantina on the other side of town. We will go there and I will buy you a drink while you tell me your names and how I can repay you for what you have done for me."

I led them across the sleeping town to the Cantina Juanita, far and away on the other side, at the very western out-skirts, and for this I had more reasons than one. In the first place I suspected that Raoul Hermoso would be out in search of us with a special squad of policias at his back, and he would not rest until he had at least ransacked all the better-known places in the center of the city. If by any chance he came as far as this place I knew that the proprie-tress, Juanita, herself — a buxom, full-bodied, vigorous wench, and my very good friend — would be happy to con-ceal us from him in her own bedroom, since she had small love for the authorities, and I flattered myself, much for me!

Moreover, I knew that Juanita took great pride in her fine, private stock of smuggled whiskies and aguardiente; a stock whose existence was not even generally suspected, for Juanita was particular for whom she brought out her best! She had never refused me, however, and I wanted my benefactors to have the very finest that was obtainable in that place.

When we arrived Juanita made a great to-doing over

26

me, though I noticed that her eye strayed often and with a light of roguish calculation toward the tall, dark Yanqui, so that I was a little jealous, and almost wished that I had not brought them!

But, then! It was done, and whatever was to happen was without doubt already written in the good Lord's book! I explained what had happened at the Águila, at the mention of which she sniffed contemptuously.

"Serves you right, chambón, for going to such a place!"

"For that," I told her, laughing, "I will punish you, chica mia!"

And I reached across the bar and pinched her mildly where her breasts thrust loose and free beneath her low-cut rebozo.

She squealed with delight, and flicked at my hand with pretended modesty.

"Go, thou!" she simpered, although I knew very well that she was pleased. "Stop, chivato!"

"Go, go, go! Ho, ho, ho!" I mocked. "I will do no such a thing, chica mia, for if I did you would be sad, and that I would not want. Moreover, if I had not gone to the Cantina Águila I would not have had the honor of being befriended by these two fine gentlemen!"

Whereupon I told her the rest of the story, and her eyes popped so admiringly that I was almost sorry that I had. When I was done, however, she clapped her hands.

"Ai-ee, then!" she cried. "I see that this calls for the best. Excuse me, señores, while I step to the back of the house for the most special!"

While she was gone I led my two new friends to a table at the back, near enough to the door of Juanita's quarters that we might slip through if need be. There I explained both her errand and the excellence of her stock, at which they grinned at one another.

"Looks like we lit on our feet!" the blond one said.

"That's quite a gal," retorted the lean, dark one.

"I think you will find Juanita ready for any occasion," I told them, perhaps a little smugly.

For some reason the dark one did not seem pleased.

"You're a kinda a pompous — " he began.

But the curly-haired, thickset one cut in quickly.

"Tut, tut, tut, Jode!" he exclaimed. "Remember, he's talkin' a language that's not his own. What's more he's puttin' himself out o' th' way t' be polite. Don't go flyin' off th' handle!"

The admonition seemed to have a soothing effect, though he eyed me narrowly.

"Yore wife?" he asked.

"God forbid!" I replied. "Juanita is but a fine friend!"

They exchanged glances with raised eyebrows, and the dark one chuckled.

"Señores," I said, "it seems to me time that we introduced ourselves. I am José Herrero Alfonso Francisco Pereda Galindo y Ruiz. My friends call me Currito — Currito Ruiz, señores — su servidor!"

For some reason they both laughed, and I might have taken offense had not the blue-eyed one thrust in quickly.

"Now, there," he grinned. "That's a mouthful all right. No wonder folks shorten it to 'Currito'! I'm afraid we can't offer ye any such highfalutin handles. Me, I'm Yancey Cahoon, o' Tennessee by way o' Texas. Tall, dark an' hyan'-some, hyar, is Jode — Jedediah, he was born — Lassiter, also

28

o' Tennessee, same as me. In fact we were born within half
a mile o' each other, an' I expect within half an hour o' th'
same time. We've been together since!"

I acknowledged with a bow, at which they seemed
startled.

"Señor José!" I said to the lean, dark one.

"Jode's the name," he interrupted, looking embarrassed.
"Jest Jode."

"Señor Don Jode, then," I said soberly, "and Señor Don
Yancey, will you sit, then, and allow me . . . ?"

Juanita returned from the back storeroom, giggling and
with her arms laden with bottles of fine things. I introduced
her properly, naming my new friends, and calling upon
them to select their choice.

I had in mind that each would name a drink and accept
a glass. But instead each chose a bottle, a thimbleful of
which would have laid me in the sheets. Yet when the
evening was done I could not see that either was in the
least affected by it!

Still, who was I to quibble? I suggested to Juanita that
a lookout might be wise, and she snapped her fingers for
the mozo, an ancient Indian who had cause, as had everyone
who knew her, to be aware of the kind bounty of her
house. He would sit at the corner, three squares away, and
unobtrusively report any unusual police activity in the
neighborhood.

Thus guarded, I sought conversation. Claro, in some way
I must reward these, my benefactors.

"You spoke of Texas?" I asked the blue-eyed one —
Yancey.

He looked a little embarrassed.

"Perhaps I should not have mentioned it," he replied.

I shrugged. To be sure there were some among us who resented the recent loss of the province. But these were mostly among the old Spaniards. The rest of us would have preferred to see Texas remain a part of Mexico. But if Texas wished independence, and was willing to fight for it, who were we to object?

"No matter," I assured him. "Texas has chosen her own way, just as the rest of us have chosen ours. At least, it is enough that she is independent — not a part of Spain, or of your country."

How naïve is youth, that I did not see which way the wind was blowing! Certainly, at this point, I have no objection to Texas, or even New Mexico, being a part of the United States. But then I did. How foolish!

A people must choose for themselves. I would no more ask the Mexican states of Chihuahua or Zacatecas or Sonora to become a part of this country today, than I would ask Oregon or Montana or Maine to turn Canadian! Or Ontario to come to us, for that matter!

But all this is beside the point. Wise or not, I believe my attitude set my new-found companions a little bit more at ease.

"She's goin' her own way, all right," the dark one, Jode, remarked.

"What do you mean?" I demanded. "I'm surprised that you señores should have come away, now that the battle is won."

"Oh, shore — 'th' battle's won, but just begun!' " the curly-haired one, Yancey, remarked. "Seems to me I've read that somewhere, though I couldn't just say where.

When fightin' goes out politics comes in. That'd seem t' be th' way o' it, friend."

"I don't quite follow," I said.

He glanced at the dark one, Jode, and shrugged.

"I cain't see no harm in tellin'," he said. "Old Sam — Old Sam Houston, that is — wants Texas a part o' th' U.S. He's pitchin' off England agin us in th' hope t' prod us into action. Same time there's a crowd — you know, Lamar an' Burnet — that have a different notion. They fancy theirselves as Presidents, an' they're opposin' Old Sam. Well . . ."

He glanced at the lean, dark man, who nodded.

"Go ahead," he said. "We can't be worse off!"

"Well, sir," the blue-eyed man went on, not in any way apologetically, but in explanation. "Me an' Jode were Houston men. After San Jack there didn't seem much for us to do. Certain, we'd no mind to settle, an' all th' shootin' was done. We drifted up along past San Anton', an' after a bit come to a place called Guadalupe. All we aimed to do was spell a bit overnight. But it seems that most of the folks thereabout were Lamar men. Comes an argument an' . . . an', well, anyway, hyar we are! I think you get the picture. The's a couple o' Lamar voters less, anyways!"

I smiled.

"So," I said, "the internal troubles of Texas are the least of my worries. Let them solve their own problems. What do you intend now?"

They looked at one another and grinned.

"Shoot!" Jode laughed. "You name it."

"Got a suggestion?" the blond Yancey chuckled. "Fact is we hain't made no plans. We got this far, but we just been driftin'. Looks like we're gonna have to settle down to work

31

pretty soon — that is, if we aim to go on eatin'. You don't know of anythin' like that around here, do you?"

"Well," I mused. It was the truth that gainful employment for Yanquis was not plentiful in Santa Fe. Still there were a few possibilities. "There will be a new wagon train organizing to go up the Trail to Missouri within a day or two. They'll take all the guards they can get."

Jode frowned.

"I don't much cotton to the notion," he said.

"Me neither," Yancey added, running his fingers through his curly hair and smiling a little ruefully. "O' course there's no reason why we shouldn't, but it just sorta seems t' me like givin' up an' goin' back home with our tails draggin'. I reckon me an' Jode was just borned with a powerful curiosity. We're always a-hankerin' to see what lays up ahead."

Jode nodded.

"It's always been that way," he said. "Ever since we was shavers."

"We grew up together," Yancey explained. "I can't remember the time when we weren't in hollerin' distance o' one another."

As he talked the old Indian mozo, who had been sent out to act as lookout for us, came sidling in and glanced at me significantly. I looked up in some alarm, and put out my hand to interrupt them.

"Excuse me, señores!" I said and beckoned the Indian to me.

"What is it, Pablo?" I demanded.

The old man's expression did not change. His beady black eyes were impassive. I could not tell from looking at him what nature of news he brought — whether it was good or bad.

"Two men," he said, "look you."

"Soplónes — policia?" I cried.

He shook his head.

"Gringo!" he replied. "Creo que no son malos — I do not believe they are bad."

"But what can they want?" I asked, puzzled.

"They not tell," he grunted.

I shrugged.

"Very well," I said. "If you are sure they are not policia, bring them here."

He padded out, and my companions glanced at me inquiringly. I explained to them as best I could, and I could see that they were as mystified as I at the interruption. But apparently seeing that I was not alarmed, they, too, relaxed. I had complete confidence in Pablo.

Almost before I had finished explaining to Don Jode and Don Yancey he was back, and in his tracks came two of the Yanquis I had seen at the Cantina Águila. I rose, stiffening a little for I was not sure what their appearance might mean, although I recognized them, of course. The first was the short, stocky, grizzled, blue-eyed man, who had stood at the left of the "Coronel's" group. The other was his sad-eyed, drooped-nosed companion.

"Señores!" I said as I moved to meet them. "You seek for me?"

The middle-aged, blue-eyed one was clearly the spokesman.

"Take it easy, son," he replied. "Sorry t' disturb ye, but me an' my pardner, here, couldn't help overhearin' yer

**33**

argyment with th' black-hearted ape, back yonder, an' it
come t' us that ye might be th' very man for us. We thought
we'd git t' ye afore anyone else."

"But — but, I do not understand, señores," I said. "How
did you find me? And — "

He chuckled.

"Jorge, at the Águila, had an idee ye might be over this
way," he said. "I ast him to keep it confidential."

So Jorge knew, I reflected. In that case there were undoubtedly plenty of others! I told myself that I must make
an effort to be more discreet in my indiscretions!

"You are sure you did not lead any others here?" I demanded. "I want no more trouble."

He chuckled dryly.

"You won't git none," he retorted. "They carried th'
black bugger out feet first — I reckon young Lassiter, here,
tended t' that — "

"He's not seriously hurt?" I cried, with some alarm.
After all, the "Coronel" wielded enough influence in that
place to make it most uncomfortable for any who had
really hurt him.

But the grizzled man shook his head.

"Nothin' bad," he said. "He'll have a sore jaw an' a
mouse, come mornin', but nothin' worse. Meantime, he
won't be lodgin' any complaints tonight! Somebody put
a stout fist t' his gundy-guts friend's breadbasket, too, but
they never could find out who!"

I swelled a little with pride at that, for I knew who!

"Señores," I said. "Please to name your pleasure, and
what can I do for you?"

The sad-eyed man spoke for the first time.

34

"Don't mostly take nothin' but milk," he said lugubriously. "But the' ain't no milk, yerabout. I'll settle fer brandy — if you got any?"

I assured him that whatever he wished was available, and signaled to Juanita as I led them toward the table. Obviously they were already well acquainted with my Tennessee friends. They nodded, and the blue-eyed man turned to me.

"I expect we oughta introduce ourselves 'fore we ask if ye're interested," he said. "My name's Wilson — Ben Wilson. An' this here's Charley Kemp. We got a bunch o' us — trappers — that had a mind to go down on the Gila. They tell us th' beaver's good down thataway. Now, from what we heerd o' your argyment, ye're a guide 'n scout by perfeshion — an' we heerd enough t' know ye're a good'n. How about it? Ye can name yer price. If it's too high, we'll say so."

I glanced at my two new-found friends. Yancey grinned.

"Like I said," he told me, "we've got a yen for over beyond. You suit yerself, though."

I turned back to Wilson.

"How many?" I asked. "I usually rate by the head."

He nodded.

"Fair enough," he replied. "I reckon the's about twenty-five, thutty of us. You know trappin' conditions down thataway?"

I smiled.

"I know enough to know that they're good," I told him. "I'm no trapper myself — only a guide. But I'll take you as far as Santa Rita, and put you on the river. After that it's up to you. All I can do is show you the way."

35

He smiled and wagged his head up and down.

"That's fair enough," he said. "Figgered on a minimum of twenty-five, then, let's say ye'll take us t' Santa Rita, guide n' found, fer twenty pesos a head. I think that's th' goin' rate, ain't it?"

"That's usual," I nodded.

"Good enough, then," he assured me. "We'll offer ye two fifty pesos down, an' two fifty at Santa Rita. If ye want t' take others ye c'n name yer own price. There's safety in numbers, an' we'll not argue about that. If ye don't want t' go with us to th' trappin' grounds, we'll make th' same bargain for th' return from Santa Rita t' Santa Fe. What d'ye say?"

I looked at the two tall Yanquis, Jode and Yancey. In my current situation, in debt to them as I felt myself, I did not believe that I should move without their approval.

Yancey shrugged.

"Shucks!" he replied. "We ain't got twenty pesos between us."

"Ay, Dios, hombre!" I cried. "Does this matter? Be my guests!"

But he shook his head.

"Thanks, Currito," he said dryly. "We appreciate th' offer, but I reckon Jode 'n me'd ruther work for our livin' — hey, Jode?"

The dark young giant nodded.

"Very well, then," I persisted, understanding a little, at least, their independence. "I will offer you work as scouts and packers. Will that satisfy? I will pay at the regular rate, and if I may I will point out to you that if you do not accept the jobs I will have to hire someone else. You will permit?"

They glanced at one another with obvious interest.

"Well-l-ll, since ye put it that way," said Yancey slowly. "What d'ye say, Jode?"

Jode grinned.

"I never did no trappin'," he replied, "but I reckon the's no harm in tryin'. At least we won't be lookin' back. Count me in!"

I felt that I had managed in some small way to repay in part what I owed to these new friends.

"Done!" I said. "Then it is agreed?"

"It's a bargain!" added Ben Wilson.

And we shook hands all around on it.

# Chapter 3

THE PREPARATIONS for such a journey as we proposed were far from as simple as might appear on the surface. There were mounts and pack mules to be procured, stores of food and ammunition to be gathered — for while all the Indians in the country toward which we were headed were not hostile, still it was the land of the unpredictable Apache, and no one could foresee when they might take to the warpath. One band, at least, through whose territory we must pass — that of Cuchillo Negro and his Warm Springs Indians — was definitely deadly, and at any moment the Navajos or Gileños or Chiricahuas or Mogollones or Tontos or Faraones might break out in a rash of warlike fervor in revenge for some slight, real or fancied. And of course the Indians of Chihuahua and Sonora — the Pimas and Tarahumares, the Yaquis and Maricopas, were always hostile. Although we would not pass through their territory, if the Apaches could raid southward, as they were constantly doing, so could these savages come north, and it was wise to be prepared!

This is but to name a few of the mass of details needed to make ready for such an expedition. To be sure, none of it came out of my pocket, it being the rule that voyagers themselves must defray all expenses in addition to the guide's fee. But it was also the rule that the contractor, as the chief guide, scout and packer was called, bore the responsibility for gathering and organizing and overseeing the undertaking. Since I was that individual it was I who was so burdened. In addition there was all that equipment and accouterment peculiar to the trade of trapping to be mustered and packed. And there was also the matter of selection and purchase of the most demanded, and therefore profitable, trade goods — primarily liquor and hardware — for my own private venture at Santa Rita, for since I was going that way I had every intention of turning an extra penny if I could.

Strictly speaking, such trade was forbidden, and quite illegal, for when Don Francisco Elguea had opened the mines, some fifteen years before, it had been stipulated in his treaty with the Mimbres Apaches, who claimed the site, that the mining settlement might be supplied only by bimonthly conductas, or mule trains, from Chihuahua and Sonora, and that no access would be permitted from the north, the direction of Santa Fe. In the years, however, Juan José, the Mimbreño chief, and his people had grown lax. They grew to be as fond of our northern luxuries as the miners themselves, and consequently a thriving trade in contraband had grown up — and was winked at by everyone.

In all this my new-found friends, Jode and Yancey, were worth a carretaful of gold. Señores y señoras, Yanqui energy and drive are traditional, and I admit that I find them amazing even now. But never have I seen such zest, such zeal, such cheerful enthusiasm for work as those two displayed.

39

I take my oath to you, it left me literally tired just to watch them! I had but to speak and they were away — and, mind you, not lugubriously or down in the mouth about it, but always laughing, always happy, always playing jokes upon one another — and upon me and the rest of our party.

At the same time, in their own way, I found that Ben Wilson and Charley Kemp were almost as helpful. They took upon themselves the task of gathering and seeing packed properly all that was necessary for their trapping on the Gila, after we had reached Santa Rita. Moreover, it was they who arranged the needed permits and papers — quite illegal, as I have said, but nonetheless necessary for any movement in that country.

There were others, of a certainty, who were both helpful and amusing — there proved to be twenty-eight in all in our party, not including myself or my two assistants, Jode and Yancey. Naturally, if it were given to me of God to remember all their names, I could scarcely list them here. But a few, at least, I should name. Ben Wilson and Charley Kemp, of course, I have described. Don Ben was a curious combination of earnestness and energy and good humor. I have been told lately that he was the first American mayor of the city of the Angels, in California — which, of course, is quite beside the point, but of interest nevertheless, I think. As you will see, he was one of a very few! Charley Kemp was no less earnest, no less industrious. But there was nothing of the spirit of play or good humor about him. He was lugubrious — it is the only word that I can find to describe him. Nothing was well; nothing was good to Charley Kemp, and, indeed, there were times when I wondered why he bothered to live. Not, mind you, señores y señoras, that he was a bad man. On the contrary, I think he was thoroughly good. But there was no happiness in him; and there was nothing happy in his life, from the beginning, I gathered, to the end. Bartalomeo — Bart — Corbin should not be ignored, nor should the camp clown, Dody Hicks. Corbin was a quiet one, keeping himself well bottled up inside, but every now and again tearing loose on an entirely unpredictable howler. There was nothing hurtful about the man. Always he was anxious to help; anxious to do everything there was to be done. Unfortunately he was singularly inept. Everything he touched seemed to turn wrong. We spent much of our time trying to steer him away from tasks which we knew we could do better ourselves.

Hicks, on the other hand, was a great, lean, shaggy dog of a man, unshaven, unkempt, filthy in mind and body, lazy as the day, and yet somehow lovable. His bulbous nose and blotched cheeks, his little green eyes and pursed lips, gave him a repulsive look. But his soul was the soul of the world, and his nature was as sweet as that of Christ. Yet he was as earthy as ever a man could be, and his turn of humor was hardly what could be called quixotic!

So much for our people. As soon as our bargain was sealed I moved out to the camp of the trappers, a mile or so to the south of the town, in order to be at hand to supervise preparations. Nonetheless I had some apprehensions as to reprisals on the part of Raoul Hermose y Maravilla. If I knew the man, and I thought I did, he would leave no stone unturned to take revenge, and surely he must know that I was there and what I was about! In a city the size of our Santa Fe it was hardly possible to keep secret such an expedition as we proposed. Within a matter of hours our destination, our route and our purpose — let alone our personnel — would be known in every cantina and home and even in the governor's palace and the cuartel of the guardia. It would not have surprised me, indeed, to learn that already our impending approach were known in Santa Rita! Thus swiftly does news travel in this land. How then could I keep my presence or plans a secret? The answer was that I could not, and I did not even try.

Yet curiously all was ominously quiet. Claro, there was a reason. But this I did not understand until later — much later, in truth.

At the camp I plunged at once into the work ahead. One day, two, three passed before anything out of the ordinary happened, and then it was hardly what I anticipated. It came in the middle of a moonlit night, when my new-found friends and I were sitting about the campfire, lazily picking our teeth and wondering who would do the dishes.

Out of the night, into the ring of firelight, came three strangers — Yanquis all; or at the least they were not Latins nor Indians. One was tall, almost as tall as Jode or Yancey, but so lean and cadaverous that one wondered if there was anything but a fleshless skeleton underneath his loosely hung buckskins. His nose was hooked and his cheeks sunken, and his mouth had a mean, downward droop at the corners. On his head he wore the most enormous fur cap I had ever seen. His companions were less remarkable in appearance, yet each had about him something that set him apart. One was enormously fat, with rolls of quaking flesh all the way from his paunch to his eyes, which seemed to be stuck into the folds of his face like little red raisins.

The other was deceptively youthful in appearance, with a great, round moon of a face and enormous, guileless-seeming, big brown eyes.

I daresay I should have observed my companions' rather cool reception of the newcomers. But I was tired myself, and if I thought of it at all I judged that they were probably equally so. The tall, skeletal one seemed to be their spokesman.

"Howdy, boys," he said, with what appeared to be an effort to be jovial. "Howdy, Wilson — Kemp. Evenin', Lassiter — Cahoon."

My companions merely nodded in reply, but the newcomers did not seem abashed. They came up to the fire and sat down between Kemp and Wilson and myself. It seemed to me only polite to make some gesture of welcome, and there, I suppose, I made my first mistake.

"Buenas tardes, señores," I said. "May I offer you coffee and a dash of spirits?"

"Thank ye," replied the lean man.

But not until I had filled their mugs did he come to the point of their visit. He glanced at me over the rim of his cup then.

"Yore name Ruiz?" he demanded.

"Yes, señor," I replied. "What can I do for you?"

"Flung yerself around a mite th' other night, I 'ear," he said flatly, ignoring my question.

"So?" I shrugged, but the tone of my voice said plainly that it was none of his business.

"No offense, friend, no offense!" he said hastily. "I just wanted ye t' know we get about. My nyme's Johnson — 'Enry Johnson, an' these 'ere" — he nodded first at the fat

43

man and then at his younger companion — "are Joe Gleason an' Eli Eames, o' Missouri."

I nodded silently, waiting.

"We got a propersition t' myke t' ye," he went on.

"What is it?" I demanded, suspiciously.

"No need t' get 'ackled up," he said a little testily. "Hit's legitermate."

"What is it?" I repeated.

"We understand ye're talkin' o' takin' a party down t' Santa Rita," he continued evasively.

"It's not just talk, señor," I assured him. "Come to the point."

"We want t' go with ye," he told me.

I did not reply at once, but sat silently studying him. I was beginning to sense my companions' hostility for the trio, and I had to admit that there was something unwholesome, almost repulsive about them.

"Why?" I said at length.

"Well-l-ll," he said. "First off we want t' git there. There's a bunch o' us goin' down t' Sonora t' trap, an' we reasoned there's safety in numbers. If we can combine forces that far it'll see us over a touchy bit o' country."

"How many?" I asked.

"Oh, thirty — thirty-five," he replied.

"What's the matter — aren't you sure?" I asked.

"There's three — four others might come hin with us," he told me. "They ayn't made hup their minds yet."

I was fascinated by his accent, which was like nothing I had ever heard before. It was only much later that I learned he was an Englishman, although he had been in

America long enough to have picked up some overtones of a Yanqui drawl. The combination was distinctly strange.

"We'll pay ye th' goin' ryte," he put in, misinterpreting my hesitation. "Fact we'll do better, an' if ye wants t' guide us on beyont Santa Rita, I imagyne we'll be able t' strike a bargain there, too."

I glanced at my companions who listened stolidly, with wooden expressions.

"I'll have to sleep on it," I said. "I'll let you know in the morning."

"Right-o!" he said, no whit abashed. "Come t' th' Fonda. I'll be waitin' for ye."

When they were gone I looked at my comrades again.

"Well, señores," I said. "You heard. What do you think?"

Dody Hicks merely spat eloquently into the fire. Ben Wilson frowned. Charley Kemp shook his head.

"I don't like it," he said. "I don't trust them fellers as fur as I c'n spit!"

"No more do I, señor," I replied, "and as for going on with them beyond Santa Rita, I can tell you right now I have not the least intention of it. I have no wish to enter the country of the Tarahumares or the Pimas. But — "

"But you are thinkin' o' takin' 'em as far as Santa Rita, is that it?" Yancey Cahoon put in.

I grinned at him.

"I fear I must plead guilty, Don Yancey," I replied.

"What's th' matter, ain't th' boys payin' you enough?" Jode demanded.

"It is not the question of that, Don Jode," I told him, "but one of numbers. It must be admitted that the man made an important point there, and thirty additional guns are not to be ignored on such a journey as we are about to take. That is the reason why I think seriously of it."

Ben Wilson spoke up almost sharply.

"I don't see what call we got t' horn in," he said. "You'll mind, gents, that when we offered Currito th' job we told him he'd have a free hand t' take on any others he'd a mind to. I don't like Johnson an' his pals any better'n you do, but it appears t' me it's up to Currito."

"And I say that the doubling of our party will more than offset any small discomfort," I put in.

"It's all one to me," Yancey shrugged. "I'm not worried about anythin' they might do."

"That goes for me, too," Jode added.

"So be it, then," I said. "At least, señores, our company will have an assortment of characters!"

How much of an assortment, however, even I did not realize until I went in to the Fonda the following morning. Johnson was waiting for me, as were a number of his friends, and I must say my heart sank a little at sight of them. Never have I seen such a villainous-seeming band of cutthroats. Almost would I have withdrawn from my decision, but it was too late now. I was already too far committed.

"H'I didn't think ye'd say no," Johnson told me sourly when I gave him my answer. "Our money's as good as any, I expect, hey?"

"I'll tell you better after we reach Santa Rita, señor," I replied coldly.

"Suit yerself," he shrugged.

He started to turn away, then swung back.

46

"Oh, by th' way," he said. "Them chaps made up their minds t' go with us. Th' chief o' 'em's in th' bar now if ye want t' meet him."

I decided that I might as well have it over with. Inside the long bar it was dark and dusky, and it was a moment before my eyes could become accustomed to the gloom. Save for a single figure at the end of the bar the place appeared to be deserted. Johnson led the way directly toward the man.

" 'Ere ye are, mister," he said. " 'Ere's our man. I told ye I'd h'arrange it, an' I did."

The man at the bar turned around slowly, and for a minute I thought the floor would open up and swallow me.

It was the "Coronel" Raoul Hermoso y Maravilla in the all too solid flesh — and seeming much bigger in that gloomy place than I liked!

# Chapter 4

*I* BRACED myself, as you may imagine, señores, fearing the worst. But, to my amazement, nothing happened. The "Coronel" only leered at me.

"So! We meet again, pelón!" he growled.

"We meet again, señor," I retorted coldly. "And if I may add, I do not like people who call me 'pelón,' and who would push me about. If I had know who was to be the mysterious member of our party, who dared not show himself first, I would have refused the hire."

He scowled angrily at that, for he knew well what I meant; and, furthermore, he knew that I knew that he knew — and made no move to resent it, which was an even greater insult. I began to feel the knots go out of my muscles, and became a little easier.

"Do you wish to withdraw?" he demanded gruffly.

But I intended to make no show of timidity before him. He was not one to distinguish between prudence and cowardice. I shrugged.

"That is immaterial to me, señor," I replied. "It makes no difference to me who rides with the party."

"But you just said . . ." he cried in surprise. It was clear that he had thought that he had me.

"No, señor," I retorted. "I only said that if I had known

48

who was to be our last addition I would have refused. That is a matter of personal distaste — not fear."

He glowered at me as if he might attack after all, for a long moment. Then, at last he relaxed and leaned back against the bar with a twisted smile.

"Very well, pelón," he said. "You may continue to dislike me — and I will continue to do as I please. It is more important to me to reach Santa Rita del Cobre than it is to quarrel with such as you. I will give you my word to keep the peace if you will keep yours."

"That is good enough for me," I said shortly, and ignoring him further I turned to Johnson, who had missed nothing of the exchange.

"We will ride tomorrow at dawn," I told him flatly. "Be there with your men and mules."

"But — " He looked distressed, and I knew that they were far from ready.

But I was in no mood to argue. They could take it or leave it.

"Be there!" I repeated. "If you want to ride with us."

And on that last note I left.

When I got back to the camp my companions greeted me with expressions of inquiry.

"Get it all settled?" Yancey Cahoon asked.

"I don't know," I replied, perhaps a little tartly, for I was still fuming inside.

"You don't know?" He looked surprised.

"I told them we'd ride at dawn," I said, "and that they'd better be here if they wanted to go with us. I got the impression that they weren't ready. Maybe they won't come."

"They'll be here," Jode put in dryly.

"Another thing," I went on. "Do you recall that Johnson said there were several others who had not made up their minds, but might join also?"

"I remember that," Ben Wilson said.

"And who do you suppose is among them, señores?" I asked.

"How th' devil would we know?" demanded Jode testily. "Unless — unless . . . ?"

I nodded grimly.

"Si, Señor Don Jode — the 'Coronel' Raoul Hermoso y Maravilla!"

They looked as if I had all at once started throwing stones at them.

"You ain't goin' t' take 'im?" Charley Kemp cried.

I drew myself up to my full height of five feet four.

"But, certainly, señor!" I retorted. "I had already pledged my promise, and besides I do not think he will give trouble."

I told them, then, what had happened at the Fonda, and concluded with a shrug.

"So, you see, señores, it would seem that he is more anxious, for some reason, to reach Santa Rita than he is to fight with me. And if he does make trouble," I shrugged once more — "can I help it if it is our way? I think there are enough of us — no?"

Yancey Cahoon squinted at me, grinning.

"Ain't you afraid of anything, Currito?" he demanded.

"But, sí, señor!" I assured him. "Rattlesnakes, Gila lizards, Apaches, Tarahumares, mountain lions, woman — many things, but Raoul Hermoso y Maravilla — No!"

I devoted that evening, since everything was packed and ready and we were prepared to leave at dawn, to saying my farewells to Juanita — for I never believed in spoiling a good thing by neglect. At first she wept upon my shoulder and declared that she was desolated; that she could no longer live if I left. But when she saw that this would not sway me, she turned to vituperation, calling me "cabrón" and "sin vergüenza" and "un mecate." But I only laughed at her, and at that she reversed herself again and sought to beguile me with a bottle — and in other ways, until I had had my fill of her company and went my way.

But as I left her cantina I realized that it had all been with the idea of speeding me on, for as I rounded the corner, feeling quite comfortably at peace with all the world, I saw, out of the edge of my eye, the señor Don Jode slip in at the door.

Vaya! Que sin vergüenza! Que hombre! He was a veritable Don Juan among the ladies. Claro! All of my comfortable feeling of well-being and amiable will to all men was cast down — shattered. My feelings were hurt! My pride was destroyed! What could I do but seek out Chucha to have the damage repaired?

As a consequence, as one can plainly see, that it was hardly an evening of much rest is a most solemn fact, and when the dawn at last kissed the backs of the mountains and drew a silver rim along the edges of the Sangre de Cristos, I was scarcely in the mood for a day's riding. To tell the honest truth, at this late date — which would never have done then — I wished heartily that I had given Henry Johnson and his comrades an extra day of grace. But it was too late then. I had said my say, and I must keep my word!

Even if they did not come, to delay would be to lose presence with my own companions!

51

But as Jode Lassiter had predicted they came — and a number, counting themselves and their arrieros, or muleteers, and the "Coronel's" additional group, that nearly doubled our own and was close to tripling the original expedition. I was more than a little apprehensive of that, for though I would never have admitted as much to my companions, I was not nearly as sanguine as I had pretended. These men, I was sure, were no ordinary hard cases. They were men who would not hesitate to stoop to any villainy, provided they thought they could get away with it, and I cursed myself for having ignored my friends' premonitions.

However, they seemed docile enough at the moment, and even well-behaved, and since I could do nothing about it I might as well make the best of it! I counted heads and collected my half portion of pay for the journey — taking great pains to let them see me turn it over Don Diego Baca, who maintained the depot and kept the accounts of most of the guides and packers, and admonish him to keep it for me until such time as I should call for it myself, in person. After that we mounted and rode out, trailing a mighty cloud of dust and a tail of barking dogs and screaming, whooping, half-naked children.

As we rode along for a little, however, and came to a rocky, less smotheringly dusty section of El Camino Real, leaving the town and the dogs and the small boys behind us; as the sun came up and warmed my back and I felt myself sinking deeper in the saddle and more into the familiar routine of the trail, I looked back along the line of march, noting that with all our mules and mounts and rich packs — considering, at least, what was in my own — we most assuredly offered a tempting prize. However, with all our outriders — their arrieros and our own, the guides and packers and scouts and cooks — to say nothing of some sixty guns in the main party, we made a most imposing cavalcade. I doubted if any Indian party we might encounter would be so bold as to attack us; and I dared hope that our companions would give us as little trouble.

Our way lay over a route of some three hundred miles, more or less, which I calculated would take us twelve or fifteen days. At first we were to go a little to the southwest, toward Albuquerque and the Rio Grande. From there we would continue southward, along El Camino Real, through Las Lunas and Belen and El Bosque — where we would first come into the country of hostile Indians. We would pass close to Sabinal, not far from Ladron, where the most notorious of Indian horse thieves hid. If we had no trouble there we would then cross the dusty miles near Polvadera, where men's tempers sometimes frayed, to Socorro. From this point we would turn off along the terrible Jornada del Muerto — the dreaded Journey of Death — and it was here that I looked for trouble from our companions, if we were to have it. Fortunately we had only about halfway to go along this scorching road. A little past the Ojo del Muerto — which, as you may recall, was where we had the skirmish with the Indians on the way north — we would turn off and pass between the mountains, the Fray Cristobal, where there were said to be many mines of fine gold, and the Sierra de los Caballos, which were as barren, believe me, as the others were said to be rich.

Here we would find our most difficult traveling, for this piece seemed to be a land that was as if set on edge, slashed

**53**

by creeks and arroyos and barrancas, chopped by cliffs and cul-de-sacs; we would be riding as often as not up or down as we would be across.

Fortunately it was only a little distance, not more than a day's journey with effort, until we reached the Rio Grande once more. There, at the hot springs of Las Palomas, we would cross and turn south again to Caballo. But at this point we would turn our faces west, leaving the valley of the Rio and the Sierra de los Caballos behind. From here the way would not be so troublesome, trailwise, although it would carry us past three bad spots; across the Sierra Negro and up through the Percha Canyon and through the Mimbres Mountains, almost within whispering distance of the Mimbres Hot Springs, which was the home of the notorious and implacable Cuchillo Negro and his band.

As I say, this was not so difficult, from the standpoint of travel. But this was Indian country — some of the worst that we must pass. And I believe that I dreaded it more than any other section of the way, for here the country was wooded as well as rocky. Great pine and thick, gnarled piñons and cedars and all manner of sad green things hung over the trail in many places; and it was for me to plan how we must pass these!

Beyond, in a cup of the mountains, with the steep peaks rising sharp behind, lay Santa Rita, with its huge copper mines and its friendly Indians and its naked children squalling in the dust — and its garrison and gobernador and regular twice-a-month mule train from the south with still more soldiers! Is it any wonder, gentes, that I hoped that we would come there without trouble or difficulty?

54

Ay de mí! Perhaps I should have wished differently, at least for myself. But how was I to know?

Would you believe it, señores y señoras? I had my fears for nothing! Not more than half a dozen times did anything of any serious consequence threaten us, and surely most of these are worth little more than passing mention! Our villains, who came with us, despite my apprehensions, behaved themselves like lambs. Was I to suspect that they were after bigger game?

Well, perhaps! But, recall, my mind was occupied — and rightly so — with each day's business and dangers on the trail. It was for me to try to anticipate what might happen; not to evaluate what occurred.

Let me tell you.

It is somewhat laughable.

The first day we traveled as far as Bajada, where the Camino drops down to the Rio Grande Plain. This is a respectable day's journey — some twenty-six or twenty-eight miles. Our people were weary, as much from the night before — as I must admit was I — as from the unaccustomed day in the saddle, and since we were yet in comparatively settled country no one sat up late. Their snores were enough to assure me that there would be no mischief that night.

On the second day trappers, traders, arrieros, scouts, packers people, and — I must admit — the guide — rode hard to cover the long day to Albuquerque, but when we got there — Ha, ha! I laugh at myself as well as at others! — we were so tired that we fell into our blankets and were glad of the sleep, although I think there were some who were resentful, although surely they could not blame it on me!

I would have stopped at Bernalillo if anyone had been willing to listen!

The next day we rode on to Belen, and I admit I drove them, for I sensed an aggrievement against me for their own haste of the day before. The next day we went only as far as El Bosque, which is no more than eight or ten miles. As may be imagined, there was a great outcry when I called a halt.

A delegation came to me, including Jode Lassiter and Yancey Cahoon, Ben Wilson, Henry Johnson and the "Coronel." It appeared that the "Coronel" constituted himself the spokesman, though I think Ben Wilson would have taken the lead if the "Coronel" had not leaped in before him.

"What is the meaning of this?" he demanded. "We have gone no more than a half a day's ride — not even that, por Dios! And you say we must stop! Why?"

I looked at him a little out of patience. After all . . . !

"Señor," I said. "I think we should stop. Whether we do or not is your problem. Beyond here lies the Ladron Country. We cannot pass through it before night. If you wish to camp in it, that is your decision. You have met these Indians, and it may be that you liked it. I think the rest of us would prefer not to . . . at least, at night . . . ?"

Jode glowered at me.

"What'd ye take us so far for?" he demanded. "Why didn't ye space it out better?"

"I didn't take you so far," I retorted. "If you remember you wanted to make long rides to begin with. Now we've reached a point where we have to make a short ride in order

56

to get through hostile country in daylight. Is there anything wrong with that?"

Yancey Cahoon put in a word on my side.

"I reckon we ought to stop here," he said. "No use askin' for trouble. Seems like Currito knows best about this stuff — else why'd ye hire him?"

I nodded at the backhanded compliment.

"Thank you, Don Yancey," I remarked.

He said nothing.

"Tomorrow," I said, "I think you will have as long a ride as you want. If we do not reach Socorro we must stop in the dust plains of Polvadera, and I think you would not like that. After that I hope you will trust me to arrange the day's march. There are places where we must go far — others where we will not. I am paid to know the way. Enough, señores?"

Ben Wilson chuckled.

"I think we have a hard taskmaster," he said.

And to that extent at least I think I won my first skirmish.

Perhaps I should not name it so. It was no more than a disagreement for a moment. The next was not even that.

The campfires were alight, and dusk had fallen. A few only, for sure, could group around a single fire and it was but natural that we of the original party — not all of us, but a dozen or so who were most responsible — should gather at one spot. We were surprised — and on guard — when Johnson and Gleason, the "Coronel" and Eames joined us.

"Ye might as well sit," said Wilson. "Coffee? What's on yer mind?"

The "Coronel" smiled unctuously. I will admit that for the moment he appeared almost human. I believed that there was more here than met our view, and I decided upon a challenge of sorts.

"Señor Don Coronel," I spoke out boldly. "When I agreed to guide you to Santa Rita, along with the rest of my party, you said that it was more important to you to reach that place than it was to quarrel with me. Believe me, it is not conceit, but I am wondering why?"

He looked at me coldly.

"You said that you would keep the peace," he growled.

"I am not seeking a fight," I retorted, "only information."

"It is my business!" he barked.

"Claro!" I replied. "That is understood!"

For a long instant he seemed uncertain how to reply. But then, all at once, he broke into a broad smile.

"Very well, then," he said. "I will tell you. I have received word that my brother has bought the mines, and is probably there at this moment. Naturally, I have a wish to see him."

"Claro!" I said again, agreeing. But my belly bucketed to my boots. If his brother was the new owner — for the last I had heard Don Francisco Elguea was in possession — how popular would I be in such a place?

"By the way," he went on in a most conversational way, as if he were merely passing the time of day, "did I tell you of the new law that has been passed in Chihuahua? I meant to mention it on our way north."

I shook my head, wondering what he was driving at.

"They call it the 'Proyecto de la Guerra,'" he said blandly, "and all it really means is a war to the death against

58

all hostile Indians. The state will pay one hundred dollars for the scalp of every hostile male delivered to the authorities; fifty dollars for the scalp of a woman; and twenty-five dollars for that of every child."

I stared at him in horror, at the same time sensing the ripple of revulsion that ran through my companions.

"But that is barbarous!" I cried.

He shrugged, smiling broadly.

"It is the law," he said, "and they have had much the same thing in Sonora for years."

"But — but how is one to tell . . . ?" I protested.

He put down his coffee mug and rose. Behind him Johnson also rose, with a gleam in his eye and a speculative expression that made me wonder later if he had not heard all this before and already had some notion worked out to profit by it.

"Exactly!" said the "Coronel," and I thought he glanced significantly at my own scalp.

After all, since I am part Indian my hair is straight and black. I think no one could tell, if my face were not under it, whether it came from the head of a friendly brave or a hostile!

The skin of my skull crawled and tingled, and you may be sure, my friends, that I took good care of my hair from that point on.

# Chapter 5

$Y$ET to my astonishment and relief the days passed with little more ominous or untoward than this. Once, on the ridges west of the Ojo del Muerto, a considerable war party, well armed and mounted, obviously for the purpose of attacking us, appeared and kept pace with us, paralleling our route on the heights above, as we followed the trail that wound through the bottoms. They followed us for almost a full day, but in the end they apparently decided that we were too formidable a foe, and they withdrew. We never saw them again. Crossing the Rio Grande, near the hot springs of Las Palomas, several of our mules became bogged in the quicksands, but even these we were able to rescue without damage either to the animals or the gear they carried. Again, as we crossed over the Mimbres Mountains, passing close to Cuchillo Negro's village, we saw many signal smokes, indicating our approach and passing. But again we were not molested. Indeed, in all that dread passage, from the Rio Grande to Santa Rita, we saw not a single living thing.

Nevertheless, gentes, you may believe well that when I lay down in my blankets to sleep, I did so always with one eye open and one ear cocked to catch the slightest rustle of sound — and with a pistol under my saddle-pillow. But if they had intended anything that night, when they came to our campfire with their tales and talk, I gradually came to think that it was only to frighten me out of my wits.

As I believe I have shown, gentes, they did not succeed in this, and perhaps in consequence, late in the afternoon of one fine spring day, we passed in safety — all of us — through the notch at the side of the mountain called the Kneeling Nun, and dropped down along the chuckling creek to the basin below, where sprawled the little village and presidio of Santa Rita del Cobre.

Perhaps at this point a few words about this Santa Rita would not be out of the order.

Long years ago all of this country, from the Mogollons on the north to the Sierra de los Caballos on the east; from the country of the Chiricahuas on the west, down into Chihuahua on the south, was the land of the Mimbreños Apaches. The word "mimbres," in our language, means "willows," and the name of these Indians, therefore, might be freely translated "people of the willows." It is curious that they should have been given such a bucolic name, for much of the land was covered with pine and fir and cedar — evergreen forests — and only the creek bottoms were thick with willows. But perhaps, señores y señoras, it meant only that they were woods Indians — as distinct from desert Indians.

In any case, do not let the name deceive you. The word "Apache" in itself is Indian for "the enemy" — and the Mimbreños were Apaches, no different from any of the other tribes, the Chiricahuas, the Mescaleros, the Jicarillas, and a score of others. They were enemies of all men, except, curiously enough, the Pinda-lick-o-ye — the White Eyes — as they called the Yanquis, the men from the north. All others they preyed upon and hated — the Pueblos, the Pimas, the Zuñi — which are properly, so I am told, a branch of the Pueblos, the Tarahumares, the Comanches, even the Navajos until the time came when it was needful to recognize that they, too, were Apaches!

Needless to say there were a host of other, lesser tribes who felt their hostility. From all of these they stole — women and horses and food, for to steal, in the Apache code, was an honorable thing; and the most accomplished thief was like to be the chief man among them. Their raids were constant and uncounted. But most of all they hated and despised the Spaniard — and after him the Mexican; and it was against them, into Chihuahua and Sonora, that the greatest number of their raids were directed.

This, as I say, was all many, many years ago. There came a change — indeed, several changes, and it is on one of these that this story hangs!

In the heart of the country of the Mimbres Apaches there was a sacred place — the council rocks at Santa Rita. For as long as the oldest padre could remember it had been suspected that these rocks covered a fabulously rich deposit of copper — which is not as fine as gold or silver, but which makes pennies. Many men tried to reach the rocks, but all were caught and killed — killed in the ways that the Apache knew best; staked out, with legs and arms spread, in the beating sun, and perhaps a small fire kindled on their stomachs, or, others, bound and hung head down above a slow fire — not so close that their hair would singe and the sizzling fat of their scalps would catch fire and kill them quickly, but just high enough so that the heat of the coals beneath would eventually reach their brains and crack their skulls! The art was not a lost one, even when I was young.

How the Coronel Manuel Carrisco, who was the military comandante of all of the district of northern Chihuahua and New Mexico under Spain, managed to reach the rocks is not known. Certainly, in the light of later events, it was not with the knowledge or consent of the Mimbreños. In some way, however, he did, for he returned with ore samples which more than confirmed the wildest rumors that had been spread. He obtained a grant from the King, allowing him to work the mines and sell the ore to the royal mint, in Mexico City.

But the Mimbreños knew nothing of this king. They would not permit the Coronel, or any of his people, even to approach. This was in the year 1804.

The Coronel, and his heirs after him, made every effort to work the deposits, but without success, and at last, in 1822, they jumped at the chance to sell their royal charter and unload the disappointing deposits on Don Francisco Elgeua, of Chihuahua, whom I believe I have mentioned. Sí, por cierto! It may be that there were other reasons behind the transfer, for this was the year of Mexican independence, and Don Francisco was a Mexican, while the Coronel Don Manuel was a Spaniard! But whatever the reason, in that year the change was made.

Now, señores y señoras, one might think that Don Francisco Elguea, of Chihuahua, would have no better luck than Coronel Don Manuel Carrisco, of Spain, in persuading the Indians to permit him to enter the sacred council rocks and carry away the ore. But this is to reckon without several factors!

In the first place, Don Francisco was a very different man from Don Manuel. He was a Chihuahuan born, and no Spaniard. He knew Indians and how best to deal with them. Probably, too, he was no more scrupulous in those dealings than was necessary. In the second place, there were different conditions among the Indians themselves. Twenty years before the chief of the Mimbres, Juan José, had been in the prime of life. He loved the excitements of war and the raiding trail. He could ride with the youngest and best of his warriors; stay longer in the saddle, go farther without food or drink, run for hours through the arid desert without stopping, take to himself as many scalps and ponies and women as any.

But now Juan José was aging — and with the eyes of age, perhaps, he recognized the inevitable coming of the white men — both Mexicans and Yanquis. He was tired of fighting against something he could not stop, and he longed for peace. He had others on the tribal council — subchiefs, who did not agree with him. Cuchillo Negro, with the long, bandy legs and short body and wizened, puckered-up face, so that he looked like some sort of an evil spider, was one — probably the most outspoken. Another was Mangas Colorado — Red Sleeves — an enormous man, even among big people, but a veritable giant among the Apaches, who incline to be short and wiry. Mangas stood nearly seven feet in his moccasins. His arms were long, reaching almost to his knees, his hands enormous in proportion to the rest of him. His body was big and square, like a hogshead with corners, and his legs were short and gnarled, and thick as the trunk of a piñon. His head, it is said, was large enough to fill a whiskey cask when he was finally killed, and having seen the man alive I can well believe it.

Yet Mangas was far from stupid. He was, I think — for what my small opinion may be worth — the most intelligent and far-seeing of Juan José's chiefs. This was before the days of his fame — or his infamy, as you prefer. Yet even then he had the foresight to recognize what even Juan José could see but vaguely; that one day, inevitably, the white man would outnumber the Indian by ten, a hundred — even a thousand. With Juan José he agreed that peace was to be preferred. But not for the same reasons. To his way of thinking a conqueror with overwhelmingly superior force was to be met with peaceful dignity. So long as whites and Indians could live together, respecting one another's pride, the land was large enough for all — though it might shrink a little for each man. But when a man's pride is trampled upon — be he red or white or blue or green! — he must fight back; he must fight for himself, even though he knows he cannot win!

That was Mangas Colorado. Even after the events of this story, after the heat of his first fury passed, he sought friendship. But senseless, thoughtless men would not accept. There were other incidents, not to be described here, until the last — his savage flogging with a bullwhip by a party of drunken miners, bound for the gold fields of California; and that only because he offered to lead them into Chihuahua and show them where they might find gold in fabulous quantities!

From that day he was the implacable enemy of all whites — Yanquis, Mexicans, or any who might come. And do you know his end, señores y señoras? Ciertamente, a price was put upon his head, and in the course of time — it is only a matter of four or five years ago — he was lured into the Yanqui camp by promises of a treaty. Yet when he came he was seized and bound, and it is quoted of the commanding officer, when he saw his prisoner, that he said: "I want him dead!"

He turned and walked away without looking back, but his soldiers could take a hint. One of them began quietly to heat his bayonet in the coals of the campfire. When it turned red and then white he plucked it out suddenly and thrust it into Mangas's leg. Would you leap up, señores? So did Mangas Colorado. And as he did so a dozen rifles cracked!

So he died! But that is not the end. The official report said that he was shot "while trying to escape." It does not explain why the head was cut off and carried into headquarters in a whiskey cask! Perhaps that, too, was "trying to escape!"

Ay, hombres! You think all this beside the point? Perhaps! But the reason why I tell it is to show that it was not only the Indian who was the savage. There have been others, who ought to have known better, who have fanned his anger and given it food to feed upon. After this, I think, it will be long before we know peace with the Apaches!

But enough! Forgive me, gentes, if I seem to have strayed. Let us return to Don Francisco Elguea and his newly acquired possessions at Santa Rita del Cobre.

The day came — in the year 1822, as white men count — when a vast conducta of mules and men appeared far to the southward of Santa Rita, upon the Antelope Plains. The scouts and watchers from the village could plainly see, and the smokes so signaled, that the mules were heavily laden, and the young men of the village began to gird themselves for a raid.

At the same time, however, it was evident that the conducta was heavily guarded. Indeed, it was formidable, and Juan José bade his warriors hold their peace for the time being and wait and see what this was all about.

To everyone's surprise the conducta made no attempt to approach the village — although it was in plain sight from the point where they stopped and camped, well below on the plain. Not until the strangers' camp had been made did three riders from among them approach the Indian stronghold, unarmed and bearing their right hands above their heads in sign of peace. They brought word that Don Francisco Elguea himself had come to parley with them, and that he was even then preparing a feast for the chiefs of the Mimbreños. He hoped that they would honor him with their presence.

Not to dwell in too much detail upon what followed, señores, many of the chiefs and most of the warriors objected. But Juan José overrode their protests and insisted that the subchiefs accompany him in accepting Don Francisco's invitation. So Don Francisco obtained his first object!

Once they were assembled, and the pipe had been carefully passed, Don Francisco gave to each chief a small cask of aguardiente and a large sack of socorro — which is the ground meal of the Indian corn, the principal article of food apart from game in that part of the country; a gift equivalent to an entire sheep or a half a beef — plus a barrel of flour. These he told them to take back to their families. Nor would he permit them to open the casks on the spot. There was plenty more, he said, for hospitality, in his own stock. And this he proceeded to demonstrate.

He offered them first aguardiente in generous quantity. After that he feasted them until they were fair on to bursting, and had scarcely enough energy to lick their own greasy fingers. While they ate he served them with wines which were strange in flavor and of a kind that they had never tasted before, but which were delicious. And so that they might not feel ill at ease he also set before them their own more familiar pulque and mescal. When the eating was done there was more smoking and more aguardiente, until at last they were all so comfortable and surfeited that they yawned for sleep and their blankets, and were ready to listen to anything for the sake of a few hours of peace.

Then — and not until then — did Don Francisco tell them the true purpose of his visit.

"My brothers!" he said. "It has long been known that here, at Santa Rita, amid your council rocks, there is a great store of the metal which we call copper. I need not tell you this, for you have long been troubled by men who sought to take away that metal with neither your permission nor gain for you."

The chiefs all nodded solemnly and refilled their mugs.

"I have talked with these men," Don Francisco went on, "and paid them not to try to come back here again, so that they will not trouble you further."

Juan José nodded gravely.

"We thank you, brother," he said. "But why have you done this?"

68

Don Francisco smiled.

"Naturally," he replied, "I did not do it out of simple charity. I will be truthful with you, my brothers — not lying, like those others. I do not speak with the forked tongue! I did it because I, too, would like to dig in your rocks and take away the copper."

The chiefs looked startled at this frankness. Cuchillo Negro scowled.

"Then we have only exchanged one robber for another!" he growled.

But Don Francisco held up his hand.

"Not at all!" he replied. "They would have taken your copper, if they could, without your consent and given you nothing in return. I, on the other hand, come to you with a treaty of friendship in my pocket, to ask you to allow me to dig among your rocks and to take away the metal to Chihuahua, where it will be melted and made into money to be used to buy food and clothes and blankets and horses and sheep and cattle and aguardiente. You see, brothers, the copper does no one any good here in the ground. But if you will allow me to take it away it will have many uses. And for this I am willing to pay!"

"No!" cried Cuchillo Negro. "The Gods will be angry!"

Mangas Colorado shifted uneasily. But Juan José pretended he had not heard.

"How will you pay, brother?" he asked. "We have no use for your money."

"I will pay you in things that money will buy," Don Francisco replied promptly, "in all those things I have just spoken of — and others besides."

There is no need here, señores, to go into detail of the

long-drawn out negotiations that followed. Cuchillo Negro was steadfastly against it from the beginning. Indeed, so bitterly was he opposed to any concession to the Mexican that in the end he angrily withdrew from the tribal council and, with some three hundred others of the band, who agreed with him, removed to the Warm Springs of the Gila — as I believe I have already mentioned.

Juan José, however, was in favor of the plan. After all, he argued, Don Francisco was right. The metal did no one any good so long as it was underground, and if they permitted the Mexicans to remove it they would be paid for it with things which they could only obtain now through raiding and warfare and hardship and deadly danger. Let it be remembered, he pointed out shrewdly, that they would not be required to dig in the mines. That would be up to the miners, whom the Mexicans would import. All that would be necessary for the Indians would be to sit on their blankets all day long, drinking mescal and playing games and counting their wealth as it poured in! What other tribe, he asked, could boast such luxury?

Of a certainty, there were a number of conditions. After all Juan José had to maintain his dignity and prestige among his own people! Only so many miners would be allowed in Santa Rita at a time. These men might bring their families, and there might be an alcalde to represent the government; a manager to represent Don Francisco. The Mexicans would be permitted to build a small presidio, but the garrison must at no time exceed thirty men and the comandante. They would be permitted to build a church, but only one padre would be allowed. These, and no more, could be at the copper mines, with the single exception of those times when the thrice monthly conductas, or supply trains, from the south arrived. Such might come twice each month from Chihuahua — bearing supplies — and the stipulated tribute for the Indians — and once a month, when necessary, from Sonora. There was to be no approach from any other direction, as I have already said, and any miners or officials who left the village for the outside must accompany one of the returning conductas when it went southward with the produce of the mines. Further, it was written into the treaty, the inhabitants of the village would be permitted to hunt only within a radius of five leagues.

To all of this Don Francisco agreed quite cheerfully, knowing full well that the important thing at that point was to obtain the treaty. Once that was done, and the mines were opened, most if not all of these stringent regulations would be relaxed or entirely forgotten.

In the meantime he was willing to wait!

Now, it must be remembered, señores, that all of this was in the year 1822 — fifteen years before our arrival. During that time miners came and miners went, and three times each month the conductas arrived so regularly and on schedule that it was said the padres could set their clock by them. They brought with them supplies for the village and the mines, for the miners were far too busy digging in the rocks to do much hunting or to plant vegetable gardens. They also brought trade goods — and, regularly, three times a month they brought the "present" for the Indians; a present, at first, of horses and blankets and socorro and mescal and aguardiente, in that order, but as the years passed it tended to be less and less horses and blankets and socorro and more and more mescal and aguardiente, for that was one of the blessings of civilization of which the Indians could not get enough.

Indeed, all worked out almost exactly as Don Francisco had foreseen. The stringent stipulations of the treaty were gradually eased and ultimately all but forgotten. Thus it happened that when the conductas came, more often than not, they also brought with them more miners and their families to swell the growing population — as well as a good many women who were no better than they should have been, to serve the wants of those miners who were not married or who preferred to spice their lives with a dash of variety. The original treaty had limited the size of the place to three hundred persons. By 1837, the year in which we came, there were more than six hundred, and it was still growing. There were four padres in the little church — which they called the cathedral — by now. There was a full company of fifty soldados in garrison at the cuartel beside the presidio, commanded by a capitán-comandante with a teniente under him. There were four or five cantinas, where drunken Indians lay in rows against the sunlit walls, every day and all day, moving only as the sun moved and brought them into the shade. There were two or three fondas, and an uncounted number of whorehouses.

And what, you ask, were the Indians doing all this while?

Señores, excuse me, but it is my poor opinion that only one of the lot either saw or cared what was happening. That one was Mangas Colorado. He remembered the great council with Don Francisco; and he remembered the treaty. He could see how openly it was being flaunted; and seeing it made him sullen and uneasy, watchful and silent, so that he earned the name of proud and surly among the villagers.

He would have joined Cuchillo Negro long before our coming, but Juan José was his chief, and in his curious way he felt that so long as Juan José lived his first loyalty lay there — even though, by now, as often as not, Juan José, who was growing old and fat and all but senile, spent his days and nights in a drunken stupor.

For the rest — gentes! — here was the world's best bargain! Everything had happened just as Juan José had said it would! There was nothing for the Indios to do; nothing, that is, except to lie around in the sun and gamble and procreate — preferably with a Mexican woman — and relieve themselves when nature demanded and get as drunk as possible on Conducta Day — and beg as many drinks as they might in between! They did not even bother to go hunting any more. Why should they when begging was so much easier? Poh! They would not go back to their old way of life for a carretaful of the best aguardiente — no, not even for twice that amount!

Why, for a small flask of mescal there were few in the Indian village, above the town, who would not sell their souls — let alone their bodies; and often a single drink would do. As for the men, they were seldom refused when they wheedled, and some, who were especially stalwart and handsome in their Apache way, were able to profit alcoholically from the Mexican women, as were their sisters from the men!

Que lástima! What a pity! I say it, not, señores, because I have myself Indian blood in my veins, but because I hate to see any peoples do to one another what was happening there in the guise of friendship. If the Mexicans debauched the Indians, so, in their way, did the Indians pollute the

73

newcomers! A whole new race of fatherless, motherless brats came into being — "half Mexican, half Indian, and whole son-of-a-bitch!" one Yanqui put it, and if it is not inevitably true, or even the rule, it was surely so in this case!

In the beginning, the first miners and their families regarded the Indians with a certain awe and respect. But as they discovered the red man's failing they became first amused, and then condescending and finally disgusted. What had once seemed funny to them became a nuisance to bear patiently. They forgot that they had started it all. If they had not first given Juan José and his people as much drink as they could hold, the Indians would not now be under their feet, begging and demanding and brimming with indigent insolence.

At the same time, although they were hardly aware of it, just as the Indians absorbed all of the vices of the white men, so did the Mexicans begin to take on some of the characteristics of the Apaches. They became cruel and heartless and crafty, and thievery became the Alcalde's greatest problem.

But enough of this! I believe I have said plenty to give you a notion of the place and the conditions that obtained there. I will not overburden you with a redundancy of details! This, señores, was that Santa Rita into which we rode that late spring afternoon.

Now let us get on with our tale!

# Chapter 6

$A$S WE DRIFTED down the flank of the Kneeling Nun I was conscious of that twinge of slight disappointment that I always felt when I came back to Santa Rita after a long stay away. It was as if I had half expected it to change while I was gone; to take a tuck in its belly and spruce up — at least, to wash its face and hands, one might say. But Santa Rita never changed except, perhaps, to become a little larger and more crowded and dirtier.

It was always a source of considerable wonder to me that with all the space at their command, theirs for the taking if they wanted it, men should huddle together in such squalor as they did at Santa Rita. And huddled is the word, señores. The houses — hovels is a better description — clustered all together in an aimless sort of a knot, a warren of blind alleys and littered pathways, foul with trash and garbage, through which goats browsed and cats hunted, rats scurried and children played and a thousand mangy, mongrel dogs fought and howled and yammered continuously. The mines which were the sole excuse for the existence of the place were located a little above the village, between the thighs, so to speak, of the Nun, and the little town itself huddled higgledy-piggledy about a long, wide, dusty plaza, which was, to my way of thinking, the only truly bearable, livable part. This took the form of a rough rectangle, some fifty by a hundred and fifty yards. Perhaps this was why I liked it, for it was the only spacious thing about the place!

This plaza stretched more or less from the northwest to the southeast, so that the buildings along the northeastern side — the Palacio del Gobierno, the cuartel and the tiny presidio — looked out over the roofs of the huddled hovels, between the squat belfries of the tiny "cathedral," to the shimmering expanse of the Antelope Plains, stretching away to the southwest. At the southeastern end was a structure of poles, thatched with brush, and usually at night enclosed with brush mats. This was the mercado — the market — and it is well to remember, señores, exactly where it stood. As I have suggested, the little cathedral stood on the southwestern side of the plaza, facing the palacio and the presidio, and in between, around the church side and the northwestern end, were clustered the two fondas and several cantinas, and curiously enough, clustered close by the church itself, a number of the town's brothels! It was almost as if the prostitutes expected holy sanction for their trade by such a closeness; and perhaps they did, señores! Who am I to say? At that age I scarcely knew how to ask, and if I had I would have been embarrassed! Now I am an honorably married man and a member of the territorial legislature. I am not supposed to mention such things.

Be all that as it may, señores, we made a brave showing as we rode into the squalid little village, and I confess that at that moment such thoughts were farthest from my mind. I had not said so to my companions, but one thing had been nagging at my mind, worryingly, for several days. This was the problem of the disposition of our various groups. To expect any one, or even all, of the fondas to accommodate so many was out of the question. I preferred to make camp *above* the town a little distance — for God alone knew what refuse went into the creek that flowed through the lower part of the village, and it had always been my experience that it was wise to camp on the upstream side of any settlement. Do not ask me why.

However, I did not want to pitch camp in the same place as Johnson and Eames and Gleason and the "Coronel." Technically I was finished with them. I had guided them to Santa Rita, and there I could wash my hands of them, and I wanted nothing better. On the other hand I had agreed to put Don Ben Wilson and Don Charley Kemp on the Gila, and to that extent I was still under obligation to them. At the same time it was customary, upon entering or approaching a town where it was proposed to camp, to pay respects to the local alcalde and inquire if he had any particular preferences as to campsite. Accordingly I held my tongue and rode in silence through the little level glade, about a half a mile above the mines. Perhaps a quarter of a mile below the mines we came upon the first scattered hovels of the village, and within a moment thereafter we had entered the Calle de Santa Fe, by which the alley along which we approached was called. This wound for some two or three hundred yards, dropping in sharp loops and turns down from the shoulder of the Nun's knee, with the houses all the way hunching closer and closer to one another, and the stench growing more and more overpowering, until all at once we burst in at the northeastern corner of the plaza, right beside the Palacio del Gobierno.

77

I had thought the narrow, winding lane that led down from the hills behind had seemed singularly deserted, and as soon as we entered the plaza the reason became apparent. Everyone in the village, it seemed to me, must be packed into the square, and we were forced to work our way around to the right, behind the crowd, almost to the steps of the cathedral before we were able to turn again and force our way through to the verandah of the "Palace."

"Hey, now!" Don Jode reined up his horse as we broke into the square. "Big doin's! What's up, Currito?"

"It's sure some kind of a do," Don Yancey agreed. "What is it, young'un, one o' them Saints' days?"

I was surprised myself. So far as I knew — and I thought I knew them all — there was no day in the calendar that called for such a celebration. Still, I could be wrong.

"I don't know," I replied. "But I will find out."

I looked around and saw a girl leaning in the doorway of one of the hutches that ringed the plaza, standing between the fondas and cantinas and the church and the other public places.

I think, señores, in any case I would have ridden up and asked her the occasion of all this excitement. But in this case I was doubly pleased that I had looked first and acted after, for this was such a thing as I had not before seen!

Of a truth, señores, I have been often in Santa Rita — yet never before had I seen her, or anything like her. She was no taller than I — indeed, she was an inch or two shorter. Her feet were bare and plain for everyone to see, but small and of exquisite form, as were her legs, up to the middle of her calves, beyond which place her bright, full multicolored skirt covered them. Still, one could guess! And, surely, such

78

legs as those could not grow fat or ugly above; not without being deformed, and there was no indication of any such about the rest of her. Her hips were sufficient to give fullness to the many-colored skirt that she wore, and her waist was slim enough even for my small hands to fit around. Above that she wore a huipil — a, how is it we say, shirtwaist — some call it a blouse, but this is not exact. In any case, it was a sort of shapeless waist, white decorated in green and red, with a little of cheap lace about the top, but very loose, lying low upon her shoulders and arms, and hinting surely at the strong young breasts that lay unhampered beneath.

She stood in the door, with one arm upraised against the jamb, and the back of her hand resting upon her forehead, so that one young breast was more lifted and emphasized than the other; and by only so much, I think, any man would be surely enchanted. But there was more, as I discovered as I swung down from my horse before her. Her mouth was small and red and shaped as if always poised for a kiss; and her eyes were large and dark and a little troubled. Her nose was small but straight, and her cheeks were olive dark with the tint of roses on them.

I think I startled her as I slid down from my saddle before her, for she blinked, and drew her eyes from the milling crowd in the plaza with an effort.

I pulled off my hat with a flourish and bowed — just low enough.

"Chica!" I cried. "You are new here?"

She looked at me coldly — yet, I could see, not without interest.

"I have been here since I was born," she replied.

79

"You must have been hiding, Paquita — Maruca — Tónica!" I exclaimed. "I have been here often, but I have not seen you! If I had . . . !"

"My name is Pepita — Josefa María de las Dolores Perez — and if you had been looking I think you would have seen me before now. My age is seventeen, and I was born here in Santa Rita. What is it you wish, señor?"

"Pardon, señorita!" I exclaimed, you may believe it, well bewildered by my own bewilderment. As a rule I was not thus flustered. "I sought only information. But now that I see you — Caray . . . !"

She gave her hips a sort of a whip and lifted her head sharply, at the same time giving me a look that was both icy and inviting.

"You wish, señor?" she demanded.

"But certainly I wish — Pepita! Is that the name?"

I felt that I was progressing well — and that certainly with the best that I had yet seen in Santa Rita. But a voice interrupted me.

"Introduce me!"

I spun about and saw that Señor Don Jode had dismounted behind me, and stood there grinning expectantly. Behind him Don Yancey still remained mounted. But there was no question of the girl's interest. Already she had forgotten me, and was eying them speculatively.

I felt a flicker of irritation, curiously directed as much at Don Yancey as at Don Jode, for it was at him that she looked the longest and with the most evident admiration. Madre de Dios! I thought to myself, are these my friends or enemies that they can leave me nothing for myself? Still, I could scarcely ignore them now. I made the introductions

80

somewhat coolly, and I think that Don Yancey, at least, had the sensitivity to see that I was displeased. But that Jode — Pouf! He was never a one to see what he did not wish to see! He swept off his hat and gave her a low bow.

"I kiss your feet, Señorita Pepita!" he grinned, and his dark eyes sparkled and his teeth flashed in his sun-tanned face.

I saw her hide one foot almost shyly behind the other, as if she were afraid that he might do so literally, and I made haste to intervene before he could walk off with my prize from under my very nose.

"And now, señorita," I said, "that I have presented my friends, perhaps I should introduce myself, no? I am Currito Ruiz, and I was about to ask you why all the excitement?"

Apparently I could not have chosen a better way to attract her attention, for she turned a look of surprise upon me.

"Eh, excitement?" she replied. "You do not know? Are you not of the conducta, then?"

I shook my head. So that was it! Of course, I knew that Conducta Day was always a great occasion in Santa Rita, though it seemed to me that there was considerably more to-do than usual today.

"No, Pepita," I told her, "we have just come from the north — from Santa Fe. But I am astonished at all this fuss over the conducta. Is it usual?"

"No, señor," she smiled — and I felt suddenly gay and happy, as if the sun had all at once burst through a bank of lowering clouds — "it is not usual. But, then, neither is it the usual conducta. This time there is a difference."

"So?" I managed to blurt. "What difference?"

81

"This time, señor," she replied, "it brings with it the new owner of the mines and his family, in a magnificent carriage, all the way from Chihuahua. Surely, this is a great thing!"

"The new owner!" I exclaimed, suddenly remembering.

"And his family," she reminded me. "Three fine ladies — his wife and daughter and his sister, his daughter's dueña!"

That was indeed something out of the ordinary, but I was by far too concerned with my own startling recollection to think of that just then.

"The new owner!" I cried again. "Tell me, Pepita! His name! What is his name?"

She looked at me as if I had gone mad.

"Por qué no?" she replied. "It is the señor Don Urbano Hermoso y Maravilla, of Mexico City. Why?"

"Hermoso y Maravilla!" I exclaimed, too startled to heed her question.

I stared around at my two companions incredulously.

"Looks like he wasn't lyin'!" Don Yancey grinned dryly.

I glanced away across the plaza, toward the palacio, and saw that the column of our party had swung and turned in directly toward the wide, shaded verandah that fronted the long building. What was more, I noticed, when we three had dropped from the line the one who had ridden ahead to take the lead was no other than the "Coronel" Raoul Hermoso y Maravilla. It was perfectly evident to all of us that he intended to make himself — at least in his brother's eyes — the head of the whole party!

Don Yancey swung his horse sharply, while Jode scrambled into the saddle.

"Come on!" he called.

I scarcely needed to be urged, but there was one thing I intended to do first. I swung quickly toward the girl, and before she could realize what I was about, caught her in my arms and kissed her soundly, squarely on the lips. To my surprise and, I might add, my great delight, she did not resist, but on the contrary responded with unexpected fervor.

"Thank you, my chiquita Pepita!" I gasped. "We must go now, but I will come to see you later, this evening, eh?"

Her fingers brushed my cheek.

"But, sí!" she replied. "Tonight there will be the grand fiesta in honor of the new owner and his ladies. There will surely be the big baile — the great dance and fandango — here in the plaza. You will come, Currito mio, and dance with me?"

"Of course, Pepita!" I cried, overjoyed.

"And you will bring the tall ones?" she wheedled.

Little witch! So that was what she had been about all the time!

"As you wish!" I replied shortly. "Adiós amiga — hasta la noche!"

I mounted, spinning my horse as I did so toward the palacio, but even as the animal whirled I saw, out of the corner of my eye, the enormous, jut-jawed, hawk-nosed Indian who stood in the shadow of the portico at the top of the cathedral steps. He had been watching us, and the way he looked at me I did not like. I did not turn my head as I rode across the square, but all the way across it seemed to me that I could feel the venom in his little black eyes boring into my back.

To the devil with him, I thought. He doesn't own the

wench, and if he's jealous of me, wait until he lays eyes on Jode and Yancey dancing with her!

The others were already arrived at the palace verandah by the time I reached the steps, and back in the shadows I could see that some sort of presentation was going forward. As the guide and nominal leader of the party, it was properly my place to present the respects of all to the Alcalde, and brother or no brother, I did not intend to be done out of this much of my right by Don Raoul. I slipped from my horse and handed the reins to Charley Kemp, who stood nearby.

"You ain't goin' up there?" he whispered aghast.

"Seguro — certainly!" I assured him. "Why not?"

"All them bigwigs!" he replied.

"Anda!" I scoffed. "I notice that Don Jode and Don Yancey were not backward about it!"

In the shadows of the verandah I could see the two tall figures bowing politely. I could also see the "Coronel" Don Raoul and Johnson, and a number of others whom I could not make out, for the glare of the sun upon the dust of the plaza made the shade of the verandah almost as deep as night.

I turned and hastened up the steps, and as I came into the shadow my eyes quickly became accustomed to the comparative gloom which was not as black as it had appeared from below. There were two almost distinct groups, I saw, standing a little distance apart. In one I noticed three ladies, and the two tall Tennesseeans, and I grinned to myself. Trust them, I thought, to find out the women first crack out of the box! In the other group I recognized the Alcalde, Don Emilio Bustamente, whom I had met on previous occasions, the Capitán-Comandante, Don Tito Morales, Henry Johnson and Joe Gleason. There were also two strangers. One, who was short and stout and young, like a small tub of lard, was an officer. I took him to be the teniente currently on duty at Santa Rita. The other was something else again. He was a tall man, almost as tall as Jode or Yancey, but much older, for I could see that his hair was graying and his mustachios were quite grizzled. He was dressed entirely in white — white Mexican trousers, tight at the top, a white buckskin vaquero's jacket, white hat with a broad brim, a great cascade of ruffles down his shirt front and white lace at his cuffs; and all of this, señores, of the finest, both as to material and cut. All in all, he was a handsome and rather dashing figure, yet he carried himself erectly and with much dignity.

Between the two groups, smirking and smiling and preening himself, as if he had just come into great wealth, stood the "Coronel" Raoul Hermoso y Maravilla. Since it was my duty to present myself first to the Alcalde and the Capitán-Comandante, it was toward them that I turned first. At sight of me the pompous little Alcalde, who seemed somewhat overwhelmed by all of this sudden descent from all directions, brightened and passed his hand across his shiny bald head with its three long strands of hair. Mine, at least, was a familiar face.

"Aha! Currito! Bienvenido — welcome!" he cried, and pumped my hand. "I wondered who it was that brought us all this great crowd of gringos!"

"You may blame me, Don Emilio," I laughed. "Although they are not all of the same party we have traveled together for safety's sake."

85

"Qué? What do you say — different parties?" Don Emilio appeared disturbed, and I could understand, for it would mean that we would probably camp in different places, which would make it more difficult for him to keep watch on us.

But there was nothing I could do about that. I nodded.

"Just so, Don Emilio," I assured him. "Señor Johnson, here, heads one group — about half our number — and Señor Don Ben — where is Don Ben?"

I looked around, but Ben Wilson, shy and self-effacing, had slipped away and lost himself in the crowd. Nor could I even see Charley Kemp, who seemed to have faded back and lost himself in the crowd. I laughed.

"I do not see him," I said. "Ah, well, my friends yonder, talking with the ladies — Don Jode and Don Yancey — and myself will have to serve for the present — we represent the original group. And then, of course, the "Coronel" Don Raoul, and his friends —"

" 'Coronel'?" The tall man in white raised one fine, grizzled eyebrow and cocked it in the direction of the obviously discomfited Raoul Hermoso y Maravilla. "You have come up in the world since we saw you last, Raoul! When were you ever a 'Coronel'?"

Don Raoul glowered furiously at me, his face pink with anger and embarrassment.

"Caray! Don't blame me," I said. "It is the only way I have ever known you, señor, and you will recall that you presented yourself to me in El Paso del Norte as such!"

The tall man chuckled dryly. Already it was clear that there was little love lost between them.

"Válgame Dios!" he exclaimed. "Your man appears to

know how to use his weapons, Raoul! I daresay you've crossed swords before, eh?"

He turned toward me.

"Your pardon, señor!" he said. "Allow me to present myself. I am the señor Don Urbano Hermoso y Maravilla, your — er — 'Coronel's' elder brother."

He did not say "unfortunately," but it seemed to me he might as well have done so. For the second time in as many minutes I felt the coolness, if not downright hostility that existed between these two, and it occurred to me to wonder, señores, why this Raoul had been in such a lather to get to Santa Rita.

But this was scarcely a topic of small talk! I shook hands with Don Urbano — cordially, for I could find it in my heart to like any man who was at odds with Don Raoul.

"And the new owner here, as well, so I am told, señor," I said.

"I had hoped there might be one man in the world who did not know it yet!" he chuckled ruefully, then studied me soberly. "You are Spanish?" he asked.

I looked him straight in the eye.

"I am of Spanish descent, señor," I replied. "Also of French, Indian, Mexican, English — and I daresay a dash of gringo as well."

Perhaps I should explain at this point, having used it twice, that at that time there was not yet any meaning of contempt to be read into the word 'gringo.' It was simply a slang word designating our Yanqui neighbors, and intended no disrespect. That only became attached to it later.

Behind me a girl's voice spoke clearly.

"Caramba! Papa, he is even more mixed up than we are!"

I turned — and gulped. In acknowledging Don Urbano's self-introduction I had somehow managed to get my back toward the other group, and they seeing me in conversation with the tall man had drifted over. Possibly Don Yancey or Don Jode had offered to present me, though that is something that I never discovered. I doubt if I would have heard them if they did, so stunned was I, for what I saw before me was as astonishing in that wild, rough place as if all the rocky hills and all the stony desert plains below had suddenly become carpeted with wild flowers.

I do not refer to the two older women with whom I found myself face to face, although, of a surety, their presence there was almost as extraordinary. What caused me to gasp and stammer — and, I fear, turn brick red — was the girl.

She was fairly tall — taller than I, alas — standing perhaps five feet seven or eight in her traveling slippers. Yet even through the heavy stuff of the gown she had obviously worn for the trail it was plainly apparent that there was nothing disproportionate about her figure, though neither had she any need for stays! But this was only a part, and a small part, of her incredible beauty. Her hair was a deep, dark, coppery red, with little lights of gold dancing through it; little lights that seemed to be reflected in the tawny-green depths of her eyes. Her face was oval, almost heart-shaped, but a shade fuller in the chin, which showed a surprising strength of character in one so dainty and so young. Her brows were finely drawn, but not so much so as to seem artificial, and her complexion was a sort of rich cameo-cream delicately flushed with roses; her lips were full, but not too full, deep red and gently curved to easy

88

laughter. Just at the moment they were slightly, almost breathlessly parted in a smile of lively interest.

I forgot Juanita! I forgot Chucha! Ay, por Dios, for a moment I even forgot the luscious, earthy little bundle of life across the plaza, Pepita! For the space of a half a dozen breaths I even dared to hope that her smile was meant for me alone. But then I realized that it was quite impersonal. It meant only that she was interested in everyone and everything around her.

In the meantime Don Urbano leaped forward.

"Diantre!" he cried. "The journey has taken my wits! A thousand pardons, my dear! This is my daughter, Doña María de la Luz Hermoso y Clark, Señor —— ?"

He broke off. Already he had forgotten my name! But his oversight served to arouse me to life once more. I started.

"Eh?" I blinked. "Oh, my name is José Herrero Alfonso Francisco Pereda Galindo y Ruiz — but everyone calls me Currito!"

"My! I should think so, with all that!" she replied, but the way she smiled when she said it took out any sting that may have been in it, and she added matter-of-factly, "I can sympathize with you, Currito, for no one wants to say 'María de la Luz' every time they speak to me. I am called 'Lucita,' or more often simply 'Luz.' "

"I throw myself at your feet, Doña Luz!" I managed to stammer the trite acknowledgment, but there was nothing of derision in her grave smile or still graver and equally formal reply.

"Beso a usted la mano, Currito — I kiss your hand, Currito!"

In the background Don Urbano coughed discreetly, and I realized abruptly that he was trying to catch my attention in order to present the other two ladies. Don Jode and Don Yancey were grinning like a pair of mountain bobcats, and I could have kicked their shins.

It is far easier, señores, to describe those other two. They were old, quite old. Indeed, they were both old enough to be my mother and have a little bit to spare.

The first to whom Don Urbano presented me was taller than Doña Luz, and of excellent figure despite the fact that she must have been over forty. Like Doña Luz her eyes were a tawny green, and it was easy to see the relationship between them, though her hair was much lighter, being more of a straw-gold.

"This is my wife, Currito," he smiled. "I hope you will forgive me — I cannot say all that! Doña Elena Luisa Clark de Hermoso. My dear, this is Currito, who has just come down from Santa Fe, with Raoul and a party of Yanquis."

I bowed as well as I knew how, and tried to put my best foot forward. I began to understand, now, the unusual coloring, for the Spanish way of adding surnames rather than dropping one told me much. I gathered, for instance, that Doña Elena's maiden name had been Clark, and from this I surmised that she herself was probably originally a Yanqui, though of a surety I could not express my curiosity at that moment.

The other lady proved to be less interesting. She, too, was fairly tall, but she was spare and dressed all in black — a mode that seemed to emphasize her own darkness. Indeed, I would almost say that she was ugly, for she had a thin mouth and a scattering of hairs on her upper lip and her hair grew low on her forehead. I thought I detected a resemblance in her to Don Raoul, and surely enough I was right, for she proved to be the Doña Beatriz de Hermoso, Don Urbano's sister and dueña to Doña Luz, and therefore sister also to Raoul.

I could not help thinking, as I bowed to her, that of a certainty Don Urbano had been blessed with all the good looks in their family!

I would have given much, just then, to remain in the shade of the wide verandah and just bask in the presence of Doña Luz, but no sooner had Don Urbano finished his introductions than the Capitán-Comandante jerked pompously at his splendid tunic and harrumphed loudly, twirling his mustachios in his most official manner.

"Humph, harraw! Well, well, señores!" he bumbled. "All of this has been most interesting, most interesting, indeed! It is not often that we are visited by a conducta and a party from the north, both in the same day; and it is even rarer that we are honored with the presence of the owner and his family — indeed, I cannot remember that it has ever happened before! However, I daresay that Don Urbano and the ladies will wish to rest and refresh themselves after their long journey, and as for you other gentes, I am sure you have your camps to make — eh? If there is any way that I can help you, do not hesitate to ask."

In the face of such a hint what could we do? We said our farewells unhappily and moved toward the steps, while the Doña Beatriz began herding Doña Luz toward the door.

"Momento, señores!" called out the Alcalde impulsively, I daresay trying in a measure to offset the brusqueness of the Capitán-Comandante. "Un momento! This evening

91

there will be a grand fiesta and baile here in the plaza, in honor of our distinguished guests. I hope that you will all come, señores. You will be welcome!"

Doña Luz clapped her hands gaily.

"Oh, what fun!" she cried. "You will come, won't you?"

She looked first at Don Yancey, who nodded.

"You bet!" he assured her.

She looked at Don Jode, who laughed showing his strong white teeth.

"A regiment o' artillery couldn't keep me away, Miss Luz!" he said.

And then, almost as an afterthought it seemed to me, she looked at me.

"And you, too, Currito?" she said.

"But of course!" I replied somewhat sadly.

# Chapter 7

*I* HAD some difficulty with Johnson and his friends, for they had apparently expected that our two groups would camp together. But I soon made it clear that that was not my idea. With Don Ben Wilson and Charley Kemp and Don Jode and Don Yancey all backing me up silently, in the center of the plaza, claro! There was little they could say or do. Johnson wanted to know where they should camp. They were new to that part of the world, he said. I told him to go southwest, down along the creek, below the village. There, I said, in about half a mile or so they would find several good places.

After that I collected the rest of my pay from him, and watched them file out along the trail that led toward Sonora and Chihuahua. I knew that they would probably find the best campsites down that way already pre-empted by the arrieros and guards who had come in that day with the conducta, but I cared nothing for that. It was a relief to be rid of them. The "Coronel" Raoul, of course, remained with his brother at the palacio, so it was with a sense of immense freedom that I mounted and led the way back across the plaza in the direction from which we had come, heading for the little level glade above the mines that I had earmarked for our camp earlier in the day.

While all this was going on the crowds in the plaza had gradually thinned, returning to the shacks and hovels to prepare their evening meal. A man could see now, from side to side and from one end to the other, and as I mounted I glanced, for some reason, over toward the tiny cathedral on the far side. The huge Indian was still there, and he was still watching us in the same cold, almost snake-like way. This time, however, I did not look away and pretend that I had not seen him. Instead I returned him stare for stare, and to my astonishment, as our eyes met and locked across the dusty plaza, his expression softened ever so slightly, and he seemed to come as near to a smile as I had ever seen an Apache give.

"Qué pasa?" I muttered to myself. "Now, what the devil? Who is he, and what comes over him? Seguro, when he saw me before he was not so amiable. What makes him so friendly now?"

I pondered this as we rode up to the campground — this among other things, such as why should the "Coronel" be so anxious to see his brother who was certainly not anxious to see him? Or why had Raoul told me that his brother was already at Santa Rita when, of a truth, Don Urbano had not yet reached the place? As to the last, to be sure, it could be that he had thought the older man was already there, but for the rest I could find no satisfactory answers at all.

We were yet a little distance from the campground when I heard Don Jode and Don Yancey exchanging words behind me. I could not hear all of the argument, of course, but I did catch a snatch of it.

"I saw her first!" snapped Yancey.

"Th' hell you did!" retorted Jode.

"Then it's every man for himself, I reckon," said Yancey.
"If that's th' way you want it," Jode growled.

I was astonished. I was amazed. I was doubly astonished
and amazed, for in the first place I had never seen the
mighty Yancey show the slightest interest in any woman —
at least, not in any serious way — while in the second, never
before had I heard an angry word pass between them!

"Jesús mil veces!" I said to myself. "Qué día — what a
day! Everything happens all at once. Perhaps it is as well
for me that nobody thinks anything about little Currito!"

We made our camp in the place I had chosen, and I
showed my companions a pool in the creek a little above,
where they could water our animals and later bathe themselves, washing away the stains of the trail, in preparation
for the evening. We pitched our tents — those of us who
used them — and spread our blankets, picketed our pack
animals and corralled our mounts, gathered firewood,
cooked and ate supper, and in general first tended to all
the thousand and one chores that had to be done. When
that was finished we took to the pool with whoops of pleasure, for the way had been hot and dusty, and I was pleased
to see that for the moment, at least, Don Jode and Don
Yancey appeared to have forgotten their difference. When
we were clean at last we withdrew to our tents to put on
our best finery, and it may be that I was a little slow in
getting ready for I was at pains to be extra careful. I, at
least, could not lose, I told myself, for if I did not make an
impression on Doña Luz I should most certainly do so on
Pepita — and there I should have a clear field if my two
friends were going to vie with one another for the owner's
daughter. After all, it was my philosophy that if I could

not have the best I would not refuse the next best! Indeed,
I even went so far as to tell myself that I really preferred
Pepita, anyway — and almost made myself believe it!

I had come to this stage in my thinking when there came
a scratching at the tent door, and Yancey, splendid in a
fresh suit of white buckskins and a broad-brimmed black
hat which I had never suspected he owned, stepped in.

"Ready?" he said, and then looked surprised. "Where's
Jode?"

"I haven't seen him," I replied.

"But he said he was comin' over here," he protested.

"No," I said. "He hasn't been here."

"But he — " he began, and then dawning comprehension
spread over his face like a rising moon, and his jaw set angrily. "Why — why, that low down, sneakin' — t' pull a
stunt like that on a pardner! C'mon, Currito! We got t'
get goin'!"

"All right, all right, caray!" I replied. "I will be with
you as quickly as I can. But remember, I must make sure
first that the camp is secure!"

He fussed and fumed while I sought out Ben Wilson and
Charley Kemp to see who would keep watch while we were
gone, and I think I was relieved as much because it eased
his impatience, as for any reason, to find that neither of
them cared to go into town. They were both quiet men,
and fiestas held little attraction for them. So we left them
in charge, along with a half a dozen others, and came away.

A lopsided moon was rising over the shoulder of the
Kneeling Nun as we rode into town, and I was pleased to
note that a platform for dancing had been rigged in the
center of the plaza, and that the square had quickly refilled

once more as soon as the supper hour was over. It seemed to me that it gave good promise of an active, indeed, a pleasant and perhaps somewhat exciting evening. My spirits rose and my pulses stirred as we turned our horses' heads toward the palacio and pushed our way through the crowd.

We were unlucky. The crowd was thick, and our progress was slow. We had no more than turned our mounts into the corral between the palace and the presidio when the band from the barracks struck up a rattling fandango. We had just reached the corner of the palacio when the first dancers climbed up on the platform, and Don Yancey, who was in the lead, stopped so abruptly that I almost ran into him. Because he bulked so large before me I had to peer around him, between his side and his elbow, to see what had brought him up so short, and at once it was obvious.

Caray! There they were, up among the dancers, swaying and stamping, Doña Luz ravishing in a gown of green silk, that set off the glint of her hair and the color of her eyes magnificently, and Don Jode gay in a suit of fawn-colored buckskin and no hat at all to cover the glossy sheen of his sleek hair. I stole a sidewise glance, up at Don Yancey's face, and was startled at what I saw. His jaw was set and his eyes were blazing, and it was clear to me that he considered his friend's behaviour inexcusable; that he intended to do his mightiest to win the girl away from him.

Little chance would there be for poor Currito this night, I thought. Later, perhaps, I might step in and claim a dance or two, at which time I might shine a little, for it was clear that Don Jode knew nothing of the dance he was doing. He made up in energy what he lacked in skill, or at least

97

he tried to, and I had no doubt that Don Yancey would be even more clumsy. Don Jode, at least, had a certain natural grace, but Don Yancey was likely to be all bull strength.

From where I stood it looked to me as if this were like to be a battle of the titans, and being no titan myself I wanted no part of it. Accordingly I mumbled a few hasty words to excuse myself and I slipped away across the plaza in search of Pepita Perez.

I found her at the very spot where I had first seen her — in the doorway of the house between the fonda and the cathedral; nor was she alone, although she seemed to be waiting for someone or something. Leaning over her, breathing down her dainty neck, was that fat lard-pot of a Teniente Flores — I learned later that was his name. At the sight of me she dimpled and came all alive. Teniente Flores scowled bleakly and gnawed at his dirty fingernails.

"Currito!" she cried, as if we had been sweethearts since we were little children. "You have come!"

"Would I not, chiquita Pepita?" I retorted.

But when she peered around me and did not see my two tall companions she pouted and drew back from my arms.

"You did not bring them!" she said accusingly.

"Do not blame me, chiquita," I replied. "Mira — look! There is competition."

I nodded toward the platform, where Don Jode and Doña Luz still danced and twirled. Following my nod, she looked first as if she could not believe her eyes, then furious and outraged, and finally as if she would burst into tears, and without a word she turned and fled into the dark depths of the house, the more to hide her feelings, I think, than for any other reason. Her going, however, gave Flores the opportunity he awaited.

"Now see what you have done!" he cried petulantly. "She will not be out again tonight!"

I doubted that. If I judged right Pepita could not stay long away from such gaiety as this. However, I kept my own counsel as to that. Instead I said, in a tone of injured innocence, "Me? Señor Teniente, you know that it was not until she saw the tall one, yonder, dancing with Doña Luz, that she went into her tantrum! I tell you, señor, those two are the very devil with the women. Every wench who looks at them swoons with desire! Anda! I ask you, what is an ordinary man to do?"

"Phtui!" He spat loudly in the dust at his feet, glowering sullenly at the dancers, but said nothing, and from that and his stinking pomade and gilded best tunic and shiny boots I gathered that he, too, had had hopes of catching her eye. I came near to laughing in his face. To think that such as he might hope to ride away with such a prize.

I say I did not laugh, yet the ghost of a smile of derision must have shown on my lips, for at that instant he turned his resentful glance back at me and must have surprised it there. He turned first white, and then a flaming red with rage, and swore at me.

"Cabrón! He goat! What chance has any decent man when you and these gringo friends of yours come to town — ?"

This I did not like, nor was I intimidated by his uniform. I moved toward him and cocked my fist, as the Yanquis had taught me to do. He saw that I was not to be bullied, and slid away a little, along the wall.

99

"Have a care, Teniente!" I warned him.

"Fuera! Fuera, asesino! Get out! Go away, assassin!" he cried in some alarm. "I do not propose to engage in a low street brawl with you! I will call the guards first, and they will throw you in the guardhouse!"

"If you do," I retorted, "my Yanqui friends will take this flea trap apart!"

I had no idea, of course, whether or not they would come to my rescue — but, then, neither did he, and apparently he was not willing to take a chance, for he changed his tack swiftly.

"Very well, then, you bandit," he snarled. "But let me warn you — keep away from this one! She at least is mine!"

"Oh, you are married, then, señor?" I cried.

That stopped him in his tracks, as I knew it would.

"Certainly not!" he retorted in shocked tones. "I mean — I mean she is my guayaba — my sweetheart!"

I laughed, mocking him.

"That I will believe, señor, when I hear it from her," I told him. "In the meantime, for your information, I do not think that any woman belongs alone to any man until she is his wife. If Pepita wishes to dance with me I will dance with her."

He turned and flung away.

"Bah!" he snorted. "Wait, then, if you like. She will not be back tonight!"

I watched him disappear in the crowd in the direction of the palace, then settled myself against the doorpost to wait. One minute, two, three passed slowly. Out of the corner of my eye I saw that the big Indian was back — or perhaps he had not moved from his position. He was still watching me, though in the dusky light of the flaming flambeaux I could not make out his expression. It made me uneasy.

I was about to concede that perhaps I had been wrong when the rustle of petticoats sounded at my elbow and Pepita peered cautiously out of the door.

"Is he gone?" she whispered.

"He is gone, Pepita chiquita," I assured her.

She gave a sigh of relief.

"Caray!" she exclaimed. "What a slug! He is always after me, and he makes my skin crawl!"

I offered her my hand.

"No matter," I reassured her. "He won't bother you any more tonight. I think we have both insulted him enough to send him sulking to the cuartel. Shall we dance?"

Ay, Dios, caballeros! She could dance, that Pepita, better than I suspected! When we came to the platform the band was butchering a bolero, yet the crudities of the music seemed to make no difference to her. She swung into it with lithe ease and a lissome grace that surprised even me — and which set off my own skill to perfection, for I will say that dancing was one thing that I could do very well indeed, nor am I ashamed to own it!

I noticed, as we swept around the platform, that Don Yancey had at last claimed his turn and was stumbling through the figures with Doña Luz with all the grace of an elephant. I must say I felt sorry for him, for the bolero must be one of the most difficult of dances for him. Yet he kept at it grimly, and Doña Luz as bravely kept pace with him. As we swung past I was momentarily pleased to think I noticed a touch of envy in her eyes, and certainly she was all sweetness as she nodded and greeted me.

"Good evening, Currito!"

I returned her nod as gallantly as I could, and still keep time to the music.

"A delightful evening, Doña Luz," I replied. "May I claim a dance later?"

"I wish you would, Currito!" It was almost a cry for help, it seemed to me.

We whirled away, and Pepita looked up at me, pouting and reproachful.

"You, too, Currito?" she demanded.

"She is a very nice girl," I said smugly.

She sniffed.

"But not my style at all, Pepita chiquita!"

Her smile flashed through the clouds.

"Ay, Currito!" she sighed happily, then added as a sober afterthought: "But you asked her for a dance!"

"You would not want me to be rude, would you, chiquita?" I asked.

But to that she made no reply, and I judged that one way or another I was better off than I had thought!

The next dance was a seguidilla, and again Pepita and I floated through it like feathers on a cloud, while Don Jode thumped around the platform with Doña Luz a little more lightly than Don Yancey, but yet with something of the tread of a young buffalo. The seguidilla was followed by a short intermission, while the musicians caught their wind, and as I piloted Pepita back toward her own door I noticed that the big Indian had not moved.

"Ay, Currito!" she breathed. "You are a magnificent dancer. Almost I could — "

"Who's the big fellow?" I interrupted her before I could

catch myself. "Up there, on the cathedral steps? He keeps watching us."

She shivered and lowered her voice to a whisper.

"That is Mangas Colorado," she replied. "For weeks he has been watching me, and I am afraid, Currito! Already he has three women in his lodge, and what he wants he takes. With his bare hands he has broken the backs of three warriors who dared to protest when he took a Mexican girl to live with him as his wife, and now I — I wonder — ! You will protect me, won't you Currito mio? Promise me!"

"I — against him?" I'm afraid my laugh was a little flat. But then I saw that she was in deadly earnest, and I sought to reassure her as best I could. "Of course I will, chiquita!" I blustered boldly for her benefit. "If he comes near you I will knock him over with my little slingshot!"

"Your — your what?" she asked, not understanding.

Fortunately I did not have to try to explain to her the story of David and Goliath, for at that instant a hand touched my arm. I whirled, thinking it might be the Teniente Flores. But instead, there was Don Jode.

"Easy, wildcat!" he laughed holding out his hand. "You young rascal! You put one over on us and picked the best dancer in the place. How about giving me a turn, eh?"

I could have told him that it wasn't his partner that made the difference, but I did not. Instead I glanced at Pepita and saw that she was gazing up at him in a way that suggested that I was already all but forgotten.

"Fair exchange is no robbery!" I told him in English, which I knew she would not understand, and he flung back his head and laughed gaily.

I leaned over and touched her arm.

"He would dance with you, Pepita," I told her. "Perhaps if you tell him about Mangas Colorado you will find him a better match for the Indian than I."

I turned away then and strode across the way to the verandah of the palacio, where Don Urbano and the Alcalde and the ladies were. As I climbed the steps and greeted the assembly I was conscious of a little flutter of interest. Well, at least my dancing had been noticed, I thought.

I found Doña Luz and Don Yancey a little removed from the others, standing by the railing and deep in earnest conversation. I do not know what flores — what compliments — he was pouring in her ear, but I do know that whatever he was saying she was not displeased, and he looked almost angry when I appeared to interrupt them. At that instant, however, the music began again, and he forgot whatever it was that he was about to say to me and reached for her hand. But she drew it away almost hastily.

"No, Don Yancey," she said. "I am sorry, but this one is already promised to Currito."

From the opening bars of the music it was impossible to tell what they were about to play, but by the time we had reached the platform I found, to my disappointment, that it was a staid waltz — or vals, as we call it, which is perhaps a little more bouncy than yours. Still, I consoled myself, if it was hardly my favorite dance, the gentler tempo would give us a chance to talk. Jode and Pepita were already there, swirling away — Jode doing a little better with the more familiar rhythm, but still being far from graceful. In amusement, I noticed that there was a look of perplexity on Jode's face.

104

Doña Luz lifted her arms, and we swung away; and all at once, to my chagrin, now that we were fairly launched upon the floor together, I found that I had nothing to say. I was quite tongue-tied.

I smiled. And she smiled. She was an excellent dancer, but as nothing compared to Pepita, though I cannot say why. She was light and graceful, but it seemed to me that she lacked the fire, the abandon of the little half-Indian. As we dipped and swirled I racked my brain to find something to say, but found it only going round and round in circles like the dance we did! And all the while she looked down at me with those deep green eyes, and a little, almost teasing smile.

At last I found a topic, for I saw Don Yancey leading out Doña Elena for a round. He was not doing badly, either, for the music was more what he was accustomed to, and she had doubtless danced with partners like him before, so that she managed him well.

"Your mother is a Yanqui, Doña Luz?" I blurted.

"Mamma *was* a Yanqui, Currito," she corrected me with a smile that told me she was not offended. "Her father was from Kentucky; her mother, French of New Orleans. My father met her there while passing through on a diplomatic mission, and carried her back with him to Mexico."

"Oh," I said. That seemed to exhaust the subject.

But now she came a little to my aid.

"Your friends are enthusiastic dancers, Currito," she said.

"They are energetic," I agreed.

"You dance very well, Currito," she told me.

"I know," I replied, "and so do you."

She seemed amused.

"But not as well as you, Currito," she said.

"Oh, yes!" I insisted.

"Oh, no!" she replied.

"I insist!" I said dogmatically.

There was little point in continuing that argument. Claro! She tried another gambit.

"I wish I could teach your friends to dance the way you do," she said, and then blushed, realizing what she had said.

I pretended not to have caught the point.

"Don Jode might learn — a little," I said glumly. "He is light on his feet. Don Yancey would never learn."

"Oh, but he is so big, so strong, so virile — so — so much the man!" she cried impulsively.

"I suppose so," I grumbled, a shade jealously, I daresay, and that ended the conversation for that dance.

Not until the music had stopped and we were strolling off the platform did she speak again. Then she laid her hand upon my arm and smiled at me gently.

"Poor Currito!" she said.

There is little enough more to tell of that fiesta. I did not linger at the palacio, but said my thanks and slipped back across the way to my little Pepita. Nor did I return again that night to the verandah. For me, señores, I know when I have had enough!

The dancing went on far into the night, and Don Jode did not return either! I could be easy and gay and carefree, at least, with Pepita, and in a way it was somehow a relief. I think she must have felt it, too. At any rate when we said farewell in the brightening light of dawn, she clung to me at her door and would scarcely let me go.

# Chapter 8

*W*E LAY three days in the camp in the glade, above the mines at Santa Rita, before anyone made a serious move to continue our journey toward the trapping grounds on the Gila. Ostensibly we were resting, both ourselves and our animals. Actually we were detained by invisible chains that bound the hearts of three men!

Of the three, I believe it is safe to say, señores, that I was the most fortunate, for certainly my problem was the least. After that first evening, at the fiesta, I found that I had little difficulty in discarding my momentary infatuation for Doña Luz. It is true that she was a gracious and cultivated lady. She was also a beautiful and desirable woman, and I had no doubt that she would be for someone a passionate and devoted wife; a fine and devoted mother.

But she was not for me! In the first place she was taller than I, and this I could never bear, no matter how lovely she might be. In the second, she made me feel, somehow — how should I say it? un chambón — a lunkhead, a stupid and inferior. No, señores, had I been so unlucky as to have won her I would have spent the rest of my life trailing around after her on a lead, so to say, to be shown off like a nice little dog! Gracias a Dios, I had the good sense to see it and withdraw before it was too late!

Besides, Pepita Perez was far more to my taste. She, too, was pretty, but in a different, provocative way; and she was alive and gay and full of unpredictable little impulses. A man never knew whether she would kiss him — or bite him or slap him. But always she ended up in my arms, making no secret of her hunger. Moreover, she was not so much in demand. There was the big Indian, Mangas Colorado, but during those first days at Santa Rita it seemed to me that he never moved from his place under the portico of the cathedral. There was also the Teniente Flores, but he was a fat babieca, a silly fool, and I had no fear of him. As for my companions, Don Jode and Don Yancey, I daresay she might have welcomed their advances, but it was my good fortune that they were occupied elsewhere.

Ay, my good fortune, perhaps yes — but their misfortune! Señores, have you ever seen it — how a woman can set two men at one another's throats? I do not mean two men who are complete strangers, or at best only passing acquaintances. That is but the everyday way of things. I mean two men who have been like brothers, like twins, like parts of one another, until the moment when she steps between. Por Dios, amigos! It is like the difference between the thunderstorm and the hurricane. It is a thing of horror and of fascination and of pity and pain. It is a thing of wonder that so much hate can be born of love. And it does no good to blame the woman in the matter, often as not, for usually she can only stand helplessly by and no more stop it than you or I! One might as well howl at the wild wind, for all the good it will do.

108

Such a thing does not happen all at once, señores. It begins in small taunts and chaff, that start out to be good-natured, but which prickle and soon draw blood. The taunts grow bitter and sharp and in time give way to bickering, and bickering to the outright quarrel, which in turn leads to hate. And through it all runs the constant rivalry to monopolize the woman's attention, until, in the end, it becomes quite literally each one for himself, just as Don Jode had said, on that first day of our arrival.

So it was in this case, and, señores, will it surprise you if I say that it troubled me? Perhaps you will say that it was no business of mine, yet it was not so that I looked upon it. In a way I was responsible. It was I who had brought them there. I liked them both. I did not want to see either of them hurt, but it seemed to me that one was bound to have his fingers burned before the thing was done.

I watched it unfold, even in those few days. If Don Jode took Doña Luz riding, Don Yancey sulked in camp and was not fit to be spoken to. If Don Yancey sat on the palacio verandah of an evening with her, Don Jode went roistering through the cantinas, being nasty and insulting to all he met. It seemed to me that if one were not shot the other would end with a knife between his ribs before it was over, and I worried about it.

In the meantime I knew well that Don Ben Wilson and Charley Kemp and the rest were fretting to be off, and my conscience troubled me about that. But I made up my mind that I would let them say the first word, and until they did I would sit close and hold hard. During that time I caught only occasional glimpses of Henry Johnson or others of his group, although I knew that they were still encamped southwestward of the town. Despite the fact that they had told me they were bound for Sonora they made no move to leave.

It was on the third evening in camp, and Don Jode and Don Yancey and I were still munching our supper of frijoles and enchiladas in silence around the campfire which we shared, when Ben Wilson and Charley Kemp and Dody Hicks came stumbling through the dusk.

"Aha! Caught ye this time!" Ben Wilson grinned. "Ye young bucks git off t' town so early these days we hain't been able t' lay a finger on ye. Currito, we'd like a word with ye."

"Sit down, señores," I said, "and tell me, what is your pleasure?"

Ben Wilson came straight to the point.

"We been figgerin'," he said, "that th' animals must be pretty well rested by now, an' we-all're kinda hankerin' t' be gittin' on. Th' pelts won't be no good if we wait too long, an' you agreed, ye recollect, to put us down on th' Gila?"

"I did," I nodded. "I've just been waiting for you to say the word. We'll go whenever you're ready. Is that all right with you two — Jode? Yancey?"

There was a moment of silence. Then Jode growled almost defiantly.

"Count me out!"

I stared at him in surprise.

"Count you — wait a momento, amigo!" I cried. "You hired on for the whole show!"

"All right! All right!" he flared so vehemently that I was rocked back. "So, what if I did? That's no sign I ain't changed my mind. I'm not goin', I tell ya. I'm quittin'. D'ye understand?"

I stared at him hotly for a long moment, feeling the bubbling anger rise within me. I wanted to take him by the back of the neck and shake him until his teeth rattled, shouting at him as I did that he was being a plain, bullheaded, stupid fool. And yet, how could I? Even if I had been able to nudge him out of his complacency, he was a man grown and would go his own way, in spite of anything I might say.

"Yes — I understand!" I retorted finally, and something of what I felt must have been in my voice, for he had the grace to redden. But at the same time his mouth and jaw simply took on a more determined set.

I turned to Yancey, almost belligerently.

"What about you?" I demanded, although I already suspected what his answer would be.

He hesitated and shot a quick glance at Jode; then looked back at me.

"I'm sorry, Currito," he said slowly, "but I reckon you'd best get along without me, too."

I snorted contemptuously.

"I had an idea you'd say that," I growled. "So you're both — "

He interrupted me with a weary wave of his hand.

"I wouldn't leave him here alone — with her!" he said.

I was angry — very angry. I stood up and kicked childishly at the fire, overturning the pot of beans and the pan of enchiladas and scattering coals halfway to the creek. Having relieved my spleen to that extent, then, I turned to Ben Wilson and Charley Kemp.

"Very well, señores," I snapped, "since these two love-sick fools choose to abandon us, I will take you on to the Gila alone — provided some of you will help me with the packing and wrangling and such when need be. Give me tomorrow to get ready. If we leave at dawn, day after tomorrow, I can put you on the river in two days' time."

I was in a foul, ugly temper all through the following day as we prepared to move. Fortunately I had already disposed of the trade goods that I had brought down with me, for if I had had to go out and find a buyer that morning I would probably have insulted him. As it was I drove my own personal mules at a merciless clip down the trail and into the town, scattering Indians and other pedestrians along the narrow way, left and right, willy-nilly. At the plaza I drove them at a smoking gallop into the public corral, in front of the cuartel and between the palacio and the presidio, and snarled at the mozo who had charge of them that he would be paid when I returned — if he had fed and cared for them properly. As I rode back to camp, around the front of the palacio, Doña Luz, who was on the verandah, called out to me by name, chiding me for not having come to see her. But though it was obvious that I must have heard, I did not even look around, but rode on, stiff-backed, up the trail.

Back at the camp both Yancey and Jode came to me separately and somewhat sheepishly and offered to help us break camp. But I was cool to them.

"My thanks to you," I said to each, in effect, "but since you have left it to me to do it all alone on the trail, I might as well start now. I can do without your help!"

After that they went away, and did not make their offer

again. Indeed, those were the only words that passed between us before I left.

Later, however, when half a dozen volunteers from Wilson and Kemp's party came forward to offer a hand, I accepted readily enough.

That night when I went down to say farewell to Pepita I was even curt with her. Indeed, so savage was I that she put aside her pert sauciness and became almost meek.

"Ay, Currito querido," she whispered. "I do not like to see you go!"

"I don't want to go," I retorted.

"You will be back, amado mio?"

"Within the week," I growled. "That is — if I get back!"

"Why do you say that, my lover?" she cried.

"Hay Indios — there are Indians in that country," I replied.

She nodded soberly.

"Cuchillo Negro and his band are said to be working up toward the forks," she mused. "Mangas Colorado is friendly to Cuchillo. Perhaps if I asked him — "

"You keep away from him!" I cried savagely, shaken out of my gloom for an instant by my concern for her. "I don't trust that Indian. Any time you talk to him I want to be close by!"

Nevertheless, I filed away her information in my memory.

She smiled and kissed me fiercely.

"You are sweet, alma mia," she told me, "to be troubled for me. But you must not worry for my sake. You must promise me that you will take care of yourself!"

"Hah!" I snorted. "I promise! I will take care of myself, have no fear, chiquita! Do you think I am not attached to this fur I wear on my head? You may be sure I will have a care!"

She nodded, apparently satisfied.

"And your friends, Currito mio," she asked, "do they go too?"

"No!" I grumbled. "They stay here — to carry on their pursuit of the Doña Luz!"

"So?" She looked mildly interested. Then she sighed. "Ay, Currito! I wish you would stay here, too — and pursue me."

"I wish I could, Pepita chiquita," I told her, touched in spite of myself. "But I have promised."

Thus she drew me out, little by little, until she had coaxed from me at least a measure of ardency. But, even so, I did not linger much past midnight. I had said that we would be away by dawn, and this time the responsibility was all mine. I was not disposed to take risks with it.

After I took my leave of her I crossed the empty plaza to the corral, where I had left my horse. The palacio was completely dark, and I smiled a little in the night to myself. If I knew anything about Doña Beatriz she had long since rescued Doña Luz from whichever suitor had the verandah that night, and bustled her off to bed.

There was one light in the presidio, however. It shone from the quarters of the Capitán-Comandante, in the corner overlooking the corral, and since it was a balmy evening the shutters stood thrown wide, and the murmur of voices came sliding down along the yellow rays. As I moved to catch my horse I could not hear all that was said

— or even most of it. Nor did I make any effort to listen, but some of the words must have been spoken more loudly than others, for they seemed to penetrate my ear, without my being aware of it, and engraved themselves upon my memory.

First there was the sound of a man's voice arguing. That would be the Capitán-Comandante himself. I could tell that much by the pompous cadence, though the words were blurred. I heard him say something about "hostile," and again "friendly," and still later "the law." When he stopped speaking there was a burst of laughter, and then Raoul Hermoso y Maravilla spoke, loudly, so that this one sentence came booming out complete:

"But, Capitán, now we have the Proyecto!"

On the heels of that several voices seemed to interrupt all at once, and I heard only the words "Nuisances!" and "What difference . . . ?" and "How's t' tell . . . ?"

At that point I whirled my reata and made my throw, catching my nag easily. But the swing of the loop set the rest of the horses in the corral to galloping around the fence, as it always does, and the thud of their hoofs must have been plainly audible in the room above, for the drone of voices stopped abruptly, and after an instant Henry Johnson's sharp face was framed in the window.

"Who's thet?" he bawled. "Who's down thar?"

"Just me — Currito," I called back. "I'm catching my horse."

"Yer've ben listenin'!" he snarled accusingly.

I was in no mood for insults from him.

"Oye, cabrón!" I called up. "Hark to me, old he-goat!

When you have anything to say worth listening to I'll come inside to hear it. I won't go skulking around under windows!"

I turned away from him then and went on saddling my horse, and after glaring at my back for a few moments he drew in his head and slammed the shutters behind him and I heard no more.

But that one brief exchange was enough to undo all the good work of Pepita's skillful cajolery and fling me back into my ugly mood of the day. When I had left her house I had been in a reasonably cheerful frame of mind, thanks to her. I had put aside my cares and worries, and was willing to accept the world as it was. But now, as I rode back toward the camp, I found myself again growing irritated and angry; and instead of directing this anger against Johnson, as by every right I should, I found myself turning it, unreasoningly, against Jode and Yancey.

The truth, of course, was that I was fond of them and worried for them. If I only realized it I had counted heavily upon getting them away to the Gila with Wilson and Kemp long enough to allow them to catch their breath and come to their senses. Once they had done that, I was sure, they would see that there were other ways of settling the problem. Let them put it squarely up to the girl to choose between them — and abide by her decision. That would have been the fairest thing to do all around. Or they could draw straws for her, for all I cared about that. The main thing, as I saw it, was that there was no sense in smashing a friendship of years. When they had elected to remain in the forest, instead of coming out where they could see the trees, so to say, I can see now that I was distressed and disappointed and angry, and I vented my anger on them.

By morning, however, I was more sad than angry. I did not see them to say good-by. If I had I would have shaken hands and told them that I held no hard feelings. As it was I was plagued throughout that journey with the vague feeling that it might be too late to apologize or offer amends by the time I got back.

Perhaps that feeling accounts in some measure for the speed with which the trip was made — or perhaps it was just that I was anxious to get back to Pepita. In any case there is no need to dwell at length upon it. We set out in a general northwesterly direction, and perhaps because I did drive them harder than I thought I was doing, we reached the river early on the afternoon of the second day. As we pulled up at the edge of the bluff and looked down upon its winding, willow-lined course, I looked toward Ben and pointed.

"Well, Señor Don Ben," I said. "There flows the Gila. I guess you can get along without me from here on."

He looked surprised.

"Ain't you goin' t' light 'n camp?" he demanded. "No use startin' back t'night."

I shook my head. That had been my original intention, but now, for some inexplicable reason, I was almost frantic to get back to Santa Rita.

"I've got four or five hours of daylight left," I told him. "I don't want to waste it. I am anxious to return, señor."

"Ho, ho!" he chuckled. "An' what was it I heerd ye call Yance Cahoon an' Jodey Lassiter? Ye young cock! I'll warrant ye've a wench o' yer own back there a-waitin' ye!"

I don't know. It may have been that which impelled me to such haste. At any rate I could not deny it. I merely flushed and said nothing.

"All right, then," he said. " 'Tis skin off yer tail, not mine, will be left in th' saddle! Have it as ye will! Here — catch! I've been carryin' yer pay in that till I'm round in th' shoulders. I'm glad t' be rid o' it. Ye better count it."

I caught the buckskin sack of doblónes that he tossed me and dropped it into my pocket.

"I'll take your word for it, Don Ben," I replied. "Good luck, then — and good trapping! When you are finished come back to Santa Rita, and I will buy your pelts. It will save you a long journey back to Santa Fe."

"We'll do that, boy," he said, and lifted his hand in salute.

I started to turn away.

"Hold on a minute!" he called, as if by afterthought. "Which way sh'ld we trap?"

"Downstream!" I replied promptly.

"That was quick," he remarked dryly. "What makes ye so sure?"

I told him.

"It is said that Cuchillo Negro and his band are out on the upper river, Señor Don Ben," I said, "somewhere around the Forks. I would not want you to meet them."

"How fur's that?" he asked.

I shrugged.

"One day — maybe two," I replied.

He scratched his head thoughtfully.

"But th' beaver'd be better up there — toward th' mountains, wouldn't they?" he asked.

"I think they would," I said.

"Where'd ye get this news?" he asked.

I told him it was Pepita's remark, and he snorted.

"A wench!" he laughed. "Well-l-ll, I reckon I'll take a chance an' head thataway, if anyone else'll go with me."

"It's your party from here on, señor," I told him, and after cutting out my lone baggage mule from the line I gave them farewell again and started on my way back to Santa Rita.

I never saw any of them alive again, and I have often wondered.

Now that I was turned around and headed back, it occurred to me that perhaps it was as well that Jode and Yancey had not come along, after all. I had had no trouble going out, and since I was in a hurry it was probably better this way. They were both good men in a scrape, but this was Apache country, and they knew nothing of Apaches or their ways. Knowing nothing of the country or its people they would only have slowed me down, since I would have had to stick to the main trail, well out in the open. As it was, I could follow a short cut, swinging over eastward against the Pinos Altos Mountains, and approaching Santa Rita more directly from the north.

Besides, even if they knew the country, one man could travel more swiftly than three. By nightfall I had reached Nopal Canyon, a good third of the way back, and the sun had not yet set when I rode into Santa Rita late on the following afternoon.

As I dropped down out of the hills toward the village it occurred to me that there was little sense in returning to our campground above the mines. The main camp was gone, and there was little likelihood that Jode and Yancey had remained to eye one another alone across the campfire like a pair of snarling dogs. No, they had undoubtedly moved down into the town, and I might as well do the same. Since I did not know just where they might have found quarters I could not go there directly, but I did not need to think twice about that. At the northwest corner of the plaza, on the same side as the cathedral, and close by Pepita's house, was one of the better fondas, and nothing could be more convenient for me.

My spirits were a good deal lighter now than they had been when I went away, and I even sang a little to myself as I rode. After I began to come into the warren of alleyways and paths that radiated from the plaza I was surprised to meet at least a half a dozen of Johnson's men at intervals; all carrying jugs, all roaring drunk, and each offering to all and sundry a pull at the cork. Understand me, I was not surprised that they were all so drunk. But it seemed to me that they were far afield, to be over on this side of town. And for them to be offering to drink from the same jug with the Indians, whom they affected to despise, was to me astonishing. At almost the same time, however, I noticed that there was a sort of general drift in the direction of the plaza, and it occurred to me then that something was afoot.

That thought was well confirmed when I rode into the square. The place was as crowded as it had been the day of our arrival, except that this time it seemed to me that there was a predominance of Indians in the throng. I noticed many who never came down from the Indian village above the mines except for some special occasion, and in the center was the old chief himself, old Juan José, as fat as a hog and drunk as a lord, haranguing his people from a low, board platform — something like the one that had been rigged for dancing, save that it was not more than a few inches high. In and out among the throng I noticed Johnson's men weaving, singing and shouting. I had not seen so many of them all at once since we arrived, and I wondered if they had been waiting for us to leave before they came out.

Over on the verandah of the palacio I noticed Don Urbano and his ladies — and in the background Don Yancey — turned out as if to watch a spectacle and witness some sort of ceremony, after which, doubtless, there would be the usual dancing and fiesta. The fact that Don Yancey was with them, I reflected wryly, probably meant that Don Jode was somewhere, drunk, about the town.

I rode directly to the fonda, and around behind it, where I put my animals into the corral there for the time being. Then I gathered up my gear and deposited it just inside the back door. There would be time enough later, I told myself, to arrange for quarters. Just then my throat was parched, and I wanted something to cut the dust away. I went into the bar and found it packed. Here and there I noticed one of Johnson's company, but in the main the crowd was made up of miners and Indians. I elbowed my way through to the rail and ordered a glassful of mescal, and was just raising it to my lips, when an enormous hand thumped me on the back, so hard that I came near to spilling the drink down my shirt front. At the same time a familiar voice boomed.

"Hi-yeeeooow! Lookee who's here! 'F it ain' th' li'l ol' boy, hisself! Hiya, Currito, where'd you come f'm?"

I turned, knowing already that it was Don Jode. He blinked at me drunkenly, and rocked back on his heels.

"I made a quick trip," I said guardedly. With Don Jode, especially when he'd had a few too many, there was never any telling which way he would swing. "I just got in."

"Jus'n time!" he assured me solemnly. "Jus'n time! Big doin's! Joh — hup — Joshesh — feed'n Injuns — hic!" He stopped abruptly and squinted at me, trying to focus his gaze on my face. "Hey! Way minna! Lash time I shaw you — hic — you call m' namesh! Ido' like people call me namesh!"

I wanted no trouble with anyone, least of all with Don Jode. I decided I'd better get out of there.

"Forget it!" I said. "I didn't mean it. Here, I'll buy!"

I signaled the barman for two drinks and flipped a coin across to him. While he was pouring them out I touched Jode on the arm.

"Keep your eye on mine, will you?" I said. "I've got to tend my horse. He's out back."

I turned and started away, and he called after me.

"C'm'on back when y'r finish, 'member!"

I waved to him and kept going.

Outside, in the air, I drew a deep breath of relief. It was a mean trick, I supposed, but I wanted no arguments, and I could see he was spoiling for one. I slipped around to the front of the inn and went along the row of hovels, toward the cathedral, until I came to Pepita's house. There I paused and looked around quickly. The crowd in the square seemed to have thickened. I guessed there must be four or five hundred Indians, in addition to the miners, who seemed to be crowded back all around the edges. At the southern end the mercado, usually open until sunset, was closed; covered all around by its screens of brush. It lacked almost an hour of sundown yet, but I thought little of that. If there was to be a fiesta it was not unnatural that it would shut down early. I noticed Henry Johnson, hawk-faced and predatory-seeming, leaning against one of the corner posts, but he did not see me. He was watching the crowd, and he seemed quite pleased about something. Up under the portico of the cathedral stood the big Indian, Mangas Colorado. But he, too, was surveying the throng with brooding eyes, and he did not look my way.

Quietly I lifted the latch and stepped inside the little one-room hut.

I had meant to surprise her, but not quite in the way I did. To my embarrassment she was dressing. She wore her party skirt, but not a stitch above the waist, and she was standing in front of her cracked mirror, brushing her long, black hair.

At the sound of the closing door behind me she spun around, and I had a breath-taking glimpse of firm, young breasts, ruby-tipped, and soft, parted lips to match.

"Currito!" she cried out, all unself-conscious, and in the next instant she was in my arms, pressing herself against me, crushing my lips with hers.

When I could hold my breath no longer I lifted my head away and laughed down at her. She held up her face, her lips pouted for more.

"Wait!" I gasped. "Wait a moment, chiquita! Let me catch my breath!"

"You are back so soon!" she said, as she nestled against me. "You are hardly gone and you are back!"

"Did you think I could stay away long?" I asked. "I went out and came back as quickly as I could, alma mia."

"And you come just in time, Currito mio," she told me. "It is the big affair tonight!"

"I can see something is going on, amada mia," I replied. "The plaza is packed, and here you are putting on all your best finery. What is it?"

"It is the thin-faced Yanqui — the señor Johnson," she said.

"Uh?" In my surprise I could not even pronounce an intelligible word.

"But, yes!" She nodded violently. "Soon he and his people will go on, and he says that he would first make the fiesta in return for our hospitality — the gran' fiesta!"

"Johnson said that?" I demanded incredulously. I couldn't imagine it.

She nodded again, and then twirled away from me and went dancing across the floor to start brushing her hair again before the mirror — and at the sight of her lithe, young body I almost forgot what she was saying. But she went chattering on.

"Es verdad — it is true!" she assured me. "There will be a special parade of the soldiers, and a fine gift just for the Indians —"

Something seemed to tick in the back of my mind — something I could not quite put my finger upon. Yet it was something! Surely it would come to me! What was it? Voices. Yes, voices in the night! What was it they had said? Something about "hostile" and "friendly" — and then a lot of laughter. Then someone had mentioned the "Proyecto," and someone else . . .

It nagged at me like a toothache.

"Do you mean to tell me, chiquita," I demanded, still only half believing, "that this Johnson — this dog of a pinchpenny — this miser — this skinflint — do you mean to say to me, querida mia, that this one, of his own free will, is offering the Indios a special, free gift?"

"Seguro, mi vida — certainly, my sweetheart!" she insisted. "What is so strange about that? First, as I say, the soldiers will parade. Then, exactly at sunset, the carretas will be brought out, laden with socorro, which they will dump in a pile on the platform which you saw in the middle of the plaza. When this is done the Indios will be invited to help themselves. That is why you see so many. The word has gone out — "

It came to me then, all at once! I remembered the night — in the corral, under the Comandante's window — the voices! I could remember the words now, all of them; and if there were gaps in what I had heard, I could put two and two together and get a fairly accurate notion of what they had been talking about. Especially now could I remember that last phrase — "How's t' tell — ?" That had been Johnson's voice. I knew it now. And if I could supply the missing words of the rest of that sentence they probably went something like this:

"How's t' tell th' difference, once a scalp's torn from th' head?"

That was it! I was sure! "Hostile" or "friendly," how could anyone tell?

"No!" I cried. "Oh, no!"

Across the square a bugle blared, calling the men of the garrison out to fall in before the presidio.

Call it a hunch. Call it luck. Call it premonition or intuition, or what you will, señores, I still think it was none of those. I flatter myself that there was some sound, solid reasoning behind it.

Do you see? I knew this man Johnson. I had journeyed with him all the way from Santa Fe, and I had reason to be well acquainted with his meanness, and from the very beginning I had suspected that both he and his men were up to no good.

Then there was that conversation I had partially overheard. It is true that I had only heard snatches of it, and that I had thought nothing of it at the time. But it must be remembered that I was preoccupied with my own worries and those of my friends at that moment. This, I think, will explain — if it does not excuse — my neglect to add everything up at that instant.

Mira! Look you! Who was in that room and speaking? First, there was the Capitán-Comandante, and I had never had a very high opinion of him. He was not like the Alcalde, who was weak, God knows, but honest. The Comandante was a pompous ass, and none too scrupulous, as I well knew. Then, there was Raoul Hermoso y Maravilla, admittedly Don Urbano's black-sheep brother, and one who had given me every reason to suspect that he was involved in some devious skulduggery. With them was the man Johnson, of whom I think I have already said enough; and probably Eames and Gleason were there as well. Johnson never went far without them!

Then, what was it they were discussing? The Proyecto

de la Guerra, of course! The new law, out of Chihuahua, which offered a bounty for hostile scalps. I could see, now, why Johnson had looked as if he had heard it all before. He and the "Coronel" had already discussed it thoroughly, and laid their plans. We were only being sounded out to see how far we might be trusted to go along with them. At the time I had overheard them talking in the Comandante's quarters the latter had still been inclined to distinguish between hostile and friendly Indians, but the word "nuisances" — used in connection with their subject — could only refer to the Indians of Santa Rita, and I was well aware that the Capitán-Comandante regarded them as such.

In addition there were other little straws in the wind, such as the sudden, almost guilty hush that had fallen on the room at the sound of the horses' galloping hoofs; Johnson's unreasonable suspicion; the slammed and bolted shutters!

I could be wrong, of course, but I was so sure that I was right that I was willing to stake my life upon it. It was an audacious scheme — a horrible one, bloody and inhuman. The very thought of it made me feel almost physically ill. But there it was, about to become a reality — unless I could do something to stop it!

At the sound of my cry Pepita turned in astonishment from the mirror and stared at me.

"Currito!" she cried. "What is it? What is the matter?"

This was no time for argument or explanations. There was not even time for words of endearment — or time now to notice the firm, young breasts so tantalizingly yet so ingenuously exposed.

"Pepita!" I croaked. "I must go — I must go at once, and

see — what — what I can do! You do not know what you have told me! As soon as I am outside bar the door, and do not open it again until you hear me rap three times — thrice, like this — " I knocked my knuckles against the doorframe so that she would know the signal when I gave it.

She looked bewildered, and a little inclined to argue with me.

"But — but the fiesta, Currito mio!" she cried.

"Curse the fiesta!" I swore angrily. "Do as I tell you! God grant I am wrong, but if I am not this will be a fiesta of death, not one of joy! I am thinking of your life, Pepita!"

I must have sounded convincing, at least, for as I stepped outside and pulled the door shut I heard the heavy bolt slide home behind me.

Outside, in the air, in the long rays of the setting sun, with the unsuspecting crowd milling before me, it all seemed a little silly. It was incredible that anyone could be so completely inhuman. Yet, as I hesitated for an instant on the step, it all began to unfold before me, exactly as I had imagined it. The soldiers were forming ranks in front of the presidio. The crowds in the center of the plaza had fallen back a little on each side, forming a lane to allow the three creaking carretas, each laden heavily with sacked socorro and drawn by a plodding team of oxen, to pass through to the platform in the middle. I glanced at the platform, and noted again how low it was — a perfect target. And I looked down toward the mercado, enclosed in its brush screen. All of Johnson's men — where were they, by the way? — could hide behind that screen and pick off the Indians on the platform almost at leisure!

But only Johnson himself was in sight now. He was still

standing by the corner of the market, one hand holding a long, black cigar. But he had caught sight of me, and he had straightened and stiffened, and an expression almost of consternation was spread momentarily across his predatory features. Then slowly, as our eyes met and held, he relaxed once more against his post, and his thinly evil mouth curled in a grimace of derisive challenge.

"All right, Currito," he seemed to be saying. "Let's see what you can do about it now! Ye're too late!"

I threw a quick look across the way. The Alcalde was there, with Don Urbano and his family — and Don Yancey. But the crowd was dense between us. I glanced at the sun. Its rim was less than a foot from the horizon. I looked out toward the platform and the center of the plaza again and caught sight of old Juan José. But he was drunk and reeling. The whole thing could be over before I could make him understand what I was babbling about.

And then a thought struck me. It wasn't much, but it was something. It might serve to save a few. I turned and sprinted for the cathedral. As I ran I saw him. He was still there, standing back in the shadow of the portico. I took the steps two at a time and skidded to a halt in front of him.

"Mangas?" I panted. "Mangas Colorado?"

His face was impassive as his black eyes raked over me. I took hold of his arms and shook them.

"Listen!" I cried urgently. "Listen to me and believe me! This is no gift. This man — the Johnson — is no more than a murderous dog, and that socorro that he pretends to be giving your people is nothing but bait. By means of it he intends to attract as many of you as he can to your deaths, so that he may claim reward for your scalps! Look! See the

129

soldiers with their arms over against the presidio. Look around the plaza. Do you see any of Johnson's Yanquis? Where are they? I will tell you! They are behind the brush screen, inside the mercado, waiting with loaded rifles. Then look, too! Do you not see how the platform where they are dumping the socorro is directly in line with the mercado? Go, man! Go down quickly and warn your people to stand back. Do not let them near that meal. Hurry! The sun is almost set, and that is the hour. I have just learned it, or I would have come to you before!"

I stopped for breath, panting with excitement and my spate of words. Deliberately he turned his massive head and looked down at Johnson, who had stiffened again and was staring up at us with an expression that was a strange combination of puzzlement, fury and fear.

"That one?" Mangas Colorado rumbled in a voice so deep that it seemed to me the cathedral shivered.

"That is the man," I nodded. "Henry Johnson."

Mangas's eyes narrowed, but his stare did not relax its intensity. He seemed to be taking in every detail of Johnson's face and figure, so that he would never forget. Even at that distance I could see Johnson's prominent Adam's apple bob as he gulped; saw him fall back a step, then two more, as if he would hide behind the corner of the market.

Mangas Colorado did not actually spit, although he looked as if he had. Contemptuously he turned away and looked moodily out over the crowded plaza. Then, abruptly, with a single sweep of his huge arm he brushed me aside and went quickly down the steps, moving with surprising, catlike lightness for a man so big. For a moment I saw him, thrusting his way through the throng, moving toward the platform, speaking sharply, right to this one — left to that. Then I lost sight of him.

I flung a quick glance at the sun. Its rim had made contact now with the knobby peaks in the west that rose up out of the Antelope Plain, and a jagged chunk was already chewed from its underside. At the same instant I heard the squeal of the ungreased wheels of the carretas, turning on their wooden axles, as they started back toward the corner of the plaza. I looked toward where Johnson had stood, but he had vanished.

What more, I wondered, could I do now? Little enough, surely — but there was one thing. I flung down from the cathedral steps and tore my way through the dense-packed crowd, wriggling and squirming through every opening. I crossed the lane ahead of the carretas and came out on the other side of the plaza in front of the presidio, close by where the garrison company was drawn up. Mechanically I noticed that the Capitán-Comandante himself was in charge, and the Teniente Flores was nowhere to be seen. But I had no time for small details at that moment. I raced down along the front of the company — the only clear space available — leaving the Comandante bawling curses after me for such a heinous breach of military etiquette.

Beyond the soldiers I struggled again with the throng, past the corral and the corner of the palacio, until I came to the point where Don Urbano and his party stood, close by the verandah rail. There I halted, puffing and breathing hard from my exertions, planted my feet, bracing myself against the jostling of the crowd, and lifted my hand, pointing and waving to catch their attention.

"Why, it's Currito!" Doña Luz exclaimed.

But I had no time for greetings at that point. The sun had already slid halfway down the horizon.

"Don Emilio! Don Urbano!" I shouted. "Get those women inside! Hurry! Arm yourselves and bolt the doors! Don Yancey, lend them a hand if you value their lives!"

It may have been the urgency of my voice; the wildness of my eye. Whatever it was, they were docile as lambs, and did not wait to argue. Doña Elena rose swiftly and coolly, brushed me with a glance, then turned and moved quickly toward the door. Doña Beatriz went white, and I thought she was going to faint, but Don Urbano caught her arm and with a single questioning look at me, turned her and steered her back across the verandah. Doña Luz, alone of the ladies, hesitated. She stared down at me as if I had taken leave of my wits and opened her mouth to speak. But before she could say anything Don Yancey reached out and caught her by both arms and literally lifted her back, into the palace.

Don Emilio alone was left. I remember being at first surprised that Raoul was not there; and then it struck me that his very absence was by way of being confirmation of my fears. But Don Emilio was leaning down, over the verandah rail, calling to me.

"Currito! Currito, what is it? What is happening?"

"Murder!" I called back frantically. "Get inside, Don Emilio! There is nothing you can do about it now!"

I turned away and plunged back toward the opposite side of the square. If I could I wanted to get to Pepita before it happened. She would need someone when the storm came.

132

But I was not sure that I could make it. The carretas were gone, and only the thin, upper edge of the sun showed above the ragged horizon. Already the crowd of Indians was surging forward with staggering, barrel-bellied old Juan José drunkenly leading the way, scrabbling and scrambling for the grain that had been heaped in the center of the platform. Yet it was this very surge of Indians toward the center that enabled me to race across to the other side, for it drew them away from the edges, and left me room to run. Halfway over I looked back. Don Emilio was still standing by the railing, staring after me. I waved my hand gesturing frantically.

"Get back! Get inside!" I shouted, and the movement seemed to rouse him, for he turned and bolted for the door.

For my part, I lost no more time, but took to my heels as fast as I could run. I had done everything that I was able to do!

At Pepita's door I fell against the panel, panting, and knocked — three times, and again, three times, and again, three times. The door swung in, and I stumbled through. Behind me I heard Pepita slam home the bolt and I caught myself from falling and turned to face her. Any moment now it would come.

"Currito!" she cried, her back against the door. "Currito, what is it? You are pale as a ghost! Currit — "

And then it came — a clap of thunder that was yet even louder than thunder when the lightning strikes close at hand, followed by a heavy, belly-wrenching afterwhump. At the same time a flash of brilliant light showed all around the cracks of the door. The shock of it flung her forward, into my arms. The building shook — rocked, literally, and bits of dust and plaster showered down upon us and all around us where we stood — she clinging, I with my arms locked tight around her.

For a moment after there was dead silence, as if a horrified world sucked in its breath and held it. Even in that instant my mind worked in a sort of dazed, detached fashion. Cannon! One thing I had not dreamed of!

Then came the human noise; the cries, the shrieks, the wails, the animal howls of fury — pain, anguish, surprise, horror, unbelief and rage, all mingled together in one scalp-tingling babble.

But it lasted no more than the space of a drawn breath. In the next instant came the rifle fire — a volley first, and then a steady, crackling tattoo as the men in the mercado — and the soldiers, too, without doubt — tried to pick off the survivors as they sought to escape. Then presently, even this died down to a scattered popping and rippling, and gave way to triumphant, bloodthirsty yells as the murdering crew leaped forward, into the plaza, to finish their filthy work.

In my arms Pepita stirred slightly.

"Currito! Currito, what is happening?" she whispered, bewildered.

I swallowed, trying to ease the dryness of my throat so that I could reply.

"That — " I gulped. "That's it! That's what I meant — the Fiesta of Death!"

# II

## FOOLS' PARADISE

# *Chapter 1*

*T*O THIS day I cannot say how long we stood so, close-locked in one another's arms, just inside the heavy bolted door. It might have been ten minutes. It might have been two hours. I do not know. I think perhaps I suffered from some sort of a reaction to my exertions that stopped the movement of my mind for a brief period. I can only say that we remained there, Pepita, clinging to my shoulders with her face buried in my bosom, her arms on either side of her head, trying to shut out the horrid sounds of that terrible butchery beyond the door; I with my arms taut around her, protectingly.

Gradually the yells, the shouts, the shots, the hideous laughter died away in the distance; and little by little our thoughts swirled back upon us. Like most such one-room huts in our part of the world, Pepita's little house was windowless. When it was hot the door stood ajar. When the weather outside was cold it was kept closed, and such air as was needed came in through the wide crack between it and the threshold, and through the cracks between it and the frame. I looked at those cracks now, over her shoulder, and to my surprise saw that already it was dark outside. For a moment I was tempted to unbolt the door and look out.

But then I felt Pepita shudder, and she lifted her tear-wet face from my breast and looked at me with fear-ridden eyes.

"Don't leave me, Currito!" she whispered, as if she had read my thoughts. "Don't leave me alone!"

I had already made up my mind about that. Judging from the distance and direction of the shots and shouts that still rang out occasionally I gathered that the murdering band were moving up the mountain, toward the Indian village. That would be a logical move, considering their object. But it was possible that a few of them still moved about in the alleys adjoining the plaza, skulking to their hideous task, and my own hair — and Pepita's, too — would be indistinguishable from that of any pure-blooded Indian once it was torn from the skull. So far as I was concerned I prized it too highly to risk it foolishly. Discretion, I felt, was the better part of valor, and I intended to stay right where I was until I was sure that it was safe to venture out.

So I kissed her gently and patted her shoulder.

"Do not worry, chiquita mia," I told her. "I am not going anywhere — if it comforts you that I stay."

"It does, Currito! It does!" she assured me.

I slipped one arm about her waist, then, and led her to where the lone candle guttered in a wooden holder by the washbasin. After I had blown it out I drew her to the wide bed, and pulled her down beside me, and she sighed and crept close, huddling against me within the circle of my arms, so that I felt like some great protecting giant, instead of the wispy little Currito that I was.

Ay, Dios! It made me believe that there was some good in the world, after all — which was a good thing for us both just then.

138

Presently we fell into a fitful sleep, from which we would start up, every now and again, half expecting to hear those horrible yells and screams in the plaza outside. But all was quiet, and little by little Pepita settled into the cradle of my arms and was overcome by her exhaustion. Toward midnight I awoke long enough to draw a blanket up over us both, and after that I, too, fell into a deep sleep from which I was only aroused by the sound of someone banging at the door.

We both came awake with a start and sat up abruptly, Pepita clutching the blanket to her. I had a sinking feeling in the pit of my belly, but I tried not to show it.

"Who's there?" I called out, making my voice as big and brave and strong as I could but yet feeling only too conscious of its slight quaver.

"Is that ye, Currito?" came a familiar voice from the other side of the door. "It's Yancey — open up!"

I wonder if I showed the relief I felt. I rose quickly and slipped the bolt, flinging the door wide. Sunlight streamed in, making me blink and rub my eyes. I had no idea that it was so late in the morning.

The sandy-haired young giant waited on the step outside. Beyond him, in the pitiless sunlight, I could see a score of blanket-covered mounds scattered the length and breadth of the plaza, but to judge from the number of wide, wet spots, blackening in the sun, there must have been many more. At the upper end of the plaza, where the narrow trail led off toward the Indian village, there was an ox-drawn carreta, and a half a dozen stolid miners had uncovered one of the blanketed heaps and were flinging limp, human bodies up into the cart without regard to how they fell. I tried to stand so that Pepita would not see out past me. It was not a good thing for a woman to look upon.

"Come in," I said to Yancey.

He ducked for the lintel and stepped inside, and I quickly swung the door behind him to a place half ajar, so that it admitted some light and air but yet blocked the view. Since that made it gloomy I struck flint and tinder and lighted the candle.

"How — how did you know I was here?" I asked as I did so, feeling I had to say something.

Yancey smiled slightly.

"I had a notion," he replied.

He glanced toward Pepita, who seemed suddenly to remember her manners, shaking herself a little, as if she were coming out of a trance.

"Bienvenido, señor! Mi casa es la vuestra," she said. "My house is yours, though it is a sad day to make you welcome."

I realized abruptly that Yancey had never been there before, and it was obvious that his mere presence under her roof pleased her. I felt a little twinge of jealousy in spite of the time and place.

Yancey inclined his head toward her gravely, impersonally.

"Mil gracias, señorita," he acknowledged her greeting, and turned back to me.

"The ladies — we all — were worried about ye," he said. "Recollect, Don Emilio saw ye last in th' middle o' th' square, just after ye'd called t' us. We were afraid — "

Pepita gasped.

"Currito was — out there?" she cried. I felt much better when I saw the look in her eyes.

Yancey nodded.

"He came over t' warn us, miss," he told her. "I reckon if any got away it was thanks t' him."

She stared at me without saying anything, but yet with a glow in her eyes that warmed my whole being.

Yancey had swung back and was speaking to me again. With an effort I forced myself to hear him.

". . . but ye weren't at th' fonda," he was saying, "an' they didn't find yer body, so I reckoned ye might be here."

He flushed hotly as he said it, and I daresay I did, too. I snatched at the first fleeting thought that might ease his embarrassment and flung it out.

"You went to the fonda?" I asked.

He nodded. Just in time I caught myself. That was the last place I had seen Jode, and I wondered what had happened to him. I had been on the point of asking when I remembered the feud between them. This was hardly the moment to remind him of it.

It was Pepita who rescued me from that situation, quite unwittingly.

"Why?" she cried out abruptly. "Why? And, señor, who — what demonio — what devil of hell could think of such a thing?"

Yancey looked at me.

"I reckon you know more about that than I do, Currito," he said dryly, and I wondered if I caught just a tiny hint of a question as to my own part in all this.

I started to bristle, and then it occurred to me that, of course, they must wonder. I alone had brought warning! How did I know if I were not in some way involved?

The thought gave me cold shivers along the spine. I

turned to Pepita. My hunch — so you call it? — warned me
that it would be better for him to hear me explain to her,
rather than speak directly to him. That might be construed
as a pack of lies and a plea for mercy!

"I had no chance to tell you last night, chiquita mia," the
endearment slipped out before I could catch it, "but it was
you yourself who gave me the key."

"I — ?" She looked astonished. "I, Currito?"

I nodded.

"If you had not told me that it was Johnson who was
giving the fiesta and offering the socorro I would never
have guessed until too late!"

"What's that?" Yancey looked at me sharply. "Johnson?
We were given to understand that it was Raoul . . ."

That explained much!

"They were both in it," I said, and forthwith I told them
the whole story, just as I have told it here. I see no point
in enlarging upon it.

When I was done Yancey seemed to arouse himself, as
from a trance.

"So that was th' way o' it!" he remarked. "Yon's mighty
interestin', Currito. I forgot t' tell ye, Don Urbano's insisted th' Alcalde hold an inquiry into this thing. They
want your story — asked me t' bring ye over if I found ye.
Will ye come?"

"Sí, hombre!" I replied at once. "Of course!"

I wanted nothing better than to see the men who were to
blame for this seized and brought to justice. And this I
wanted quite as much for a practical as for a moral reason,
for I flatter myself that I knew my Apaches, and unless
prompt action were taken by us the Indians would take it

upon themselves to exact their own vengeance. In that case many an innocent might suffer for the crime of a few.

I tucked in my shirt and picked up my hat.

"Wait!" cried Pepita. "Do not leave me alone, Currito! I am afraid to be alone!"

"Why, chiquita!" I looked at her sympathetically, understanding that she was distraught. "It is all over. There is nothing to fear now."

"Just the same," I could see that she really was frightened, "I do not want to be alone, Currito. If you must go, let me come with you!"

I glanced inquiringly at Yancey, who nodded.

"Sure, let her come," he said, and turned to her. "We'll wait outside, miss," he told her, "whiles you put on some clothes."

Only then did I realize that she never had gotten around to putting on her shirtwaist!

As we sat on the step outside, waiting, I could feel myself going all hot and cold inside from embarrassment for what I felt he must be thinking — not for my sake, for he knew all about me, but for hers, which was a curious thing, for I had never before given a thought to her morals. Indeed, considering the town and the surroundings in which she lived I would not have been surprised to learn that she was a professional prostitute. I might have been hurt, but I would not be surprised. Nor could I, with any honesty, have blamed her. Yet now I was concerned for her. I wanted to protect her — even from thoughts!

I realized, of course, that there was no use in explaining that our night together had been entirely innocent; that we had been too utterly frightened and exhausted to be aware of one another's state of dress or undress. That would only make matters worse! No, I decided. Drastic ailments require drastic remedies. I must say something that would shake his thoughts away from her.

"What happened to Don Jode?" I said. "Have you seen him?"

The vehemence with which he spat into the dust at his feet told me that I had succeeded even better than I had intended.

"Slept through th' whole thing!" he replied with grim disgust. "Dead drunk! He never woke up till I found him in th' bar at th' fonda this mornin'."

I recalled that that was where I had left him, and I wondered if the drink I had bought for him had been the one to lull him to sleep. Whether it was or not, I felt, he was lucky. All he had missed was a horror and a nightmare, and in his condition it might well have been dangerous for him to be out and about. I found myself defending him.

"You know why he was drunk," I said. "He's in love with her, too. Just because you're rivals is no reason to break up — "

He spat again.

"He's no rival o' mine," he said coldly. "He ain't fit t' come within a mile o' her, and I aim t' see that he don't."

I felt a wave of impatience. I wanted to ask him what made him think he was so much better qualified, but I held my tongue. For the moment, at least, I had my bellyful of fighting and quarreling.

Pepita joined us with a scarf over her head, and we put her between us and hurried across the plaza. She kept her eyes averted, and did not look at the blanketed heaps or at

144

the great bloodstains in the dust. As we entered the palacio, the ladies especially appeared surprised. Doña Beatriz quite openly drew her skirts away from Pepita and went to sit on the other side of the long room, where the hearing was being held. Doña Elena was gracious but reserved. I could see that for once Doña Luz was at a loss to know how to behave. I thought I had better explain.

"Señorita Perez was alarmed at being left alone," I said, "so I thought we had better bring her with us."

Doña Elena raised her eyebrows ever so slightly, and I went brick red, all at once realizing that I had tacitly admitted having been with her, at least since the massacre. I glanced at Pepita and, silently, with my eyes, tried to beg her forgiveness. She gave me a timid little smile of reassurance, and I felt better.

It was the first time I had been inside the palacio, and even then I did not get past the big front room, or sala, where Don Emilio performed his official duties. The ladies sat at one end, and at the other end there was a long table at which the inquiry was in progress. Don Emilio presided, at the head of the table, and ranged on either side of him were Don Urbano and his brother, Raoul, and of course, the Capitán-Comandante, Don Tito. The Teniente Flores was conspicuous by his absence — I learned later that he was on duty at the cuartel — and I was astonished to see Johnson and Gleason and Eames seated there.

Don Yancey stepped forward.

"Here he is, Don Emilio," he said. "He's got an interestin' story. I reckon ye'd best hear it from him."

Don Emilio nodded to me, and I took my place at the foot of the table and told again everything, exactly as it had happened — leaving out mention of Pepita's dress, of course!

There were no interruptions, although when I bluntly accused Johnson and his friends and Raoul and the Comandante each one tried to speak out in his own defense. The Alcalde waved them to silence.

"Let him finish, señores!" he said in such a tone that I wondered what was in his mind.

I soon found out. When I was done his lips twisted in a mirthless grimace.

"You have made some rather serious charges, Señor Ruiz," he said, and so unaccustomed was I to the name that I looked around before I realized that he was addressing me. "You have witnesses, I suppose?"

I opened my mouth to reply, and then closed it again, all at once aware that I had not a living soul, except an Indian, who could substantiate any of the things I had said.

"Mangas Colorado?" I finally offered hesitantly.

"Mangas Colorado is gone, señor," Don Emilio replied frostily. "All of the Indians are gone. Their village is deserted."

"And good riddance, I say!" growled the Comandante. The Alcalde motioned him to silence and looked at me.

"Then I have no one," I said boldly. "But I think the events speak for themselves."

"Do they?" replied Don Emilio. "The Comandante — Don Tito, here — says that the Indians attacked first — "

"With cannon, I suppose?" I retorted sarcastically.

"With cannon, Señor Ruiz?" The Comandante looked up. "Did you *see* anyone use cannon?"

"I did not *see* it, Don Tito," I replied, "but I certainly *heard* it."

"Bah!" snorted the Comandante. "That was the sunset gun you heard — the one we always fire at sundown to salute the colors!"

It was a lie, I knew. But how could I dispute it?

"That was the signal for the attack," he went on. "When the gun sounded the Indians seized weapons and rushed us. My men were forced to fire in self-defense."

"That's right," Johnson chimed in. "We 'ad a gyme goin' in th' mercado, an' when we 'eard th' shootin' we grabbed our guns'n piled h'in."

I appealed to the Alcalde.

"Don Emilio!" I cried. "Are you going to let them hoodwink you like this with such a pack of lies?"

"How do I know they are lies?" he demanded, unsmiling.

"But — but, surely you could see — " I began.

He shook his head.

"I saw nothing," he replied. "By your own admission you ran close to the verandah and screamed at us to get inside. Your appearance, your whole demeanor convinced and frightened us, and we obeyed you to the letter. How could we see what happened?"

"Don Urbano — ?" I cried frantically, turning toward him.

But he could only shrug and spread his hands. Clearly he was more in sympathy with me than with these others, but he could not swear to something he had not seen.

And now the other side opened their attack. It was Johnson who began the discrediting movement.

" 'Ere, you Ruiz — Currito!" he put in. "You talk a lot

147

about seein'. Did you, yerself — did ye see h'any o' this ye tell o'?"

"I think I've already answered that," I said stiffly. "I did not."

"Why not?" he shot back at me.

"Because I — " I began, and then began to see where his line of questioning was leading. Yet I had to finish. "Because I — I took cover myself. I was indoors."

"Where?"

I did not answer that. How could I without harming Pepita? I was silent. Johnson chortled triumphantly.

"There, see?" he cried. " 'E won't answer that because 'e cawn't. I tell ye, senyors, 'e's th' one as 'as been givin' us a pack o' lies. 'E weren't no more under cover than I was. 'E was out runnin' with th' savages 'e'd been plottin' with t' cut all h'our bloody throats, that's w'at!"

I stared at him in horrified amazement. But I was even more surprised when a woman's voice rang out from the other end of the room.

"He was not!" It was Pepita, God bless her. "He was with me! He was with me the whole time! He stayed with me all night, and if it hadn't have been for him I would have died, señores! I am not ashamed to say it!"

Johnson sneered. The other ladies drew back in horror.

"Aye, a woman o' that sort'll swear t' h'anythink," he growled, "an' ye cawn't believe a word she says, either!"

I flung myself impulsively along the table, in a furious effort to get at him.

"Why, you dirty, murdering rat — " I shouted.

But Yancey and Don Urbano caught me and pulled me back.

148

"Take it easy, lad," said Yancey quietly. "I know how ye feel, but that won't do any good."

"We've had enough bloodshed to last us for a long time, Señor Ruiz," said Don Emilio. "Try to control yourself."

"Tell him to keep the filth out of his mouth, then," I retorted hotly.

"All this is beside the point," the Comandante interrupted pompously. "The main thing is that the whole affair was very cleverly planned, and I think the evidence shows that two men were involved in inciting the Indians to rebellion — Señor Ruiz, here, and — Señor Cahoon, there!"

Yancey started up out of his seat.

"Me?" he cried incredulously. "You accuse me . . . ?" Don Tito nodded.

"Exactly so, señor!" he replied. "Do not think that I have not had my eye upon you! I know, for instance, that you were with General Houston at San Jacinto. I know, too, that Texas covets this territory. I say that you were sent here by General Houston to foment trouble among our Indians, so that Texas would have an excuse to march in and annex us! I say, also, that Señor Ruiz is your assistant to that end."

At this date I am aware that such an accusation would sound farfetched. Today, as we approach 1870, these things no longer happen. But at that time it was not so unbelievable. There were a half a dozen schemes a year in those days to cut off a chunk of Mexico for this purpose or that. Just for example, it must be remembered that only the year before Texas had won her independence; and that in four years time a Texan expedition, marching on Santa Fe, was to be defeated and captured by Governor

Armijo! Oh, no! It was incredible to us, who knew it to be false. But it was not so to most of these others.

One thing, at least, Don Tito had said that was true. It was a diabolically clever scheme — and looking along the table at Raoul Hermoso y Maravilla's smirk, I thought I could guess the name of the devil!

But Yancey was standing. He, too, stared along the table. "Gentlemen — señores!" he cried. "You don't believe this?"

No one answered him. He swung about and looked toward the other end of the room.

"Luz!" he called. "Lucita! At least you don't believe it?"

But Doña Luz's face was white, and when he spoke to her she drew back a little, as if he had threatened her. Clearly she was convinced. Yancey's shoulders sagged, and though my own predicament was not good, my heart went out to him. It seemed to me that Raoul was exacting a hard vengeance.

Don Tito stirred, and glanced at Don Emilio.

"Well, Your Excellency?" he asked. "Shall I arrest them?"

My mouth was dry. Both Yancey and I stared at the Alcalde for a long moment while he cogitated. The room was silent. When he spoke I nearly fainted with surprise.

"No, Don Tito," he said. "We have had enough trouble already. There are two sides to this story. Each side accuses the other, and how do I know which is telling the truth? I do not. I can not. Since that is so, I say that it is unfortunate that all this has happened, but let us say no more of it. What is done is done! I will leave you, señores — you, Señor Johnson, Señor Gleason, Señor Eames — you, Señor Cahoon, Señor Ruiz — I will leave you free to go as you will — and the sooner the better, but in no case later than the next conducta to the south. If any of you — any of you, mind — are in Santa Rita after that I shall be forced to order your arrest. That is all, señores."

I did not stop to argue the injustice of the decision. At least he had ordered the same for Johnson and his companions as he had for Yancey and myself. I turned on my heel and walked out the door. Not until I felt her hand on my arm did I remember Pepita; I looked down and found her fallen in beside me, walking with me, and as I looked I felt her fingers tighten.

"Never mind, Currito," she whispered. "It is not true — not any of it! And I will walk with you! Anywhere!"

I smiled at her proudly.

"God bless you, chiquita!" I said. "It is good to know someone has faith in me."

We were halfway across the plaza when steps ground behind us, came abreast of us, and then slowed to our pace. I looked up to see Don Yancey at the other side of her. He grinned ruefully sidewise at me.

"Do you believe all that stuff, Currito?" he asked.

"Of course not, Don Yancey," I replied. "But it doesn't seem to matter what we believe, does it?"

He shook his head with a chuckle.

"I reckon not!" he replied.

"What now?" I asked.

He shrugged, then jerked his head back toward the palacio.

"I'm not welcome back there any more, looks like," he said. "I reckon I'll just join Jode at th' fonda till it's time t' go."

"Then perhaps this is one of those ill winds that blows to somebody some good — no?" I replied, thinking to cheer him a little.

But he only sighed heavily.

"Maybe!" he grunted. Then he glanced sidelong at us again, soberly — first at me, and then at Pepita, and his expression was wistful.

"You're lucky, Currito," he remarked. "You don't *know* how lucky!"

# Chapter 2

*W*HEN I stepped out of the little, squat, adobe palacio, that bright spring morning, I did so with the feeling that my days in Santa Rita were numbered. If Jode and Yancey insisted upon leaving at once, I told myself, I would be in honor bound to go with them. The next conducta was due within the next three or four days, and should be returning within a day or two after that. However, this was the mule train from Sonora, which was the least regular of the three, and which, indeed, might not come at all. It sometimes did skip a month. The next regular conducta from Chihuahua — one of the two which traveled so precisely on schedule — was due in exactly a fortnight, and would go south again two days after its arrival. This meant, according to my calculations, that I could count on no more than twelve more days there, and the thought left me a little depressed. Not that I was beginning to like the place, or had any affection for its officials, who I felt had treated me shabbily and cast an unpardonable slur upon my honor. But I was growing fond of Pepita — so much so that I even toyed with the idea of asking her to go with me; a circumstance that I found somewhat disconcerting, for until then I had always prided myself on my ability to take my women and leave them alone!

However, in all of this I was burning my bridges before I came to them — if I may coin another phrase. My days in Santa Rita were indeed numbered. But I miscalculated the number.

Let that be as it may, señores, I shall tell the story as it unfolded. Those were strange days — those of the next fortnight at the copper mines. In general they were strangely peaceful. Before the massacre it had been impossible for a man to move across the plaza or down an alley without being beset by arrogant beggars or drunken idlers, or solicited by some insolent red wench offering her commodities for a dram. But now they were all gone, and it was not because they had been exterminated. Henry Johnson and his comrades counted their "pelts," as they called them, and lay claim to some three hundred and sixty odd — all killed in self-defense, they still stoutly insisted, although many were the scalps of women and children.

But there had been more than eight hundred of the Indians, all told, so that it was obvious that better than half had escaped. Among them, apparently, was the giant Red Sleeves — Mangas Colorado, whom I had warned myself — for his body was not among those found and buried the next day, although Juan José's was. What had happened to them? Where had they gone? It was as if the earth had opened and swallowed them down whole!

Knowing these Indians as I did, I was disturbed. To me the silence was ominous. But if anyone else in Santa Rita shared my uneasiness I never knew of it. Even Yancey scoffed.

"You start at shadows, Currito," he told me. "I can't say I like th' way it was done, but it's sure a relief to be shut o' 'em."

"That's beside the point," I retorted. "What troubles me is that since that night we have not seen hide nor hair of them. Neither have we heard anything about them — of where they are, or what they are doing."

He grinned at me.

"I'll set your mind at ease if that's what's worryin' you," he said.

"All right!" I challenged.

"They're runnin'," he told me. "Runnin' as far and as fast as they can. They're scairt green!"

"I wish I could believe it," I replied grimly. "But I've never heard of an Apache yet who was afraid."

He gave me an almost pitying look.

"You're forgettin', Currito," he told me, "that these folk weren't Apaches any more — not real ones, anyway. They'd turned into town Injuns. Long ago they lost all th' belly they ever had for fightin'. All they was good for was layin' around in th' sun an' whorin' an' swillin' rotgut — beggin' a handout from anyone that'd be fool enough t' give it to 'em."

Clearly there was no sense in arguing with him. I only shrugged. But that did not mean that I agreed with him.

In the light of this attitude on his part, and in view of all that had happened, one would think that it would not be long before Yancey insisted upon shaking the dust of Santa Rita from our heels. Indeed, in his unhappy situation it would hardly be surprising if he felt that the sooner we were gone the better. As a matter of fact, I believe that

155

he did feel so, and that he would have lost no time in acting upon the impulse, but for one complicating factor —
Jode!

I do not know why we should have assumed that Jode
would be sympathetic; that he would be pleased to patch
up their quarrel and shake hands and let bygones be bygones. Perhaps the ordeal through which we had just passed
biased our judgment. We still felt its sting, and we forgot
that he had not been present. He could not possibly know
how sore was the wound. At the same time, I believe, in his
reaction to his treatment at the hands of Doña Luz and his
anxiety to re-establish matters between them as they had
been before ever they had come to Santa Rita, Yancey was
inclined to overlook, or at least minimize, certain facets of
his erstwhile friend's character which had only come to
light within the last few days.

The truth is that Yancey had been right and I had been
wrong, and I might as well confess it now and have done
with it. So long as things were going his way — even so
long as hardships and disasters were of a sort to be shared,
Jode was personable, likable, gay, insouciant. He was certainly handsome beyond his share, and attractive to women;
and there was never, then or later, any question as to his
courage — or perhaps bravery would be a better word, for
Jode's daring was of the reckless, devil-may-care kind,
rather than that which is quieter, more thoughtful, less
spectacular but nonetheless true.

But with all this Jode was basically selfish, hard, cruel.
So long as he was unopposed he could be companionable,
even to the point of seeming admirable. But woe to the man
who stood in his way. What he desired he took; and it made

no difference to him from whom it might be. Nor did he much care about the means. If he could get what he wanted by fair means — well and good! But he was not above stooping to foul when fair means failed.

To be sure, I knew nothing of this at that moment. In fact, if anything, during the last few days I had been rather critical of Yancey, holding him too harsh in his judgment. But it was about this time that my own eyes began to come open, and so I make note of all this at this point.

We took Pepita home first, after leaving the palacio, and there Yancey would have left us discreetly had I not called after him:

"Un momento, Don Yancey! Hold on! I will go with you to the fonda if you will wait for me just a little."

He halted and settled against the side of the building.

"Sure!" he smiled. "Take your time. I ain't in any hurry."

I stepped inside with Pepita, and in the gloom of the one low-ceilinged room she turned toward me with a look of alarm in her eyes.

"Pepita, amada mia!" I said quickly, fearing that she was about to burst into tears. "I must say my thanks to you for the way you stood up and spoke out in my defense. It was a brave thing that you did, and I am grateful."

"How brave, my lover?" she smiled shyly. "It was true."

"Yes — true," I replied seriously, for I think I had never felt more solemn than I did at that moment, "but not in the way that they thought — that they were bound to think! That was your bravery, querida mia, and that is what I will not forget."

"But now you go?" She looked all at once again as if she were about to cry.

"Uh — all of my things are at the fonda," I told her lamely.

She brightened.

"Then you only go to get them?" she cried. "You will bring them back and stay here with me?"

I shook my head.

"No, Pepita chiquita," I told her. "That would not be right. Last night there was a reason. But that is over now. It would not be right for me to come here to stay."

She looked at me blankly.

"Cómo? Why is it not right, querido mio?" she asked.

"Because it would hurt you, Pepita," I told her. "Don't you see what people would think? I would not have them — "

"Think? Pouf!" she interrupted me with an exclamation of astonishment. "Currito mio! Could you not see what those people over there think of me already? How could they think worse?"

There was certainly cold logic in that. So far as the people at the palacio were concerned she was beyond salvation, and I daresay that it would have made little difference if I had been less preciously scrupulous. It would have brought pleasure to her, even if only my company. And it might well have been the means of guarding her from more serious harm. But I remembered Johnson's remarks, and I was bound that I would not be the cause of every filthy tongue in the town wagging over her name! I shook my head.

"Please, Currito!" she begged. "I am afraid to be alone!

And, see? Is this not a nice little house? We will be happy here, and I will make you my special tortillas and enchiladas!"

But I remained stubborn as a mule.

"It *is* a nice house, Pepita chiquita," I told her. "But I cannot stay! I like it — and I like you too much to bring evil on you. I will come often to see you. I will spend every day with you. But I — "

She stamped her foot, her patience at an end.

"Don't bother yourself, pelón!" she flared. "Go — go away to the filthy fonda, since that is what you prefer. But do not take the trouble to come back. I — I will not be here!"

"Pepita — " I cried, taking a step toward her.

But she ran around to the other side of the bed and turned her back on me.

"Go away!" she commanded. "Don't you come near me, chambón! Get out of my house — that you say you like so well that you will not stay in it. Go on! Go away! Get out, and don't come back!"

She was very angry, and I had no doubt that she meant it. I sighed and put on my hat and went out. Yancey was still waiting. He took one look at my face and sobered.

"Don't tell me *she's* angry, too!" he exclaimed.

I nodded miserably.

"How come?" he demanded.

"I told her I was going over to the fonda — that I couldn't stay here," I replied glumly. "I was only thinking of her — "

He smiled wryly.

"Sure!" he said. "I know! I reckon there just ain't any

way to figure a woman — Well! Misery loves company! Come on, let's go over to th' fonda an' get Jode an' all cry in our beer together!'"

We did not have to look far for Jode. As I expected he was in the bar, but at the sight of Yancey he rose as if to leave.

"Wait a minute, Jode," the sandy-haired man called to him. "I've been lookin' for you. I want to talk to you."

Jode halted, hesitating, wooden-faced.

"Cain't say I want to talk t' you," he retorted.

Clearly he was in a foul humor, yet it was too early in the day for him to have been drinking. I guessed that he must be feeling the effects of last night's mescal, which will often leave a man with a murderous hangover. Had I been Yancey, I think I would have resented his tone, but the big Yanqui's patience was longer than mine.

"An' I can't say I blame you — th' way I've been actin'," he replied. "It took a massacree an' — an' some other things t' wake me up. But I can see now what a fool I've been, an' I'd like t' be th' first t' offer my hand an' say I'm sorry. How about it? Let's go back an' take up where we were before all this fool-headedness begun."

Jode squinted at him suspiciously, ignoring his outstretched hand. He shot a quick glance at me, and then looked back again at Yancey.

"What's got into you?" he demanded. "Has th' little peacemaker, here, been talkin' to you? Or maybe you figger you can sweet-talk me out — hey?"

Yancey sighed and dropped his hand.

"No," he said wearily, "it's neither one. Sit down, and I'll try to explain."

160

He signaled to the patrón for three drinks, and we moved to a corner table, Jode sliding into his place with a look of mistrust, as if he expected us to reach for knives at any moment.

"There's a lot happened in th' last twenty-four hours," Yancey said when the drinks had been brought.

"So I'm told," Jode growled. He looked at me. "I missed it. Slep' through the whole thing!"

"You were lucky," I told him.

"I dunno!" He shrugged. "I was in a pretty good humor t' go out an' collect a couple o' scalps o' my own, just a little while before, as I recall."

He glowered at Yancey meaningly. The sandy-haired man pretended not to notice.

"That ain't all that's happened," he said.

Jode glanced at him, interested in spite of himself.

"No?" he growled. "What else?"

"Well, for one," Yancey replied, "it's been fixed so's it looks like we were responsible for last night's dust-up. They give us till next Conducta Day t' git out!"

Jode looked surprised.

"Don't tell me anybody minded!" he remarked.

"Some did," Yancey smiled wryly.

"Oh?" Jode was definitely interested now.

Yancey nodded, as if to emphasize the fact, and launched into an account of the inquiry at the palace. So far as I could see he left nothing out, nor did Jode interrupt him again, though I saw his eyes widen when the sandy-haired giant mentioned Doña Luz's reaction to the accusation against him. When Yancey was finished Jode leaned back in his chair and stared almost triumphantly at his erstwhile friend. There was a small, sneering smile on his stubbled lips, but his eyes were cold and hard.

"Well-l-ll!" he said softly. "So, ye're a Texan agent, hey? By God, now, I never thought o' that! I wouldn't put it past ye though!"

"It's no laughin' matter," Yancey began. And then he caught sight of Jode's expression, and the front legs of his chair banged down on the floor. "Now hold on, Jode!" he cried. "You know as well as I do — "

Jode leaned forward, over the table.

"I don't know a thing, mister!" he growled flatly. "I never laid eyes on you till we met in Santa Fe!"

"That's not true!" I cried involuntarily.

Jode turned his cold eyes on me.

"Can ye prove it?" he demanded.

I gulped.

"No, but I know what you told me in Santa Fe," I retorted.

He gave me a slow, hard grin.

"They didn't believe ye this mornin'," he said. "What makes ye think they'd believe ye now?"

Yancey spoke soberly. He was eying Jode intently.

"I've already told her we came out from Tennessee together," he said.

"I'll tell her ye lied," Jode shot back. "Why wouldn't ye t' cover up?"

"But — but!" I could see that Yancey was holding hard to his temper. "But we've been ordered to leave, man! Don't you understand that?"

Jode leaned back and laughed insultingly.

"You've been ordered t' leave," he chuckled. "I ain't!"

Yancey made one more try.

"Come on, man!" he cried. "I said I didn't blame you for being angry. I'm sorry! I didn't realize I'd hurt this bad. But open your eyes now! The fight's over — "

"That's what you think!" Jode interrupted. "I'm tellin' ye it's just commenced!"

Yancey broke off abruptly and stared at him.

"You really mean it, don't you, Jode?" he said a little wistfully.

"You bet I do!" Jode leaned over the table toward him again. "Look, mister! You've had your chance. Now I'll have mine! What's more, I'll win where you lost!"

Yancey sat back in his chair and glared at his former friend, his face red and angry.

"All right!" he snapped. "If that's the way you feel about it, you can go to hell in your own handbasket! I'm sorry I ever offered my apologies. But, suppose you tell me somethin' now. She wouldn't talk t' me. What makes you think she will t' you?"

Jode grinned confidently.

"She will!" he retorted. "She will! You wait 'n see!"

He stood up and ran a hand across his chin.

"If I'm goin' a-courtin'," he said tauntingly, "I reckon I'd best go an' clean up."

For a long moment after he was gone Yancey sat and glared after him, at the door through which he had disappeared. Then abruptly he snatched up his untasted glass of mescal and tossed it off at a gulp and stood up.

"Come on, Currito!" he said grimly. "That . . . He's got this place staked out, an' I'm damned if I'll stay under th' same roof! Let's go over t' th' other fonda!"

I found my gear and joined him outside and we trudged across the angle of the plaza to the only other inn the place boasted. All the way he kept muttering angrily, and once I heard him say: "By God, if he hurts a hair o' her head — "

From that I realized that the chances for an early departure from Santa Rita were slim indeed. And to tell the truth, señores, I did not truly mind, for I hoped it would give me a chance to make my peace with Pepita.

# Chapter 3

*H*OW he managed it I do not know, since I was hardly in his confidence, but I can say that Jode's was no empty boast. I have said that he had a way about him that was attractive to women, and no doubt this had much to do with it. Yet even with this it seems to me that his incredible success was much too swift and too overwhelming to be attributed wholly to honorable means.

I do not mean by this any reflection upon Doña Luz. I believed then, as I have always believed, that she was a most remarkably level-headed young woman. But she was a woman, nevertheless. I think — indeed, I know now — that her affection for Don Yancey, was both deep and overwhelming. In fact, it was deeper and stronger than either he or she suspected. To be sure, it was swift and impulsive, but that was the Spanish side of her temperament and was certainly nothing to be decried.

But these very factors worked in Jode's favor. Don Tito had needed a scapegoat to hide his part in the brutal mass murder of the copper mines Indians. Henry Johnson and her uncle, Don Raoul, had both hungered for vengeance. Between the three of them she had been made to believe — quite wrongly, but nonetheless convincingly, so far as she was concerned — that this great, open-faced man to whom she had almost given her heart was in reality no more than a treacherous spy and a hostile agent who simply made use of her for his own ends.

Believing this, false though it was, the very depth of her budding affection made the ache in her heart more painful and more difficult to bear, while her very impulsiveness made her dejection sharper. Accordingly, when the personable Jode came hastening to her with spurious sympathy he found his work already half done. He had only to offer a few lies and innuendoes, let her take his kerchief to dry her eyes, mutter a few curses on all black-hearted villains and two-faced dogs — and then open his arms to catch her on the rebound!

I do not know that this was the technique he used, to be sure. As I say, he did not take me into his confidence. But it is my guess. I do know, however, that on that very evening he called upon her and was admitted to see her, and that they sat upon the verandah of the palace, conversing in low tones, until nearly midnight. I know this because after I had tried to see Pepita at her house and had received no answer to my repeated knocking other than a muffled command to "go away," I went and sat beside Don Yancey on the bench in the moonshade in front of the fonda and watched for him to leave.

On the next afternoon they went riding — and again on the next — which I found disturbing enough to mention.

"That should not be allowed," I said.

"You're damned right, it shouldn't!" Don Yancey agreed.

"Because of the Indians, I mean," I told him.

He gave me a half-disgusted look.

166

"I can think of worse things," he growled.

"You would not say that, señor," I said, "if you knew them as well as I."

But I could see that he was preoccupied, and that, at that point at least, he did not take either me or my fears concerning the Indians seriously. So I held my tongue, making up my mind that I would go myself to Don Urbano and warn him of the dangers that might lie in wait among the very bushes at the edge of the village. However, I had my own problems during that time, and somehow I never got around to it. By the grace of God and good luck . . . But, there! This is a part of what I am to tell. It is enough, now, to say that if such harm as I feared had come to them, I would have felt badly to blame.

As I say, though, I had much on my own mind — and much in my heart — to preoccupy me during that time. Each day brought us nearer to the moment when we must go, and even I could not tell when that might be. At the best, I believed, it could not be more than a fortnight — when the Chihuahua conducta was due. At the worst, it might be within four or five days — if the Sonora mule train was on time. In the meanwhile I was beside myself with anxiety. Pepita had offered much in my behalf — unsuccessfully, it is true, but that made it no less a sacrifice on her part — and I had responded with a slap. At least I realized that she had interpreted it so. I felt that I must see her and try to make her understand how concerned I was for her; why I had behaved as I did. In another case I would probably feel that I had made my gesture. With Pepita it was somehow different. Mine was the burden — not hers!

As I have already told, she would not respond to my

knocking on the first night. However, I did see her the next day — across the plaza! She had gone to the church and was returning, and at sight of her I started to cut across the corner of the square, hurrying, to intercept her. But she saw me coming and began to run, ducking in at her own door and slamming it in my face, just as I came up. I heard the bolt click, and though I pleaded and pounded at the panels, she did not even deign to reply.

I met with much the same results that evening, and the next day and the next evening. I will not trouble you with details, save to say that it might almost have been called a sort of a game had it not been such a serious matter to us both. After I saw her coming back from church, I too took to haunting the cathedral at all hours — although I had never been a churchman. I also took to lurking in the alleyways near her house, watching the washtubs in the back yard, hoping that there I might catch her at her household chores; even hiding behind the outdoor privy feeling sure that she could not deny the call of nature, and that I might, as a last, desperate resort, intercept her then!

But she had sharp eyes, señores, that little Pepita, and she baffled me at every trick and turn. I might hunt the timid deer or the cunning cat or the wily bear or the swift antelope with great success. But with this child, this girl, this woman, all of my stalking was to no avail!

The third day after the massacre was actually the one on which the Sonora conducta was expected — although, as I have indicated, this was the irregular mule train, and might be as much as four or five days late, or might not even come at all. It did not come on the third afternoon, and on the following morning I noticed a pair of local hustlers near the palace corral, cutting out the "Coronel" Raoul's two fine riding horses and three pack mules — for I would hardly say he traveled light! As I watched idly from the bench before the fonda they groomed the animals and gave them a feed of grain — almost an invariable sign of a forthcoming journey. There were other indications as well. His saddle was brought out and oiled and hung with his bridle and saddle blanket on the corral fence. Pack saddles were brought out and given a similar check, after which the mozos fell to making up the packs — by which I gathered that the "Coronel" was about to leave us.

I wondered if this meant that Don Urbano and his family were also planning to return to Mexico City. If they were, I thought, it could be a severe blow to Jode's schemes — as well as a sorrow to Don Yancey, for I suspected that he had not altogether abandoned hope. However, there was no sign of any such intent.

Shortly after midday the plaza — both fondas and the several cantinas facing on the square — began to fill with men from Johnson's camp, making the rounds, and I noticed a number of houses down in back of the cathedral and over near the cuartel were especially popular. Adding this to the preparations for the "Coronel" Raoul that I had witnessed in the morning, I suspected that Johnson and company were about to go on their way, and that Raoul would accompany them. That suspicion was confirmed when, later in the afternoon, I overheard some of them, in conversation with the patrón, say that they planned to ride for Chihuahua in the morning.

At the time I thought little of it save that it was a good riddance. So long as they remained I went always with the uncomfortable feeling of having to keep my chin on my shoulder and watch behind me, for I would not put it past Johnson to slip a knife between my ribs. He was that kind. A single stroke of vengeance would not satisfy him if any further opportunity offered. It also seemed to me that they were being rather childishly impatient — especially for men who had engaged to join our party from Santa Fe on the pretext that there was safety in numbers. I realized later, of course, that there was method in their madness. As a matter of fact they were anxious to be off before the Sonora train arrived, for if they should be there at that time, by virtue of Don Emilio's order they would be forced to accompany it when it left on the return trip. Sonora also had a law, similar to the Proyecto de la Guerra, offering a bounty for hostile scalps. But the Sonora bounty was much less than that of Chihuahua — ergo, it was to Chihuahua that they preferred to go, claro!

That was also the afternoon when I almost intercepted Pepita once again. Ay, por Dios, señores! Many things happened in Santa Rita on that day, that I shall be put to it to tell all of them!

It happened that I was quietly — I might almost say stealthily — slipping down the alleyway between the cathedral and her house, bent on my usual mission for those days. My objective was the back yard, where I hoped I might be able to surprise her at some chore or other, and surely enough, as I came to the corner of the house, I heard her chopping at the woodpile.

Claro, señores! To live she must eat, and to eat she must have a fire to cook by, and to cook she must have wood for the fire, and to have the wood she must chop it! It was heavy work indeed, swinging the ax, especially for one so small and fine, but she was accustomed to it. She had been doing it all her life. But I, not stopping to think of that, was horrified at the sight of her doing such work as should be left to a man, and like a great fool I cried out before ever I was close enough to catch at her.

"Pepita, por Dios! This is not for you! Here, let me!"

At the sound of my voice she dropped the ax, flung one startled glance over her shoulder and fled, ducking around the other side of the house and racing toward the door in front.

I followed, you may be sure, with wings on my heels. But as fast as I sprinted, she was faster. I was yet two steps from the door when she slammed it and shot the bolt.

This was toward the middle of the afternoon, when the plaza, and indeed, the whole town it seemed, was crowded with Henry Johnson's villainous crew. They were all about me, walking back and forth from cantina to cantina and fonda to fonda and bar to brothel, but I paid them no heed as I stood and sobbed and pounded at the door. As a matter of fact, if I had thought about it at all I would have sworn that they were equally indifferent to me.

As may well be imagined I was betwixt rage and tears at such a scurvy trick of fortune. It must have been the sixth or seventh time I had been thus balked in the four days that I had been trying to see her only long enough to beg her pardon, and I was close to the end of my patience. Indeed, I would have given it up long since had she been anyone else!

In consequence I leaned against the door and beat upon it with both fists, calling out her name and begging her to let me in, saying that I must see her, that I had something to tell her that she must know. I know well that she heard, for the house was not large, and such a thundering as I made might well have been heard by the padres at the altar in the cathedral! Yet she made no answer, and presently I began to calm down a little and to try to devise a scheme that might break down the barrier that she had built up against me. As I paused and pondered I did so all unaware that several of Johnson's choicest, attracted by my howls and pounding, had stopped to watch the fun. Such, at least, they evidently thought it.

After I had stood so for a moment, pondering, an idea came to me; an idea that might work. At least it would be a sort of last desperate resort. I swung back to the door and more quietly this time, yet more sharply, I rapped — rap, rap, rap — rap, rap, rap — rap, rap, rap — just as I had on that terrible night.

"Pepita!" I called, wheedling a little. "Pepita chiquita! It is I, Currito! Do you not remember our signal? Let me in, Pepita mia, for I have something I must tell you; something I would tell you on my knees, Pepita — and tomorrow may be too late! Tomorrow, Pepita, Señor Johnson leaves for Chihuahua, and remember Don Emilio has ordered Don Yancey and myself to leave. It may be that he will insist that we go with Señor Johnson, in which case we will have no choice but to obey. If that happens, then, we will be separated forever, and I will never be able to say to you what it is I wish to say!"

For a moment there was silence from within, and then I thought I heard a rustling and a sound of movement and steps that came close to the door. I could even swear I heard her touch the bolt! Gracias a Dios! She was going to open.

But exactly in that instant a thundering chorus of mighty boos and howls and jeers and hoots of laughter broke out behind me. I whirled, naturally, furious and red-faced, to see — four of Johnson's toughest bullies, laughing and choking and hugging their sides as if they feared they would split!

When they saw that I had turned and was glaring at them, they began to chant in hooting unison:

> Pep-PEE-tah! Pep-PEE-tah!
> Chick-KEE-tah! Chick-KEE-tah!
> Eso es tu Curr-EE-toh!
>
> Remember our tap?
> Rap — rap — rap?
>
> Let me in, Duck,
> And we will . . . !

I would not repeat the rest of it if I could. It was foul. It was filth, such as only their kind would use, and it went on for what seemed endless verses — as long as any one of them could think of a ribald rhyme! Ay, Jesús, señores! They were very funny fellows — they thought. But if I had been armed with even a stick I would have attacked them, and such was my fury that I truly believed I would have broken every skull among them. As it was I had only my bare hands, while they all carried rifles and had great dirks at their belts, and two of them carried tomahawks, as well.

So, what could I do except flatten my back against the door and scowl at them as ferociously as I knew how? At first I was so surprised that I could not seem to think. Behind me silence fell. The bolt did not slide. The door did not open. Nor could I expect it to now! Of course she heard them! How could she help it? Their hoots and shouts and ribaldry were audible from one end of the plaza to the other. I could picture her horrified expression, her stricken eyes, and more than ever I wanted to kill my — our tormentors with my bare hands.

Then it occurred to me that in staying where I was I was only prolonging her agony and embarrassment. I turned back to the door and put my lips close to the panel, calling softly through to her. I pitched my voice low, so that I hoped they would not hear. But at the same time I had to make it loud enough so that she would hear me.

"Pepita!" I called. "Are you there, Pepita? Can you hear me? Do you hear them?"

"Yes!" From the sound I could tell that she was standing as close to the door as I, and my heart leaped with pleasure. Then, she had been about to let me in! But I could hardly expect her to do so now. I spoke to her again.

"Pepita! When I go they will go, too. Do not open the door now — for anyone. Later, when they have all gone away, after it is dark, I will come back and give the same knock that I did before. If you will let me in then I will tell you what is in my heart, Pepita mia."

She did not reply, so that I could not tell whether or not she would open her door to me later. Yet I certainly meant to try, and I had a feeling that she would let me in. I paid no further attention to the still hooting, whooping quartet

174

in the plaza, but turned away and walked straight to the fonda where I was staying and went to the room I shared with Don Yancey.

As I predicted, once I was gone the four foul-mouthed bravos found no entertainment in howling at a blank wall and a locked door. Accordingly they ceased their scurrilous chant and went roistering and reeling on their way. Later I saw them at the far end of the square talking to Henry Johnson, who had evidently just come up from their camp, laughing and slapping their thighs and holding their sides. Undoubtedly, I thought, they were telling him about their mighty adventure, and for a moment I was tempted to return to my room and get my pistols and let them have a ball or two. But then I realized that Don Emilio would certainly place me under arrest, and any chance I might have of seeing Pepita would go glimmering.

Don Yancey was not in our room at the fonda when I got there. However, I thought little of that. When he did not appear in the combination bar, kitchen and dining room before supper I wondered what might be keeping him. But when he did not turn up at all during the supper hour I became genuinely concerned about him. In or out of love, Don Yancey's appetite was always excellent. Indeed, I would say that it was as big as he was, and I knew that he would not miss a meal if he could help it. As soon as I was done I strolled over to the public corral, between the presidio and the palace, and looked to see if his horse was there. It was gone and so was his saddle, so that it was evident to me that he had ridden out of town somewhere. But where — why? I was worried. The longer the Indians remained silent and unseen, the more my scalp tingled. I had no fear

for such a party as Johnson's would be. But in my judgment a lone rider — or even two — was not safe out of
sight of the town. As for myself, I would not have ventured
beyond the first clump of willows alone!

For a moment I wondered if he had just decided to leave,
and had quietly packed up and done so. But then I remembered that most of his gear was still in our room, and decided from that that he had at least intended to come back.

It was not yet sunset when I went back to sit on the
bench in front of the fonda and watch for him, for Santa
Rita supped early. But it was thick dusk — almost dark,
indeed — before he came riding in at the north corner,
which was the same way we had entered coming down
from Santa Fe. He turned his horse into the corral and came
striding through the thick, dusty gloom, toward where the
yellow light poured from the fonda door and lay like a
stripe of pale gold on the hard-packed earth.

"Hola!" I called to him as he came up. "Hombre! Where
have you been? I was growing worried about you."

For answer he cursed bitterly, savagely.

"What's the matter?" I demanded.

"That goddam Jode!" he told me. "He took Doña Luz
out early this mornin' — ridin'. Th' mozos, over at th' palace
corral, told me they was laughin' an' jokin' when they rode
out, an' they heard Jode say he was goin' t' take her up
through th' saddle, back o' th' Nun, over toward th' Hot
Springs!"

"Great God!" I cried, leaping up involuntarily. "Why
that's Cuchillo Negro's country!"

"I know," Yancey nodded somberly. "That's why I rode
after 'em. You've got me so jumpy myself with your gloom-

castin' about th' Injuns that I was feared for 'em — for her, anyway!"

"This is no joking matter, Señor Don Yancey!" I assured him gravely. "Whoever stirs from the village, even a little distance, in any direction, is in danger from the survivors of the massacre here — believe me. But to go deliberately into the country of Cuchillo Negro, who has never been friendly, is practically suicide! Didn't you bring them back?"

"I didn't find 'em!" he told me grimly. "An' believe me, hombre, I'm not jokin'!"

I stared aghast at him, limned in the shaft of light that streamed from the door of the inn, letting his news seep slowly into my consciousness. It was past dark now, and they had not yet returned! Certainly, if they were able they would try to get back by dusk — and, I told myself, there was no prize that either Cuchillo Negro or the remnants of the copper mines Indians would rather have than the beautiful daughter of the owner! They would not kill her — not at once, at least. If I knew these Indians, they would probably do it slowly, horribly, lopping off a piece at a time and sending it in to her father, so that he would know what was happening to her, and knowing be equally tortured! As for Jode, they would have their own ways of dealing with him, too — and just at that moment I felt that he richly deserved anything they might do to him!

"Do you want me to go and see Don Emilio? Don Tito?" I asked. "They might order out a search party from the garrison."

But he shook his head.

"No use now," he replied. "I must o' rode twenty miles

out an' back without seein' hide nor hair o' 'em, an' th' signal smokes was thick th' other side o' th' pass. If I couldn't find 'em in daylight, th' entire Mexican army won't turn 'em up at night. Wait till mornin'. If they ain't back by then — " he shrugged — "then we'll see. We ain't exactly welcome over thataway, you know."

I nodded soberly. He was right, of course, but I knew how hard it must be for him to wait. In view of that I found his next words utterly baffling.

"D'you reckon the's anythin' t' eat left?" he asked. "I ain't et since this mornin'. I could put away a horse!"

How any man could think of eating at such a time was beyond me. But as I say, rain or shine, in love or out, Don Yancey's appetite was always good. I suppose his size accounted for it.

As it proved the bean pot was still in the ashes, and there were some tortillas left. Don Yancey finished them, and while he ate I kept him company with a copita of aguardiente. When he was done he went out to respond to nature's demands, and for the moment I was again left alone.

The big room was not crowded for it was midweek, and few of the miners came out to make the rounds of the bars save on Saturdays and Sundays. Most of Johnson's crew had returned to their camp at supper time and there remained, doubtless making ready to depart the next day. Thus there were only four or five hangers-on at the bar when Johnson came reeling in, just drunk enough to be ugly, and apparently looking for someone.

Apparently I was that someone, for his eye lighted evilly as he caught sight of me, and he came rolling over and thrust his ugly, vulture's face down close to mine, so that I could not avoid his stinking breath.

"Ullo, Currito!" he leered. "How's yer ramera chica — 'ey? Pretty little pussy, she were! Aw-haw-haw!"

Now this is a phrase which I do not like to hear applied to any reasonably respectable woman, much less to Pepita, and I could feel myself going hot with anger. Yet I am a peaceable man — and I was not armed, while he was with the inevitable dirk. I have since wondered if he did not deliberately intend to egg me on.

"Go away, cabrón mecate!" I snarled. "Take your filth and get out of the sight of decent men, you murdering cochino!"

The fury of my voice, together with the names I called him, caused heads to turn at the bar and fetched a silence on the room. But Johnson cared nothing for that. He cackled and began to chant, derisively, a few lines of the bawdy filth that his bravos had howled at me in the plaza that afternoon.

That was too much for me. Armed or not, I had had a bellyful of that. He was taller than I, considerably. But as I think I said earlier in this account, he was skinny as a reed. I did not think he was in extraordinary condition, but he might have been tough as rawhide-covered wire. He still did not frighten me. I clenched my right fist and swung it from the floor, at the same time as I heaved myself to my feet from the three-legged stool I sat upon.

I think he did not expect me to be so easily provoked, for although I am no expert in such matters he did not have time to duck. My fist caught him squarely in the mouth with all the force at my command plus the full weight of my rising body.

This may not have been much, but in his unwariness it was enough to split his lips against his gums and loosen three of his blackened stumps of teeth. It was enough, too, to tumble him backward in a sprawling heap of spidery arms and legs in the middle of the barroom floor. But it was not enough to knock him unconscious. He was up like a cat and came streaking at me with his head down and his shoulder hunched before his bleeding mouth and his drawn knife clenched in his fist.

As I say, I was totally unarmed, and moreover, having struck the first blow and thus used up my advantage of surprise, this was a ticklish moment for me. All of the men in the room, at the bar and at the tables, were sympathetic to me, I am sure. But everything happened so swiftly that they were unable to help. I simply acted instinctively in my own defense, reaching down behind me and snatching up the heavy, three-legged stool on which I had been sitting. As he came close to me I flung it full in his face, and again he reeled back, to fetch up with a thud against the bar.

This time, however, he did not fall. Nor did he drop his knife. Instead he lay back against the bar, shaking his head a little as if to clear it, and I had the satisfaction of seeing that the blood was streaming from his nose now, as well as from his mouth, and that the heavy stool had cracked and flattened that already crooked organ so that I was sure it would be a sight to behold in days to come! The other men at the bar cheered.

"Ole, Currito! Viva! Viva! Bravo! Hit him again!"

But I was not at all sure that I would have another chance. When he came at me again it was more warily, and I skipped behind a table desperately, wondering what I should do now.

To my vast relief this was the moment at which Don Yancey chose to make his reappearance. He came in through the front door, having stepped around to the palace corral to see if Doña Luz's horse was yet there, and he took in the critical situation at a single glance. Clearly he was far more accustomed to this sort of thing than I, for he knew at once what to do, and he lost no time in doing it.

Johnson, intent on me, did not see him come up behind. Indeed, I doubt if he even knew the huge Yanqui was there until Don Yancey grasped him by the scruff of the neck and the seat of his breeches, lifted him bodily, as if he weighed no more than a child, and carried him, kicking and wriggling, to the open door, where he catapulted him out into the night, not even deigning to disarm the fellow.

"Get out!" he called after him. "Get back t' yer camp, you filthy scum, an' don't let me find you around here again! I'll be waitin' for you!"

He turned away from the door, brushing his hands together, and then came over to where I stood, still gasping at the swiftness of it all. The whole thing had taken no more than seconds.

"That's a bad habit you've got, Currito," he said.

"Habit — ?" I must have looked blank, for he grinned.

"Seguro, hombre!" he replied. "A feller your size goin' around unarmed is just askin' for trouble. Better carry a knife or a gun or somethin'."

"Pues sí, hombre!" I replied, smiling. "I daresay you are

right. In the future I will not be caught empty-handed!"

"I'm sorry I broke up your little party," he grinned.

"Are you?" I laughed. "I'm not — and my thanks to you, Don Yancey! I believe this calls for drinks all around — how do you say it — on me? After that, if you will excuse me, I have an — er — engagement."

He cocked an eye at me.

"Success?" he asked.

"Gracias a Dios! I believe!" I told him.

"Then, by all means — a drink is in order!" he cried.

We stepped to the bar and I called for aguardiente all around, and it may have taken the patrón five minutes to set them up for everyone. When the glasses were filled Don Yancey picked his up and lifted it toward me.

"Here's to — " he began.

But he never got beyond that. Outside, the early evening quiet of the plaza was abruptly rent by a hair-raising, spine-tingling, blood-curdling woman's scream.

Don Yancey started involuntarily, spilling his drink across the back of his hand.

"Jesus!" he exclaimed. "What was that?"

Why it should have done so, I do not know, but cold fear clutched at my heart. I dropped my untasted glass upon the bar and raced for the door, Don Yancey close at my heels.

Outside, in the starlit night, my worst instinctive fears seemed to be realized. Down at the far, southern end of the plaza I could see the vague, black form of a horse and rider, racing. In the still night air the sound of galloping hoofs, drumming in the dust, was as loud as a kettledrum. And looking diagonally over toward the west, toward the little house close by the cathedral, I could see that the door stood wide-agape, and the yellow light of the candles inside streamed out through the opening and cut a swath into the darkness of the night.

Square in the middle of that path of light something lay in the dust of the plaza. At that distance it was shapeless, indistinguishable, looking like nothing more than a heap of rags. But I did not need to be told what it was.

"Pepita!" I cried out in anguish. "Pepita! Ay Dios, what have they done?"

And I went racing out toward that formless huddle with Don Yancey close behind.

# *Chapter 4*

IN SPITE OF Yancey's longer legs I was the first to
reach that pitiful bundle, huddled on the ground in the
pathway of candlelight that streamed from the open door.
I flung myself down upon my knees beside it and reached
out to turn it over, hoping against hope that I was mistaken.
But I was not. It was Pepita, and I saw that there was a long
gash in her scalp and she had apparently been stabbed somewhere in the body as well, for her clothes were covered
with blood.

"Pepita!" I whispered. "Pepita mia! Can you speak? Can
you tell me? Who has done this to you? Por Dios, I will — "

Don Yancey came up and knelt at the other side of her.
Her eyelids fluttered open for an instant, and faintly I heard
her whisper my name, but she could say nothing more, and
I could see that she was no more than half conscious. I
looked across at Yancey in a sweat of agony.

"Help me!" I begged. "We must get her inside and find
out how badly she is hurt. Pray God she will not die!"

He held out an enormous hand and waved me back from
my little efforts to raise her.

"Easy, lad!" he told me. "Let me do that."

He slipped his arms under her and stood up, raising her

184

as easily as if she were no more than a feather. I followed him toward the door.

"Ay Dios!" I swore. "Who would do such a thing? By the blessed blood of Christ, if I knew — "

Yancey paused with his foot on the doorstep and the light full on him and the girl in his arms. He glanced back at me grimly and jerked his head toward the southwest corner of the dusty plaza, where the trail led off to Sonora and Chihuahua.

"He rode off thataway," he said. "I reckon that ought t' give you an idea!"

He shouldered the door wider and went on in with his precious burden. Instinctively, I imagine, he kicked the door half shut with his heel before he laid her on the bed and fell to examining her hurts.

For my part I hesitated on the step, stricken to sudden immobility by his words.

"Johnson!" I breathed sharply. "Henry Johnson!"

And at once I knew what must have happened. Earlier in the evening I had seen Johnson talking with those same bully-boys who had jeered at me in the plaza that afternoon. Obviously they had been telling him about their mighty exploit, and no doubt they had told him of the special knock that I had used to signal her. Perhaps, even, they had heard me say that I would return, and had told him that, too.

In any case, following our fight and his ejection from the fonda, he had gone out thirsting for revenge and taken out his spite upon the one person who could not fight back. Doubtless he had gone to her door and rapped — as I would rap, thrice three times. She, poor child, beyond doubt thinking it was myself, come as I had promised, opened the door, whereon he had seized her and dragged her outside and attacked her with his knife. It was nothing more than good luck, I knew, that had enabled her to scream as she had. That had frightened him away, knowing that it would bring help. But for that she might well be dead now!

I teetered where I was, upon the doorstep, before the door that was half ajar; now that I knew, one side of me bidding me ride for vengeance, the other side admonishing me to hold for love. Go after him, cried out one part, and serve him as he has served others! Wait, said the other. Stop and see. She may need you now! If she is dying could you forgive yourself if you were beyond the touch of her hand? The feel of you near could be the link that holds her to life! But if he escapes? asked anger. Let him — for the time being, replied the more sober, honest being. Time enough, later, to catch up with him wherever he may be. Right now she needs you! Don't go! Don't go!

These were imaginary voices, as I say, and it scarcely took as long for them to flash through my mind as it has for me to set them down here. Yet it was a moment or two before I started to follow Don Yancey in through the door. My hand was on the frame when a real voice, a human, woman's voice, spoke to me out of the darkness at my back.

"Well, Currito!" it remarked. "Are you even acting as guard and lookout now for your friend, Señor Cahoon?"

I whirled about, and to this day I could not say whether I was relieved or alarmed to see the Doña Luz, sitting there, sidesaddle, upon a strong gray horse. Behind her, on his red roan, Jode Lassiter leered at me like a timber wolf.

"What?" I said, for I was dazed beyond belief, and this

new development seemed only to make matters worse — though at that point I could scarcely say how. "What do you say, señorita? I do not understand — "

"Don't you, Currito?" she asked, as she slipped down from her saddle, clenching her riding crop — for she clung to that as she had her silla de mujer, her sidesaddle, as an evidence of civilization! "Don't you? It just happens that we came into the plaza as your large friend was carrying your wench into that crib. I saw that with my own eyes! I thought, at least, you had enough pride to resent that. But apparently I was wrong!"

Before I suspected what she was about she lashed out at me, catching me across the side of the face with her crop — and I cannot say I liked the taste of civilization!

I fell back against the doorframe, to be sure, not entirely flung there by the force of her blow. Surprise that she would do such a thing was as much to blame, though I have since come to know that the primitive within us will rise above all that we have been taught when we see what we truly value jeopardized.

"Señorita!" I gasped. "Doña Luz — "

Behind me, at that instant, the door swung open, and Don Yancey, with his sleeves rolled up, appeared.

"Currito — " he began, and then abruptly he stopped, staring sharply at Doña Luz and then at Jode.

"You — she — ?" I stuttered, not knowing quite what to say.

He ignored me.

"Where the hell have you been?" he flared. "In God's name, I thought you both dead an' scalped! Thank th' great Christ you're both safe!"

He swung back toward me.

" 'Tis bad — but not too bad," he told me. "She's askin' for you. . . . Here's a good thing — "

"Are you quite finished, Señor Cahoon?" Doña Luz demanded sharply. "If you are, I would like you to know that I watched you carry that woman in. . . ."

He turned cold eyes upon her.

"That woman has been stabbed an' nigh scalped," he told her. "If you've got nothin' better t' do than jaw then get away. If you've a mind t' help then fetch hot water an' cloths — an' yer pa an' Don Emilio. I think they sh'ld hear what she has t' say — if she's th' strength t' say it by th' time they get here!"

He looked again toward me.

"Come in, Currito — come in," he said with an abrupt shift from the hard to the gentle. "She's askin' for you, boy."

And though he did not speak of it I could see him eying the growing welt across the side of my face where Doña Luz's crop had struck.

I looked back at them, wondering if they realized what they had happened upon, and stepped in through the door. Behind me Yancey's voice flared:

"Will ye do as I ask — or get t' hell out?"

I looked toward the bed, and saw that the wound in her scalp was a good three inches long, and gaping, as if he had tried to cut a piece out of it.

"Looks like he tried to get another 'pelt,' " said Yancey at my elbow. "Alive, too!"

There were words in my mind, but I cannot say them here! He looked at me sympathetically.

188

"Th' cut in her side's not much," he said. "He hit for her heart, I sh'ld say, but a rib cut it off, an' it slid t' th' side. Plenty o' blood, but no danger from that, I judge. She's lucky, Currito — an' so are you."

"I ought to go after him — " I muttered.

"Never mind, now, boy!" he said easily. "I'll go down and get him myself in th' mornin'. Right now she needs you. You stay here, y' hear me?"

" I hear you," I replied, nodding without looking at him. My eyes were all for her on the bed before me. "God will overtake him if I don't!"

He smiled seriously, approving all that I implied.

"I don't blame you," he said. "Igod, I don't blame you!"

A knock at the door brought Doña Luz and a pan of boiling water and some torn-up sheets — and Don Emilio and Don Urbano, both in nightshirts that flapped around their shanks.

"What's this? What's this?" bawled Don Emilio pompously.

"See for yourself," growled Yancey. "I reckon her story'll tell you who was lyin' an' who was tellin' th' truth th' other day."

We were fortunate, I daresay, that her hurts were not worse than they were. As it was there were at least three of us — Don Yancey, Don Emilio and myself — who had some experience at binding up superficial knife and gunshot wounds. At that time and place a rudimentary knowledge of such things was essential. But I doubt if any of us could have dealt with anything more serious.

By a sort of tacit consent the others stood aside and let me wash and dress her wounds. The gash in her side, just under her breast, and along the ribs, must have been at least six inches long, but though it had bled profusely it was not deep. I pulled it together with ordinary household thread and a darning needle, then washed it well again and bound her all around the body in clean linen. The cut in her head was more difficult, mainly owing to the length and thickness of her glossy, black hair. But, working carefully, I managed finally to patch it together so that I believed it would heal without leaving her disfigured.

As I worked she opened her eyes and smiled when she saw who was her clumsy surgeon.

"Currito mio," she murmured. "I could tell by the gentleness of the touch that it was you."

"Gentle!" I growled bitterly. I never felt more clumsy. My hands seemed all thumbs — and mere stubs of them, at that. Yet she never so much as whimpered. Instead she put her hand out upon my shoulder, so that her fingers caressed my neck, and kept it there the whole time.

When he saw that she had opened her eyes and was clear in her mind, Don Emilio began to question her, and she talked to him freely as I worked over her. Essentially her story merely confirmed what I had already guessed, and there is no sense in repeating it here. When she was through Doña Luz gasped in horror and her father looked grim, and even Jode, who had followed them in, swore softly in English.

"Bandido! Asesino! Cabrón! Cochino!" Don Emilio sputtered. "I will see him hang for this! Do any of you know where he can be found?"

"I know where his camp is," Yancey told him. "I've already promised Currito I'll go down an' get him, first thing in th' mornin'."

"I'll send a file of soldiers with you, in case you have trouble," Don Emilio promised.

"I won't have no trouble," Yancey assured him quietly. He glanced at Jode. "What're you swearin' at?" he demanded. "You didn't do much better t'day, I reckon."

Jode looked surprised, but Doña Luz flared out at Don Yancey. One would think that what she had seen and heard this night would have opened her eyes, and that she might be a little contrite. But on the contrary she seemed to be angrier than ever at him. I reflected that Jode's poisoned tongue must have been even sharper than I had guessed.

"How dare you speak to Señor Lassiter that way?" she demanded. "You — you — two-faced — "

Yancey ignored her and glared at Jode.

"Th' buckeroo, over at th' corral, told me," he said, "you was takin' her over through th' saddle, toward th' Hot Springs! Ain't you got no better sense than that — ? "

"We did nothing of the kind!" Doña Luz interrupted him. "That's what we talked of doing. But I remembered that Father had told me I must not ride that way, so we went west instead, toward the mountains over beyond the plain!"

The relieved look on Yancey's face was almost comical to see, but I could not forget that he had risked his own life by riding over through the saddle in search of them. The thought infuriated me.

"To ride anywhere outside the village, alone and unarmed," I put in coldly, "is dangerous just now."

It was on the tip of my tongue to tell them of Don Yancey's risk, but at that instant Pepita called out my name in a small voice.

"Currito!"

I turned back to her.

"Yes, Pepita mia?"

"I am afraid, Currito!" she whimpered — she who had been so brave throughout my clumsy ministrations only a moment before. "I am frightened! You will not leave me now?"

Yancey glanced toward her.

"This is no place for us to be quarreling," he growled. "This girl needs rest — and quiet. Come on! Let's we get out of here!"

Pepita reached out and caught me by the sleeve, perhaps thinking he was speaking to me as well as the others.

"Do not go, Currito!" she cried.

Yancey grinned at me.

"You stay here, Currito," he commanded. "T' hell with what anyone thinks! Th' rest o' you, come on! Clear out!"

When they were gone I rose and went around to the right-hand side of the bed, so that I would not jostle her wounds, and dropped to my knees beside her, brushing her cheek, her shoulder with my lips.

"Pepita chiquita! Amada mia!" I whispered. "I am a fool! I am a great fool!"

She looked at me, wide-eyed, and lifted her hand to run her fingers through my hair.

"Why?" she asked. "Why do you say such foolishness, querido?"

"Because I angered you, Pepita mia," I told her. "I do

192

not know yet what it was that I said or did — but whatever it was, it was foolish!"

She gazed at me for a long moment in silence, and the look in her great eyes was soft and warming to my soul. But then she turned her face away, as if something had hurt her terribly.

"It was not anything you said — or did, Currito mio," she whispered.

"What then, prenda mia? How did I offend?" I was surprised.

"You did not offend me, Currito, mi amante," she said in a voice so small that I could scarcely hear it. "It was — it was — "

"What, querida chica?" I persisted.

"At — at the palacio, Currito," she said — and I could feel her stiffen, as if it were an effort to force the thought out — "you saw! You saw what those others thought. You thought it, too, and I do not blame you! Why should I not be judged in the same way as those around me? I live in a little house, close by the cathedral. I am alone. All around me — all around the church — there are other women — putas, prostitutas, rameras — whores — who earn their bread by the rhythm of their buttocks, and cover their backs with their tails, like squirrels!"

"Pepita!" I cried, ashamed then that I had ever thought that such a thing was possible — for I could hardly deny it. "Pepita, I — "

She rolled her head toward me and smiled a little, wanly, and put up her fingers to my lips.

"Let me finish, Currito mio," she said gently. "I say this because this you thought, and I could not blame you for so it must look. But it hurt me, Currito! It hurt me because never have I been so! This house was my father's, who was a miner — a buscón, a prospector — not one of these peónes in the copper, up above. My mother was an Indian, who died when I was born — which is why I have no brothers or sisters. My father was a frugal man — and a knowing one. He found places — in the mountains — where there was ore — oro and plata both — gold and silver — not much, surely, but enough for his need."

"Pepita querida," I interrupted her. "You are talking too much. You are tiring yourself. You can tell me all this — "

"No, no, Currito, mi corazón!" she insisted. "Let me tell you. I have thought much of it, and I will rest easier — "

"In my arms, Pepita mia," I broke in.

She looked at me almost pleadingly.

"If I may, Currito," she whispered.

"May!" I cried. "My heart would turn to stone and my soul to smoke if you did not!"

She smiled and touched my lips again with her finger tips.

"Hush!" she commanded. "You distract me!"

"All right," I grinned. "If it makes you feel better — talk till dawn, prenda mia!"

"I could not do much else — cut as I am," she replied, and blushed deliciously. "But, I am serious, Currito mio! Because the deposits he found were not large my father told no one where they were — even me. And he only admitted to me that he had discovered them when he lay dying, in this very bed! He would go off, into the monte — to the west, I think — for weeks at a time, and when he came back he would have a little sack that he would never let me peek into. Every six months or so he would load his mules and sit me on the packs and ride with the conducta, to Chihuahua. I did not know what he did there, then, but I did know that when we came back most of the mules carried nothing at all, and one of them carried two very small but very heavy canvas sacks."

"So?" I laughed. "Are you going to tell me you are an heiress, Pepita chiquita? "

"In a way, Currito!" She was quite serious. "It was not very much, but do you see? What Father had in those bags were coins that he received for his dust, and he did not use many of them. He saved them for me, and if you will look in the cupboard, underneath the bottom plank, you will find what is left of them. Eight hundred pesos he left. There should be almost five hundred in the cupboard."

I smiled slightly, reflecting that I had been paid half again as much only for bringing Ben Wilson's and Johnson's parties out from Santa Fe.

"I'll take your word for it, Pepita mia," I told her. "But what . . . ?"

"I do not tell you this to make you think that I am rich, Currito, mi alma," she interrupted me, "but so that you will see that I have not need to be like these others around me! In Santa Rita a little goes far. Two or three pesos a month is as much as I need, and I have used as little as I must of what he left. I dance at fiestas. I cook a little, and wash when people come who do not know how to do these things for themselves. Sometimes I wait on table at the fondas, or serve as barmaid when the patrón is busy. By this I stretch what my father left me, so that it lasts longer. But never do I sell my body! Never do I take pay for what I have to give!"

"Pepita, I — " I tried to break in, but she would not let me interrupt.

"Never!" she insisted, and went on ingenuously. "I am me, and where is the joy to be paid for something that is done only for money? Pah! I spit on it! Love is a joyful thing, Currito, not something to be bought and sold!"

I thought her wandering a little at that point, perhaps from the poison of her wounds, and I answered her gently.

"That is true, Pepita mia. It is true, true. But what . . . ?"

She smiled at me and once again ran her fingers through my hair.

"What has that to do with us?" she asked a little wryly. "This, Currito — it is this that I have been trying to say. That day, when we came back from the palacio, I could see that you thought as they thought — perhaps more kindly, for that is your way. But nevertheless you thought it, and that was why you would not stay! You did not want to be linked with such a one, and I could not blame you. But it hurt, Currito! It hurt, and I ran away from you."

"Pepita!" I cried, shocked that she could think me so callous. "Pepita mia, that is not so! Do you not see? It was just the other way 'round! For a peso I could have half the women in the village. I did not want anyone to think that of you — that is why I would not stay! Don't you see?"

She stared at me, wide-eyed.

"Truly?" she whispered. "You mean that, Currito?"

"I mean it, Pepita chiquita!" I assured her gravely.

196

"Then I have been the fool," she retorted.

"Basta!" I laughed. "Enough, woman! We have both been mistaken! You thought that I thought that they thought so I thought that . . . Ay, Dios! It could go on forever, but there is none of it true! I see only one solution!"

She looked at me, still on her back, with her strong breasts raising the blanket that covered her.

"What is that, Currito?" she asked almost anxiously.

"Marry me!" I grinned. "That will solve everything."

She bounced up on her knees on the bed, letting the blankets slide, naked but for her bandages — and winced.

"Gently! Gently, mi vida!" I cried, and eased her back. She sighed as I drew the covers up over her.

"You mean it, Currito?" she whispered.

"I mean it, alma de mi vida — soul of my life!" I assured her. "I dream of it — if you will!"

"I will!" she assured me, turning toward me and putting her arms tight about my neck. "Ay, Currito, I will!"

"One thing!" I told her, with mock gravity.

"Currito!" She looked alarmed. "What is that?"

"We will wait until your wounds are healed," I told her. "Then — I do not want to hurt you, Pepita. Nor would I wed cold stone!"

"Currito!" she whispered, burying her face in the hollow of my shoulder. "Currito mio, I will do as you wish — nor will you find that you are marrying cold stone — believe me!"

"Pepita!" I whispered. "Pepita! Alma de mi alma — soul of my soul!"

# Chapter 5

*H*A!

I do not mean that as a sneer at her love or mine. We were both sincere. But how could she or I know what the next days would bring?

Don Yancey came about midmorning, when we were both refreshed with sleep. He glanced at her.

"How do you feel?" he asked.

"Wonderful!" she told him. "If this would happen every day with the same result I would be scarred from head to foot!"

He glanced at me, with raised eyebrows.

"We're going to be married," I said, "as soon as she's up and about!"

He threw back his head and roared with laughter.

"By God!" he shouted. "You had me scared for a minute! Congratulations t' you both!"

"Did you catch Johnson?" I asked.

He sobered.

"They were gone," he said. "They must o' left long before daylight. Th' fires were cold. I would o' followed 'em, but Flores reckoned we sh'ld head back."

"Flores?" I was surprised.

"Uh-huh," he replied. "Ramón Flores — you know. The teniente, over at the cuartel — th' one that does all th' dirty work that Morales don't feel like doin' himself."

I nodded.

"I know him," I told him. "Well — he got away this time, but one of these days I will catch up with him, and when I do . . . !"

As it happened, that was to be taken out of my hands. But how was I to know that?

I look back upon those all too brief days that followed as among the happiest I have ever known. To be sure there was plenty of work to be done, for since Pepita could do nothing herself I had to take over for her. By day I cooked and cleaned, chopped wood, carried water, put ashes in the outhouse, bathed her and myself, carried out the slops and sang happily from dawn to dark. By night we lay close, wrapped in one another's arms, whispering our love, and tasting the tender-sweet agony of each other's kisses.

In the meantime the squalid little village, nestled under the Kneeling Nun, continued its complacent existence, smugly confident that nothing could ever happen to shatter its cocky assurance. Perhaps it would be dramatic of me to say that I alone, of all the people in Santa Rita, anticipated trouble. But the truth is that now that Johnson was gone I simply assumed — when I thought of it at all — that what danger had existed was over, and as the days passed and nothing happened, I too fell into the habit of complacency. Indeed, I was much too idyllically happy with Pepita to bother my head about such gloomy matters.

At the same time, however, I looked forward to the tenth

of the month — the day which would bring in the conducta from Chihuahua. Probably, in view of what had happened, an appeal to Don Emilio would have produced a pardon for me and permission to remain as long as I wished. But I had had a bellyful of Santa Rita, and I wanted nothing better than to shake its dust from my heels. By the time the conducta arrived, I judged, Pepita's wounds would be well enough healed to permit traveling, and I longed to take her away from there and give her a good long look at the outside world.

Indeed, Pepita and I even discussed it and laid our plans.

"You are sure you will not be homesick, Pepita chiquita?" I asked a little anxiously.

"For this?" She laughed gaily. "Currito mio, the only reason I did not go long since is because I know no one anywhere else, and I did not know where I would go!"

But I had to be doubly sure.

"I do not want to take you away if you are truly attached to it," I told her seriously.

"Attached to it — pooh!" she retorted. "Currito, you are a silly, blind, sweet tarantín! You are a simpleton, and I love you! Can you not see that wherever you are, that will be home to me? Go, now, and see the agente, so that we may sell this house and the furnishings that are in it before it is time for us to leave. I will take with me nothing but my clothes — and maybe one or two nicknacks, and when we get where we are going we will buy all new things together, you and I — eh, Currito, mi corazoncito?"

And another time:

"Where will we go, Currito querido? Chihuahua I have seen. I would like to go to some place new — Monterey,

200

Zacatecas, Durango, Guadalajara, Puebla, perhaps even Ciudad México? Can we go to those places, amado mío?"

"Por qué no? Why not?" I grinned. "Perhaps I will even take you to los Estados Unidos — the United States — to San Luis, in Missouri, or to Nuevo Orleans, chinita del alma mia!"

I laughed and was happy to see how her eyes lighted and shone with excitement.

To tell the truth, however, I did have one worry. I was afraid that we might not be able to dispose of her little house, with its furnishings, in the short time that was left to us. But, as it turned out, that was the very least of our problems. It was well located, especially for a certain kind of business, and I had no sooner announced it was for sale than we were besieged by a dozen or more prospective buyers — all women who had hitherto operated down back of the cathedral or on the outskirts of the village, and who scented greater profits to be made at the center of things! They each bid against the others, thus inflating the price far beyond what I had thought it would be worth. What was more each came with cash in hand. It was a revelation to me to see what sums these women could produce!

I must admit that I was perhaps a little overly squeamish about disposing of it for such a purpose. But Pepita was far more practical than I.

"Currito, my lover!" she scolded me fondly. "You are a great dolt! What difference will it make to us what becomes of the place once we are gone? You know that no one else could afford to pay such a price! I say take the money and put it in the sack, along with my little store of pesos, and keep it against the time when we will want to settle down and buy a place of our own. It will be a part of my dowry, alma de mi alma!"

Which was certainly plain common sense. Accordingly the place was sold to the highest bidder under the sole stipulation that we would continue to occupy it up to the day of departure. As soon as that was done I fell to sorting and packing everything that she wished to take with us, as well as my own gear, so that by nightfall of the ninth our packs and bundles and saddlebags were all tied up and in readiness to go. That night I crept into bed and into her arms all trembling with excitement and anticipation, and she came to me all soft and warm and strained against me, gripping me tightly with her smooth, young thighs, and fluttering her tongue against mine until I thought that my heart must burst out of my breast from the sheer ecstasy. It was only later that the thought came to me, when we were lying sweetly exhausted, side by side.

"Pepita chiquita," I whispered. "Chinita de mi alma, there is one thing we have neglected."

"What is that, my Currito?" she asked.

"To get married, amada mia," I told her. "I meant that we should do that before we left!"

"Pouf!" she laughed. "Let us wait until we get to Chihuahua, where I can be married to you in a great big, big cathedral!"

And with that she rolled over and came to me again, from which it will be seen that by now her cuts were almost entirely healed.

It was just as well, however, that when I had sold the little house for Pepita I had stipulated that we be allowed to remain in it until the day of our departure, rather than agreeing to give possession on any set date, for the tenth of the month came — and went, and no conducta came winding over the plain below from Chihuahua!

Our disappointment may be imagined. At the same time the bewildered astonishment of the Santa Ritans must be pictured! Never — not once in all the fifteen years that the mines had been in operation — had the Chihuahua conducta failed to arrive promptly at half past three in the afternoon on the tenth and twentieth of every month! Month in and month out, year in and year out, the mule trains had come and gone between Santa Rita and Chihuahua, at least, as surely and as regularly and as precisely to the minute as the sun comes up in the east and sets in the west. Indeed, I think the Santa Ritans would have been less shocked and surprised to see the sun come up out of the west and set in the east!

The first, and most immediate effect of this astonishing occurrence was to send three quarters of the village, myself and Pepita among them, scurrying to consult the calendar. No doubt, we thought, we had made some miscalculation and lost a day somewhere back along the weeks — or else had gained one. We weren't quite sure which it should be, none of us being very agile-minded when it came to such calculations! Then, when we found out that our calendars were quite in order, we smiled at one another a little sheepishly and went about telling everyone we met that there always had to be a first time for everything, and that undoubtedly that train would be along mañana. That is we said that to everyone who didn't beat us to it!

But mañana also came and went — with no conducta. So did the next day, and the next, and the next! Men began to frown and fidget, and an atmosphere of restlessness began to be noticeable about the plaza. It was not that anyone was frightened, but as is always the case when some inexplicable event or other upsets the normal routine of our lives people began to grow jumpy and irritable. So far as Pepita and I were concerned, however, we were not too terribly upset. We were disappointed, to be sure, that the start of our journey was delayed. But we could wait — and find happiness in one another while we waited. Perhaps because I was not a Santa Ritan myself, and so could not actually realize the utter incredibility of the thing, I was not so much affected by it as others, and as for Pepita, she was happy just to be with me, and it made no difference to her whether the conductas ever came or went so long as we were together.

A week passed and then two more days, and the conducta never did arrive. But before we knew it almost it was the nineteenth of the month, and men's faces brightened all around the village. The morrow would be the twentieth, the day when the second Chihuahua conducta of the month was due, and then the mystery would surely be cleared up.

That, at any rate, was the generally accepted theory, and I had no reason to doubt that it would be so. Probably when the next day's mule train arrived we would find that someone in Chihuahua had simply slipped and completely forgotten the existence of Santa Rita.

But to the consternation of everyone the twentieth of the month also came and went — with no conducta!

This time there was no dashing off to study the calendar. Neither did men delude themselves that the nonappearance of the second train was a coincidental mistake. Something, it seemed obvious, was radically wrong. But what, everyone asked everyone else, could it be? Was Mexico at war and Chihuahua besieged? It could be. In that remote corner of the world war could have engulfed all the rest of the planet, and without the conductas to carry in the news, we would never know about it! Or had there been some major disaster — a great fire or an earthquake — a flood or a volcanic eruption was hardly likely — which had wiped the city of Chihuahua from the face of the earth? That also was possible. Perhaps a plague had stricken the place, so that they were afraid to send out a conducta to us, for fear of spreading pestilence among us. We thought of everything — except the right one!

In the meantime the situation was serious. As I have indicated, there were few gardens in Santa Rita. The miners had little time to plow and hoe, and they had come to depend almost entirely on the conductas to bring in provisions from the south. It is astonishing how quickly a small reserve will disappear when six hundred hungry mouths are nibbling at it. Already, with three conductas — counting the one that never came from Sonora — missed, the larder was getting disturbingly low.

I think, perhaps, that the first, indeed just about the only, move that could be taken to alleviate the problem was to send out hunters to try and eke out the rapidly dwindling store of meat, and Yancey and Jode and I were among the fifty or more who tried our hands at it. Yancey and I went south and west, in search of antelope, with moderate success. Jode went north and insisted on taking Doña Luz with him, and I fear that his expedition was more of a lark than a hunt, for they returned empty-handed, although there was plenty of game all around. Hunting for the pot, as we were, the rest of us did fairly well, bagging more than a score of turkeys, fifteen antelope, a half a dozen deer and three bears. But even this scarcely made a dent in the demand — and seven hunters never returned at all. Some of our friends were a little bitter about that, for it was generally assumed in the town that those seven had simply set their faces toward Chihuahua and kept going.

At the same time, although I never could see what good it could do, a lookout was posted at the top of the Kneeling Nun to keep watch for the conducta and to pass down the word the moment he sighted it. That I felt from the beginning was a mistake, for even though he sighted the conducta, far off, such a one could scarcely hurry it along; and every day that he watched and did not report a mule train coming plunged the general morale to a deeper pitch of despond. But there were even worse results than I anticipated. For three days everything went quietly. But on the morning of the fourth day, when the guard climbed the mountain to relieve the soldier — a Domingo Lopez — he found the man murdered, with a knife in his back!

Yet even this, although it was regarded with horror and shock, was not considered especially significant. Lopez had been a surly, sour, quarrelsome brute, and he was known to have many enemies. It was simply assumed that one of these had seized the opportunity for revenge. Lieutenant Flores and a squad climbed up and fetched down the body in a blanket, and another soldier was assigned to the duty. That afternoon Sergeant Rojas, with sixteen men of the already slender garrison, marched out toward Chihuahua with orders to march as far as was necessary to intercept the conducta or bring aid. We never heard from them again. Two days after that the second guard on the Kneeling Nun, Diego Suarez, was found stabbed to death. This time, however, he had also been scalped!

I believe I am safe in saying, señores, that it was at this moment that those most thoughtful of us began to have an inkling of what was happening. Should it seem to some that we were perhaps a little slow to recognize the sinister pattern of events, or to understand the stealthy horror of the inexorable noose that was being drawn even tighter about our collective necks, may I point out that these things did not happen all at once, or even necessarily in the same absolute sequence. True, in the final analysis, when all things were added together they produced the inevitable. But some of the things that had happened had not yet reached a recognizable conclusion. As I have said, there were some who believed that the missing hunters had simply taken themselves off to Chihuahua or Sonora. Others thought they might have gone rather far afield, and that they would presently return with full bags. After all, a full week had not yet passed since they went out. By the same token we had no reason to be concerned for Sergeant Rojas and his men at that point. They had marched out only two days before, and such were their orders that they might have to go all the way to Chihuahua, a distance of some five hundred miles — hardly a walk that would be done in a day or two!

Indeed, had the savage murderer of Diego Suarez been able to restrain himself and left the poor devil's scalp intact, we would probably still have assumed that it was all a rather gruesome coincidence and continued in blissful ignorance and with a comforting, if utterly false, confidence in our own individual safety.

To be sure, every effort was made to conceal the matter, in order to avoid a possible public panic. At the orders of the Capitán-Comandante the Teniente Flores waited until after dark to bring in the dead man's body. Then he was wrapped from head to foot in a blanket and slipped in at the back door of the presidio. But in such a small place a secret of such a nature is impossible to keep. The word spread like wildfire, and before morning it was all over the town.

That night I found Pepita quiet and thoughtful — a little worried, for the first time since we were come back together again. When I blew out the light and we lay close in bed together, I could feel her shiver slightly in my arms.

"I am afraid, Currito mio!" she whispered. "I think the Indios have marked us all for death!"

"Nonsense, querida mia!" I scoffed, although secretly I thought she was right. I did not want her to be subjected to the constant agony of dread.

"No, no! It is true, Currito!" she insisted. "First there are the conductas which do not come and do not come. Mark my words, vida mia, they will never come! Never again will we hear the mule bells tinkle on the trail to Chihuahua or Sonora! Never! They have been stopped — ambushed — waylaid by the Indians. And when the savages have starved us until we are weak they will attack us, and kill us, too!"

"Pues mira, chica!" I snorted, trying to sound convincing. "That is silly! You are letting yourself be frightened by a shadow, chinita de mi alma!"

But she insisted still.

208

"It is not silly, amado mio! It is true, and you know it is true! You tell me that it is nonsense only so that I might not be afraid. But I am afraid! Currito mio, do you think that we should pack our things and go? You have the mules and the horses, and I can ride. We might go northward — to Santa Fe. Or we might turn west, to California."

But I quickly vetoed that idea — thereby tacitly admitting that she was right!

"No, chiquita!" I told her. "Here — so long as we are many — there is safety. But you and I alone on the trail? Pouf! We would not get two days' journey behind us before we would be taken!"

"Then you do think what I think, Currito mio!" She was quick, that one!

I sighed.

"Very well, Pepita chiquita!" I replied. "Yes, I do. But I would not have you be alarmed. I believe that right now dark eyes watch this village. I believe that not a man goes to the outhouse to relieve himself but it is noted! This I have believed since the night that Johnson and the others attacked Juan José and his people. But I do not think that we should allow ourselves to be frightened into even greater danger. Recall, querida mia, that the Sergeant Rojas is even now on his way for help. Recall that the Indios cannot intercept every conducta. Soon or late those below, in Chihuahua, will realize what is happening and will send help. As a matter of fact," I added in an effort to lighten my grim words, "I am sure that there are some men of sense in the garrison at Chihuahua who will realize our predicament as soon as they hear Johnson's story, and they will see to it that we are relieved! In the meantime, we are better off here, where there are soldiers, than we would be away, trying to escape by ourselves!"

"As you say, my Currito!" She snugged closer to me, as if for protection. "I will follow you and trust in your judgment, for you know of these things. But do you think, perhaps, if we could persuade some others — enough, say, so that we made a party strong enough to defend itself — ?"

That made more sense, and I did not hesitate to say so. Indeed, I promised to see what I could do in the way of it in the morning. But the next day I went to the palacio and there consulted with Don Urbano and Don Emilio and the Capitán-Comandante, putting the plan before them.

Fool that I was! Naturally they were against it, and even forbade me — or Pepita — to leave the place. Their responsibility was to the entire village, and any group, such as I proposed, that marched to save its own skins, would only leave them weaker! It was my mistake, not, I hasten to say, on my account, but because had I approached it somewhat differently some who are dead today would be alive. But I have yet to meet the man who has lived without error!

In any case the idea was vetoed. Indeed, it was flatly forbidden. I noticed some results, however. The guard on the Kneeling Nun was doubled, so that there was one to watch for the conducta and one to watch the one who watched. I noticed, too, that Doña Luz no longer rode out with Jode. Instead, they sat upon the verandah, close together, while Don Yancey scowled on the aguardiente at the fonda, diagonally across the way.

But this was scarcely remarkable. When the sun set the whole village of Santa Rita became unwontedly quiet. Men — and women — drew back into their homes and barred the doors, and if any found it necessary to relieve themselves they did so in a chamber pot or a tin bucket, and carried the results out to the outhouse in the morning, in broad daylight!

That, I think, will offer a hint as to the temper of the place. Every man knew, but no man would admit. There is no thought to be indecent — only to show that the most natural, human, physical acts were affected by the common, growing fear. Pepita and I grew sober, gentle. There was a quiet and a strength in our relations that was not there before. Once it was simple joy. Then it became the pledge of soul to soul. If death came to us, it could not separate us now.

But this was a thing that was close and personal to us. It was the result of the common danger, to be sure. Yet it was ours. The common cause — the open declaration of war, one might say, involving not only ourselves but everyone in Santa Rita del Cobre — and God alone can calculate how many others after — came within a few days. It happened only a moment after daybreak, in fact, while most of the village was yet asleep and Pepita's hand was warm and soft and moist against my cheek.

Across the plaza, in the light of the rising day, a woman screamed . . . and screamed . . . and screamed!

# III

## CAMINO DEL MUERTE

# *Chapter* 1

GENTES!

You have been awakened, I know, one way or another, all of a sudden — by an alarm, by a shout, by a whimper from the child's room.

Have you ever been brought up so, abruptly in the dawn, by a woman's cry of terror? Have you ever leaped, in a way you never were quite sure about, into your pants and gone racing barefooted across a dusty plaza and buckled up your belt and fumbled at the buttons of your fly as you went, in your mind trying to brush aside the cobwebs of sleep and make some sense to yourself?

I will go further. Señores, have you ever seen six severed heads set upon the posts of a verandah, all facing the door — dripping gore onto the planks, with tendrils and hacked gullets and strings of empty veins hanging like so many big and little worms toward the bloody boards under them?

Do you blame a woman that she screamed? Hombres! I would have screamed myself if I could have found my voice!

What then? What happened, you ask? I will tell you as best I can — as well as anyone knows.

Doña Beatriz — she who was the sister to Don Urbano

and the "Coronel" — had a distemper of the organs which demanded that she relieve herself frequently during the night. As a consequence, as soon as it became light it was her habit to carry out her jar of slops and empty it in the outhouse — quite naturally, taking advantage of the moment for further evacuation.

But to step out of the front door, bucket in hand, and find herself face to face with a row of slack-jawed heads; heads without bodies! Hombres! Hah! Do you think she would not yowl?

Let alone faint and scatter her offal all over the porch!

Amigos! I was not the first to reach the palacio. There were others — the guards at the presidio, the mozos from the corral behind, the padres who had been building up the calluses on their knees! Even a neighbor or two, whose pants were handier to grab. But when I came there, I will say, I was full of sympathy for her — which I think was the only time I ever did feel anything of that sort for the old buzzard!

It is difficult to imagine, señores, yet it is true. Sometime during the night the Indians — it could be no one else — had slipped down into the village, under the noses of the guards, ignoring the sleeping houses, and deliberately and grimly planted those heads upon the posts, beyond any doubt, as a warning of what they meant to do to us all.

Hombres! Have you ever seen a man scalped? I do not mean the act — I mean the result. Think! The skin of the head holds up the fat and muscles of the face. When this is gone the features sag and droop in a way that is more than frightening. It makes a man wonder if it is this that he looks like when he is in his grave. It is worse than a skull alone.

It is slack flesh and drooping, open mouth, lending a hideous idiocy of expression. The muscles of the face, no longer supported by the bridge of skin at the top of the head, sag. The cheeks drop on the jowls, and the eyes start from their sockets, while the lids hang down redly, like those of a bloodhound.

No, señores, I could not blame the woman for screaming and fainting — especially when she recognized one of those heads as that of her own brother!

# Chapter 2

*W*HOSE were the others?

Señores, I will tell you truly, it was that which I found more disturbing than that the "Coronel" — Raoul Hermoso y Maravilla — should eventually be overtaken by his crimes. To my way of thinking, especially considering the part he had played as instigator of the massacre of Juan José and his people, he had it coming. So with Johnson and Gleason — also grimly present. But the remaining three were more significant. One was the head of Sergeant Rojas — who had gone to intercept the conducta, or, failing that, to fetch aid from Chihuahua. The other two I had never seen, but this did not lessen my feeling of horror and consternation when one of the guards from the garrison whispered to me that one was a capataz and the other an arriero, both of whom had long been engaged with the Chihuahua conductas!

I was not so stupid that I could not see at once what that meant. Obviously, we were cut off indeed!

I think I have made it abundantly clear that I was hardly a welcome visitor at the palacio. Consequently I was surprised and a little concerned when that very morning, not

218

more than two hours after Doña Beatriz's discovery of the heads, a trooper from the presidio came thundering at Pepita's door with the message that my presence was demanded at once at the palace. Obviously, since they had taken the trouble to send a special messenger, the matter was one of some importance, and accordingly I lost no time in responding. This time, however, Pepita did not accompany me. Nor did I protest. I could understand perfectly her reluctance to appear again in the long sala, where the Alcalde conducted his official business.

As I walked across the plaza I racked my brain in an effort to account for the mysterious summons, and in view of my last experience in the official chambers I think I may be excused a few qualms. Of a surety, my conscience was clear. I had done nothing to merit censure. But then neither had I done any wrong before. I wondered if Don Yancey would also be present.

He was. So was Jode, which I found rather mildly surprising, for I had not thought that those two would remain in the same room with one another, such had their mutual hostility become. But for the time being, at least, they seemed to have tacitly agreed to a sort of tense truce. In addition to them there were Don Emilio, of course, and Don Urbano, and Don Tito Morales and the Teniente Flores, as well as nearly two score of others of greater or lesser prominence, whom I see no advantage in naming. From this I gathered that this was to be a conference of some sort, quite probably having to do with the gruesome event of the morning. But I was still at a loss to know why I should have been included.

I noticed, however, that none of the ladies of Don Urbano's party were present, and this led me to believe that this was a meeting at which a course of action was to be decided upon, rather than any kind of an inquiry. In the latter case they might have been admitted for their own entertainment. But where a course of action was to be chosen they would hardly be consulted. Such matters were men's problems, and their distracting presence — let alone possible critical comments — were best dispensed with.

By all right, I daresay, Don Emilio should properly have been the one to take the lead, in his official capacity. However, he did little more than preside, wielding the gavel and singling out those among us who had something to say. In the main it was Don Urbano who took the lead and carried us along in the way he thought we should go. At sight of me, as I entered the long room, he smiled with quick, flashing charm, and then sobered equally swiftly.

"Good morning, Currito," he greeted me. "I am especially glad to see you."

"You sent for me, Don Urbano?" I asked.

"I did, Currito," he nodded. "I think you can help us."

"I, señor?" I was surprised. "I do not know in what way, but certainly I will be only too happy to do what I can."

He smiled gravely.

"Thank you, Currito," he said. "You will understand presently, and when you do I believe you will agree that I had reason to call on you."

"Servidor, Don Urbano!" I replied, and he gave me a little nod of approval.

"Very well, then," he went on. "This is a meeting of our authorities and our most influential citizens to try and come to some decision as to what we must do in this crisis. I think

220

I need not remind you of what happened this morning. I believe you were one of the first to arrive on the scene after my sister, Doña Beatriz, gave the alarm?"

"I think so, Don Urbano," I said, "although there were others who were there before me."

"That is of no great importance," he replied. "What matters is that you saw for yourself those gruesome warnings — for I think you will agree with me that it was intended as a warning?"

"Claro, señor!" I replied. "But of course!"

"And however it was meant," he continued, "it was significant in two very serious ways. First, it is painfully evident that the Indians are bent on cutting us off from the world outside. There is no question now but that they were responsible for the failure of the conductas to arrive. It is clear, too, that they do not intend us to send for help."

"Pues sí, Don Urbano!" I agreed. "Yes, indeed!"

"And it is equally bad, Currito," he told me emphatically, "that they were able to slip into the village, under the very noses of the guards, and plant their terrible trophies on our very doorstep without anyone so much as suspecting their presence! At that rate we might all be murdered in our beds before ever we could cry out, unless we take precautions."

"You speak truly, Don Urbano," I agreed, "except for one thing."

He looked surprised.

"And what is that, Currito?" he asked almost hopefully.

"Nothing that will help, señor," I told him. "But it would not be as you have imagined it. On the contrary! You forget that these Indians are Apaches. I think we would all be

221

given a very considerable time to cry out. Indeed, the more we cry out, I think, the better will they be pleased!"

He frowned a little, as if he wished I had not been so outspoken. At the same time several of the others in the room stirred uneasily. Jode grinned wolfishly. Yancey looked serious.

"But I do not see, señor — " I began after a moment's silence.

"How you can help, Currito?" he asked. But he did not expect an answer. He went on. "I will come to that. Meantime we are faced with the problem of what to do. If our garrison were strong enough the logical move would be to send out a strong detachment to summon help. But the loss of Rojas and his detachment, plus the two guards on the mountain, cuts the number of soldiers in garrison here to thirty-one and two officers! That is hardly enough for defense. If we split the command, and sent part of it toward Chihuahua, there would not be enough left to pepper the first wave of attackers."

"That ain't all," put in Yancey. "We've got to remember supplies are gettin' a mite scarce — an' I don't reckon many've got a hankerin' t' go huntin' in th' hills — not after this mornin' anyway."

Don Urbano nodded.

"Now, Currito," he went on, "you came to us not long ago with a proposal to lead out a group for Chihuahua. Would you still be willing to attempt it?"

I hesitated.

"Caray, señor!" I replied. "As to that, I do not know what to say — after what has happened this morning. We must remember that there were seventeen well-armed soldados in Rojas's party, counting Rojas himself. There were thirty or more in Johnson's group — all hard-bitten frontiersmen. As for the conductas, I do not know how many there were, but I suspect there were more than there were in Johnson's and Rojas's parties combined. I am afraid, señor, that if I led out a party strong enough to be sure of getting through, it would leave the village too weak to withstand any attack that might be made before help could arrive."

"That is the danger," he admitted.

I took a deep breath and offered a suggestion of my own.

"One man, traveling alone on a fast horse, might make it," I said. "That is if he knew the country — and the ways of the Indians."

He studied me soberly.

"Could you do it, Currito?" he asked.

Heads turned. I think everyone in the room was staring at me. I thought somberly of Pepita, and reflected that she would hardly approve. But, then, if someone did not move Pepita would be no safer than anyone else! I could take comfort from that, at least.

"I can try, Don Urbano," I said.

For a long moment he did not answer, but sat drumming on the table and pondering some thought that was running through his mind. Then presently he looked up at me and smiled.

"Thank you, Currito," he said quietly. "That gesture is much appreciated — and will not be forgotten. But I am afraid we must refuse. It is too risky — not only for you, but for all of us. Suppose you did not get through? How would we, here in Santa Rita, know? We wouldn't! We would be sitting here, waiting in dreadful suspense, consuming our supplies, and watching — watching — watching for the help that would never come!"

I spread my hands and shrugged, wondering what was in his mind.

"As you wish, señor," I said. "But what . . . ? "

"No, I still incline to think that our first plan is the best for all," he mused.

I was surprised. I did not know there had been any other plan.

"What is that, Don Urbano?" I asked.

He smiled abruptly.

"Ah, yes, Currito," he said. "I forgot you had not been told. It is really quite simple. You see, we cannot send one man alone, because he might never reach Chihuahua. We cannot split our forces and send a party strong enough to make it without too seriously weakening the force that would remain behind, at the village. Therefore, my boy, there is only one answer — we will all go!"

"All?" I gaped at him. "Everyone?"

He nodded emphatically.

"Lock, stock and barrel," he assured me. "We will evacuate the village — men, women and children; young and old — with all livestock and all our provisions and belongings, too, for all of me. Such an exodus would put a very substantial army on the march — better than six hundred, all told, I would venture to say. I believe even the Apaches would hesitate before they attacked such an array!"

I said nothing, but I hoped that he remembered that at least half of that number would be little children and old men and women, incapable of fighting if we were attacked.

Indeed, I only hoped that all of them would have the strength for such a strenuous journey!

"Very well, then, here is where you come into the picture," he continued. I started, and forced myself to listen. "You are the only one among us who has had any very extensive experience in organizing such parties — "

"Nothing as large as this, Señor Don Urbano!" I protested, panic-stricken.

But a little thing like that did not even make him pause.

"No, no, I understand that, Currito," he said. "But after all it cannot be so different — only bigger and more complicated, that's all."

"Sí, señor!" I gulped.

"Very well, then!" he exclaimed again. "You will be capataz — how do they call it on the trail from Santa Fe to San Luis? — the Trail Boss. You will be in supreme command so long as we are on the trail. You will tell us where to march and how far and in what order. You will see to the deposit of all supplies in a common pool, and to their distribution. You may commandeer stock and transportation where necessary for the common good. The Capitán-Comandante, of course, will command the military — but he will be under your orders while on the march. Only in the event of attack will he assume command of defense. In other words, Currito, I ask you to take full charge of organizing this march — just as you would a party which you had been engaged to guide. Will you do it?"

"I will do it, Don Urbano," I said — but I did not like it! "I will have to name my own assistants, though."

"Certainly!" he assured me.

"Then I will name Señor Cahoon and Señor Lassiter, to

begin," I said. "I will pick others for special tasks later. But these will do to start."

I think no one will be surprised at my choice of Don Yancey to serve at my right, all things considered. My selection of Jode, however, might lead some to wonder how well balanced was my judgment. I can only reply that to my way of thinking it was not only an intelligent move, it was a rather clever one as well.

In the first place, as I already knew, Jode, when he put himself to it, was a hard worker. He had shown himself to be shrewd in his own way, and he was quicker-witted than most in Santa Rita. I have already said that his courage was unquestioned, and I knew that he was capable of intelligent action when the occasion demanded and he was not torn by petty jealousy and personal prejudices. If I knew him at all he would rise to the challenge of responsibility. After all, he would have as great an incentive to get his division through safely as would Yancey or I. On the other hand, if I picked Yancey to serve as one of my assistants, and did not choose him, it might well throw him into a fit of the sulks that would have dangerous results for us all. Indeed, it seemed to me a rather astute move that might well turn a knotty problem and a potential sore spot to an asset that would be to our advantage in the end.

I believe Yancey understood something of what was in my mind, although he never mentioned it. I noticed thereafter that he tried hard to hold himself in close restraint whenever it was necessary for us to consult together — though I can't say as much for Jode. Pepita, on the other hand, could not understand it, no matter how hard I tried to explain. She called me a fool in a dozen ways, and for two nights she would not even kiss me. Indeed, from the very beginning she disapproved of the whole plan. I argued and cajoled and pointed out to her that it was the best — in fact, the only — move that we could make, unless we chose simply to sit there amid the sun-baked rocks of Santa Rita and slowly starve to death. She did not rant or rage or declare that she would have none of it. She only spoke of it once, indeed;

"As you say, Currito mio. What you wish I will do."

After that it was a closed subject, but I could see that she was not happy, and her love-making lost much of its old fire, and became tender and unspeakably gentle, and in a strange sort of way somewhat preoccupied.

As a matter of fact, however, in those next few days there was little opportunity and less will for love play on my part. I went to my work before the dawn, and kept at it until long after dark had come again, for the need for haste grew every day more and more obvious as our piles of stores and provisions shrank. When I came home at night, to the little casita on the western side of the plaza, it was more often than not to fall into exhausted slumber before ever she had cleared the crumbs from the supper table.

You may wonder, señores, what on earth was so difficult about the undertaking; why it should require so much work by way of preparation. Pues mira, hombre! Now, see here, man! To be sure this was work that I had always done, and that I understood. But never before had I taken a party of more than sixty or seventy out on the trail. This time I was asked to lead some six hundred. Nor were all of those strong men and vigorous women in their prime years. Many — far too many for my peace of mind — were old men and

227

women; some crippled, some palsied, some blind, some lame, and not a few, especially of the women, bedridden. And then there were the children — from suckling babes in their mothers' arms to scampering, scurrying, potbellied, half-naked urchins, to prurient girls in their early teens and lusty, swaggering youths, just beginning to feel their manhood but not yet sure enough of themselves to act like men! When I came to count noses I nearly despaired, for it seemed to me that there must be six hundred and fifty children alone. Every time I would turn around, it seemed to me, another would pop up — and indeed four more were born even as we prepared to start!

Finally I gave up this maddening task of census taking, assigning it — a little maliciously, I fear — to Don Emilio, who I felt might as well be doing something, and turned my attention to more important details.

Nor were these details to be scoffed at, either. It was bad enough to contemplate moving the entire population of the place. Don Urbano, God forgive him for he knew not what he did, heaped coals of fire on my head by publicly promising that each family might take any or even all of its possessions if it wished. True, the promise was made as a preface to an appeal to family heads to use their judgment. But the damage was done. Hardly one in a hundred had the sort of judgment that he looked for, and the only result was that one and all at once began piling all of their possessions in huge mountains in the street outside their doors — patty pans and pepper boxes, pillows and the pictures on the walls, even the cracked chamber pot under the bed, to say nothing of the beds themselves. I declare there were at least forty enormous, hand-carved nuptial nests, each capa-

ble of holding a half a dozen adults! There were commodes
and cupboards, chairs, tables, candlesticks and statues of
the Virgin and figures of Christ on the Cross! I could
hardly begin to enumerate them all, but I can say that folk
forgot that all these things had been fetched out piecemeal,
and that a wagon train fifty miles long would scarcely
serve to carry them back to Chihuahua all at one time!

Clearly, I had to put my foot down somewhere, and I
pat myself on the shoulder, señores, for the way in which I
managed the matter — think me smug if you will! I simply
appointed Don Urbano himself to oversee the problem, and
turned it over to him lock, stock and barrel! He was somewhat taken aback, and I think a little put out that I should
set him to work — he having considered himself somewhat
above such things until then. But I reminded him that he
himself had agreed that I was to have a free hand in the
naming of my assistants, which he acknowledged, and
thereafter fell to the task assigned to him. I will say, too,
that he did as good a job as could be expected of anyone,
under the circumstances, though long was the niggling and
wrangling over each item, and loud were the wails of protest over every article that must be weeded out and left
behind!

This, of course, brought up the problem of transportation — and, señores — Jesús, María y José! — it was a problem! As vital as it was I saw to this myself as much as possible. First I counted. There were fifty carretas belonging
to the mines, and some thirty additional which belonged to
individuals throughout the town — and may the saints spit
on me, señores, if it was not like drawing teeth to get these
people to give up their carts and teams for the common

cause. But naturally! Each man wanted to keep his wagon to carry his own!

I do not know, señores, if you have ever seen a carreta. It is a two-wheeled cart, with a box about six and a half feet square at the bottom and seven and a half feet at the top, about four or five feet deep. Thus the capacity of each is about seven cubic yards — or a total of five hundred and sixty cubic yards of carrying space, in our case — with which I was expected to move an entire village of six hundred souls! And, remember, gentes, this meant the carrying not only of their furnishings and personal belongings, but also of the necessary supplies and provisions for the journey, as well as those poor ancients who could neither walk nor ride horseback!

Pues Dios, caballeros! Such arithmetic I never did before! Eighty carretas, with four oxen for each, gave us three hundred and twenty animals — which must be fed! My problem! I decided that we would use two ox teams rather than four. That way we could spell them, team and team, each day, and they would keep fatter if we had to slaughter some for food. Of mules I found some three hundred and seventy-two, including my own twenty-two on which I had hoped to carry out Pepita's belongings. Reluctantly I added them to the common total. Most of these were pack animals, broken only to dead weight. Some we might train, in the few days at our disposal, to riding animals. But that was a gamble. Our riding horses, including those of the military detachment, Don Urbano, Don Emilio and myself, numbered no more than one hundred eighty-eight, besides which there were the eight harness nags and two carriages — phaetons, to be exact; frail things for such rugged going — in which Don Urbano's party had arrived.

In addition there were some two hundred wheelbarrows in which some things could be trundled!

But the great problem was that of supplies. To feed everyone over such a distance — I was relieved to find that the village of Janos lay some two hundred miles closer than Chihuahua, which would be a help, if not altogether a solution — would call for a tremendous amount. We could supply some of what I calculated from the mine and public stores. But it would be far from enough, and if each householder had been fully stocked and ready to contribute to the common store we would hardly have had enough. As it was neither was the case! Everyone wondered if there would be enough to go 'round, and each man who had any sought to hold out a little for himself!

I believe, señores, you can begin to see something of my problem!

Yet, I think, we gathered in most of the supplies and most of the provisions, most of the animals and most of the vehicles, so that all could benefit. I divided the column into three divisions — roughly two hundred in each — with Don Yancey and Jode to alternate in the advance and the rear, each position being equally critical, at intervals, while I commanded the center with the bulk of the old men and women and children. I set a score of the troopers of the garrison ahead, under Don Tito Morales, thinking to flatter him so, but I fear he was hardly pleased to serve as advance guard. The Teniente Flores I sent to the rear guard with ten men, for which he gave me a surly, sullen look —

not realizing, I daresay, that his was actually a far more dangerous position than Don Tito's, and therefore by way of being a post of honor.

As I say, Don Emilio kept score — and a grimmer task than he reckoned it proved to be in the end; while Don Urbano saw to the distribution of transport. In that case I insisted only that the military be left their mounts, which might stand strongly in our defense if the need arose; that those unable to travel otherwise be given space in the vehicles, and that the weakest of the rest be mounted so far as possible. The rest of us would walk, I announced, though I made sure a horse was handy against need in case of attack. My system, there, was to permit some momentarily fatigued woman or child to ride while I led. When and if attack came I unceremoniously took over the animal. When the alarm was over I returned to my place in line, and if they were there surrendered the saddle and led off once more.

Doña Luz and Pepita and Doña Elena I gave charge of the children and old folk of each division — and I let them ride, since I expected them to be back and forth among their charges. For this alone I thought I was criticized, but I ignored complaints and let matters stand. After all, I could hardly escape some censure!

As you will understand, señores, I am sure, there was a need for haste. Already our supplies were dwindling, and no more would be received. On that account I felt I must not waste a moment. At the same time, insofar as it was possible, we must keep our plans secret. There was no doubt in my mind that the Indians kept the village under close watch. The incident of the heads was proof of that. If they had not known perfectly well that the way was clear they would hardly have dared to venture so close! Accordingly I gave orders that as much as possible our movements should be carried out under cover of darkness.

Alas for that! A man might as well have tried to keep the birth of illegitimate quintuplets, the ruination of his sister or the elopement of his mother on a desert isle a secret! It was easier for a man to be cuckold and hide it than to make believe that we were up to naught but sitting there — especially after the assembling of the carretas with their creaking and groaning and whistling and squealing on their great wooden wheels roughly doweled to raw wooden, ungreased axles! When the carts came in and gathered in the square their squeaking, groaning, grumbling progress must have been audible from the Rio Grande to the Tonto Basin, and from the Mogollons to the Casas Grandes!

I held my head in my hands. But there was nothing I could do. There was not even a pot of bear's grease in town. Exactly one week to the day from the meeting at the palacio I rose even earlier than usual and said my prayers and relieved myself at the corner of the casa. Then I crept back in bed with Pepita and gathered her in my arms, waking her with kisses, but trying not to.

"You are ready, amada mia?" I asked when she stirred.

"I am ready, Currito mio," she said quietly.

I held her close to me, and our lips met — and our bodies, and for a little while she was as ever before; warm and tender and strong and hungry.

Then after she touched my face with soft, sweet fingers.

"I love you, Currito!" she whispered. "Do not forget me!"

"Forget you, Pepita mia? Alma de mi alma!" I cried.

233

"What is this? Why should I? As if it were possible! In a few days we will be in Janos — twenty, at the most, that's an average of fifteen a day. After that we will go more swiftly, guayaba mia! Before the month is done we will be in Chihuahua, and there we will be married in the big, big cathedral — as you wished. How will I escape thee then, little soul of my soul — even if I wanted to?"

For an instant she smiled gaily, happily, adorably, as I remembered her.

"Do you think so truly, Currito?" she asked. "You are sure?"

"Why should I not be, Pepita chiquita?" I demanded. "Why should I not be? I am as certain as this!"

And I drew her to me again.

# *Chapter 3*

*I*F I WAS less sanguine than I pretended should I have said so to her?

Aiee, cojónes de Jesús sobre la cruz! Do you think me a beast, señores, that I could not share my fears with her?

But I wept as I watched them march out a few hours after — wept though I swallowed the wet and the salt. I kept the clutch on my throat, and let the tears run backwards, for I could no more let them see my doubt than I could her!

Was I one to say to the mother with the babe in her arms what I feared? Could I confide in the husband who trusted me, or the little child who did not know what it was all about? I could not, of course, so I put on a stern mouth and hardened my eyes and sat my horse in silence.

I think I have suggested what I saw. I sat, as I did, in a manner of review, and watched them pass, not because I fancied myself as a general in command of his troops, but because I had been set in charge of this movement, and I felt that it was up to me to see that we moved off in good order, if nothing else.

They gathered in the plaza, at the appointed hour — peónes from the mines and their half-caste children, who wondered what was happening, barmen, mercantes, militares and whores, who had a better notion! The people from the palacio and the presidio — Doña Luz, Doña Elena and Doña Beatriz, which last was fainting and recovering and fainting again by turns! I wished she would faint once and for all and have done with it, which was not charitable of me, but my own tension was such that I could not help it. Don Urbano was my strength and my sword. He had his duty, which I had assigned him. But how could I know that he would do his work well, and help me with all that I had to do as well? I should have turned to him then and said: "Ay, Dios, señor — take it, and welcome!"

"Why?" you ask me? Why, indeed! Para los senos de la Virgen! Would God anyone had such a responsibility but me!

They moved out in three divisions — not that I believed they would march in order, but at least it was more wieldy to divide them into three equal, or more or less equal groups. Jode commanded the first, and in this I placed the youngest men — those I considered the best fighters. In the center I put the carretas and pack animals, the carriages — and the older men, women and children — which I commanded myself, feeling that from there I could ride forward or back, as occasion demanded. In the rear I assigned the rest, including the next best fighters, as I judged them, under command of Don Yancey. The Capitán-Comandante led an advance guard of twenty men — let him go first for once, I thought! — two hundred yards ahead of the van, with a two-man connecting file in between. The rest of the militares, under Teniente Flores, fetched up the rear at one hundred yards, with no connecting files. I called for volunteers as flankers, and put the sheep and hogs, such as we had, between the first and second divisions, and the spare cattle and cows between the second and third. Doña Elena I assigned to the first division, so that there should be no hanky-panky, and Pepita I placed with the third, to attend the women and children there. Doña Luz I kept with me, in the center, so that there should be no jealous rivalry between Jode and Yancey — or so, at least, I planned it.

I sat my nag stiffly, watching from before the presidio, until even the last soldado of the rear guard was gone, and then I took a quick canter around the deserted town to make certain that no one had been left behind. It gave me an eerie, creepy feeling drubbing through those empty, echoing alleys. Smoke still rose from most of the chimneys, but the doors of the houses seemed to have an abandoned look, and nowhere, from one end to the other, did a living thing stir. When I came back to the plaza, perhaps twenty minutes later, I could still hear the tortured agony of the squeaking carretas far south on the trail. As I touched spurs to my horse and rode after them I made a wry face, for it seemed to me that that must be audible even as far away as the Ojo Caliente and Cuchillo Negro's headquarters. But then I reflected that it scarcely mattered. Without doubt the Indians had kept a close watch on the village, and they probably knew already that we were on our way.

I overtook the rear guard about a mile down the road, from which I gathered that they were moving at the approximate rate of two miles an hour — which was better than I had dared to hope. If we could maintain that pace and traveled only ten hours a day it would mean that we should reach Janos, about three hundred miles to the southward, in about two weeks' time. The thought gave me a warm feeling around the heart. In two short weeks my troubles would be ended, and I could again take my Pepita in my arms without a worry or a care in the world. Then I could take her by the hand and lead her to the altar where we would kneel together before the padre while he made us man and wife!

But if I was pleased with our progress I could not say the same for that flaccid lump of lard, the Teniente Juan Ramón Flores. As I rode up he scowled ferociously at me and growled:

"We'll never get there at this rate, chichigua capataz!"

But not even with him, not even when he called me a wet nurse could I quarrel as I felt then. I grinned at him.

"Vaya, burrito! Go on with you, jackass!" I retorted. "We are going faster than I thought we would, but if you are not satisfied I will see what I can do."

"Carajo! I wish you would," he grumbled.

"I will, then," I assured him. "But remember, mocho, we've got a lot of children and ancients up ahead, and we must take care not to outrun them."

Since he had no answer for that I rode on ahead and was surprised to find Don Yancey riding at the tail end of his division.

"Pues hombre!" I cried. "What are you doing back here? I thought you would be in the lead."

He shook his head grimly.

"No, man!" he grunted. "Up there how would I know what they're a-doin'? Back here I c'n keep 'em bunched up an' movin' — keep 'em from stragglin'."

238

"De veras!" I exclaimed. "That's so! Hombre, you are sharper than I! I never thought of that!"

Near the middle of the division I came upon Pepita, and I rode up beside her and gave her a stout squeeze and a slobbery buss, at which she blushed wonderfully and the folk around us laughed and cheered.

"Ay, chiquita mia!" I cried. "I lied to thee last night!"

She looked so stricken that I rocked with laughter in my saddle.

"Pepita chiquita," I gasped, "do not look so alarmed! At this rate we will be in Janos in two weeks instead of three, as I told you, and then I will make you the señora Josefa Pepita José Herrero Alfonso Francisco Pereda Lopez y Ruiz! Does that not please you, pichoncita mia?"

The look of adoration that she gave in answer filled my heart so near to bursting that I could scarcely sit my horse as I rode ahead. But a shadow fell across my happy mood when, midway between the second and third divisions, and just ahead of the cattle, I overtook a bent old man doggedly trundling a wheelbarrow piled to its teetering limit with household goods. He was struggling to keep up with the center, but already he was dropping behind. Sweat streamed from his head in great gobbets, and his frayed, threadbare shirt and patched trousers were plastered to his backsides. Already he was limping, and I could see that the flinty stones of the trail kept getting into his open sandals and chafed his bare feet.

"Better dump that and forget it, papacito," I told him. "You'll never get it all the way to Janos like that."

But he only gave me a grim look and shook his head stubbornly.

"All right, grandpa!" I said. "If you insist! As soon as I've checked the line ahead I'll drop back and spell you with the barrow while you ride a way."

Doña Luz rode at the rear of the second division, sitting astride a dainty, dancing white Arabian. She wore her sombrero on one shoulder, looped there by its chin strings, and she had shaken out her red-gold hair and let it float loose in the sunlight like a rippling banner of burnished copper. Her color was high, and her lips were red and moist and parted. Her man's shirt was open at the throat, and unbuttoned to the middle of the vee between her breasts and I could catch more than a hint of creamy, tantalizing bosoms. She was a lovely, a tempting, an alluring, a breathtaking vision, and I could not blame either Jode or Yancey for wanting her. Por Dios! But for my little Pepita I would have wanted her myself — still!

She flashed me a smile that rocked me in the saddle as I rode up.

"All well behind, Currito?" she asked.

Apparently she had forgotten her anger with me at least. I nodded.

"All well, Doña Luz," I assured her. "How goes it here?"

"Like a charm!" she told me.

"Let's keep it that way, doña mia," I replied, and she looked pleased at my unbending from my customary stiffly formal attitude. "Is your father up ahead?"

"He rides at the front of this division," she nodded, "in your place until you should come up."

"I will relieve him as soon as I have checked the entire line," I told her, for the moment forgetting the old man with the wheelbarrow.

240

"May I ride forward with you, Currito?" she asked.

Ay, cáspita! I thought, now I begin to understand! You would ride with me only as far as Señor Jode, and then you would leave me to go on by myself! But I will not betray my friend, Don Yancey! I shook my head.

"Better not, Doña Luz," I replied, and then bethought me of the ancient peón and was proud of my quickness of wit.

"There's a little old man with a tremendous wheelbarrowload of furniture back by the cattle," I said. "He'll never make it, but he's too stubborn for me. Maybe you can persuade him to throw it away and concentrate on saving himself?"

"I'll try," she promised.

I rode on and noted that because of the carretas and carriages and all the pack animals this was the longest part of the line. I would do well, I told myself, to take some of the younger, armed miners from the first and third divisions and post them along this stretch as guards, for I suspected that here was where the Indians would strike if they attacked us on the march. I paused beside Don Urbano and told him of my plan and he gave enthusiastic approval, after which I cantered ahead, past the first division and was gratified to find Jode riding at the front of the line.

"All right?" I asked briefly.

Although I had appointed him to command the division I felt no friendlier toward him on that account.

"It's a breeze," he sneered. "Nothin' to it!"

"Pray it doesn't change!" I retorted curtly, and started to ride ahead to check the advance guard.

"Where's Luz?" he called after me.

I jerked my head back along the line, and answered before I thought.

"Back at the end of the second division," I said and rode on.

I found the advance guard all in order, and the Capitán-Comandante reported hostilely that he had seen no sign of the Indians.

"That's good," I told him with equal chill. "But don't let that lull you to sleep. Just because you can't see them doesn't mean that they're not there."

I knew what was the matter with him. He was jealous. In his own estimation he should have been placed in command, and as a matter of fact I would just as soon he had been, for it would have lifted a world of responsibility from my shoulders. But, at the same time, it might be pointed out that if he had been placed in charge the added duties would have drawn him away from the vitally important task of guarding the column.

"I'll tend to my work," he told me coldly. "You do yours."

"I will," I assured him grimly, "including keeping tabs on you, señor!"

When I dropped back Jode was no longer at the head of the first division. His place had been taken by a moon-faced, rather dull-witted-seeming young miner. I cursed savagely under my breath, for I thought I could guess where he had gone, and I felt I had only myself to blame. I should have guessed what was in his mind when he called after me and given him his orders then to keep to his post. I clapped the spurs to my nag and went racing back, so full of fury that I did not even pause to salute Don Urbano. Indeed, so black was my scowl as I galloped past him that he turned and stared after me in astonishment and alarm.

Sure enough, when I reached the rear of the division, there was Jode, on his stout black horse, prancing and preening himself beside her. As I came up they were both laughing gaily at some sally of his, and from the way they looked at one another I gathered that he was making even greater headway than I had imagined. I thought of Yancey, and my anger rose another notch.

At sight of me they sobered abruptly, and Jode's eyes narrowed. His face looked bleak but watchful.

"What the devil are you doing back here?" I demanded furiously. "Who said you could leave your post?"

His face was wooden, completely expressionless. His dark eyes fastened themselves on mine.

"You got eyes!" His voice was hard and cold. "You c'n see what I'm a-doin'. The's no sense a man stickin' too close to th' job all th' time."

"It's just when a man turns his back that things happen," I told him savagely. "I say you'll stick to your post as long as we're on the trail. Save your social impulses for after we've made camp! Now, get back up forward, and stay there."

He made no move to obey.

"I ain't takin' orders from you," he growled.

"You are," I retorted flatly, "so long as I command this column! If you want to argue the point I'll go and fetch Don Urbano and Don Emilio so we'll have a pair of impartial judges."

243

His jaw set stubbornly, but Doña Luz glanced at him unhappily.

"You'd better go, Jodey dear," she said. "After all, they did put Currito in charge. There's no use in asking for trouble."

He flashed his dazzling smile on her.

"If you say so, honeybun!" he replied.

He kissed his fingers and reached out and patted her cheek, then put spurs to his horse and cantered ahead with a sour glance at me. When he was gone Doña Luz looked at me reproachfully. I almost felt guilty under her eyes.

"I don't think that was quite fair, Currito," she chided me. "After all, he was doing no harm, and I like to ride with him. He's so handsome and dashing, and he keeps me amused!"

"Claro!" I replied bitterly, thinking of my own true friend who loved her to distraction. I suppose I should not have mentioned it, for I suspect it only piqued her to torment him. "If you must ride with someone, why don't you give Don Yancey a chance? He's eating his heart out for you, back at the end of the column!"

She sniffed.

"That big stick!" she snorted contemptuously. "There's no charm in the man! He never has anything to say!"

I was stung to his defense.

"He has more real charm than a dozen Jodes!" I retorted. "He's genuine and honest, where Jode is false metal. And if his heartful of love makes him tongue-tied, that's better than a thousand of Jode's glib lies!"

She bristled.

"Lies?" she cried. "Lies, you say? I suppose you think

Jode's lying when he tells me that he loves me, and that he wants to marry me!"

I looked at her startled. I had no idea it had gone that far.

"I think so!" I replied quietly. "I think he's only paying court to you to strike back at Don Yancey."

That was hardly true, and I knew it, but for Yancey's sake I had to try to undermine this thing somehow.

"Pooh!" she snapped. "I don't believe it. What's more, I think your precious Don Yancey is not only a graceless stick, he's a rank coward as well! The very fact that he is skulking along at the rear of the line proves that!"

"Nothing of the kind, Doña Luz," I growled. "He is skulking along back there, as you describe it, because I ordered him there. As for it proving him a coward, I will tell you flatly that when you are dealing with hostile Apaches the tail end of the line is as dangerous as the front — and Don Yancey is well aware of it!"

She gave me no reply to that, and so I continued.

"No, Doña Luz! Believe me, I have served with them both, and I know them better than you. I say that Don Yancey not only has more charm, he is more deeply sincere and has more honest, quiet courage in his little finger than a dozen of your Jodes!"

She answered me not a word to that, whereby I guessed miserably that far from helping Don Yancey I had only made matters worse with my meddling. When she spoke her voice was chilly.

"I talked to your little man with the wheelbarrow," she told me. "But he would not listen to me."

"Diablo!" I cried. "I had forgotten him! I promised him that I would come back and help him — !"

I started to turn my nag back, but just as I did so the column ahead ground to a straggling halt.

"What's wrong?" Doña Luz demanded, her curiosity getting the better of her anger.

"I don't know," I replied. "But something's happened. I must go and see. You stay here!"

I jabbed my spurs into my horse's flanks and sent him galloping ahead at the top of his speed. When I came to the front of the line I found that the first division had come up against the rear of the halted advance guard, and both soldiers and miners were standing stock-still in the middle of the road and were staring in horror to either side of the way. They looked a little green, and several of them were vomiting in the dust. I followed their stares, and all at once I felt as if I would be ill myself.

We were halted at the beginning of a long straightaway, a gently sloping wooded stretch, that led through a last thicket of willows and cottonwoods before emerging onto the open Antelope Plains below. And here, ahead, on either side of the trail, in plain view so that they formed a gruesome corridor of death that could only be intended as a warning, hung from the heels, stark naked and head down, almost a half a hundred bodies!

I recognized them, of course, as who did not, for they were the men of Johnson's and Rojas's parties — every last one of them! But this was not all, for each body's stomach had been ripped open, and the bowels hung in grizzly, ropy festoons about them, while under each one were the gray, cold ashes of a small fire, and every skull was blackened and burst by the heat!

The Capitán-Comandante turned a gray face toward me.

"We must cut them down before the women see them," he gasped.

"Dios, hombre!" I cried out at him. "Are you mad? That's exactly what the red devils want us to do, so they can attack while we are halted. Mark me, they're not far away! Get on with it, man! Get on and march fast, for we're none of us safe until we reach the open plain!"

# Chapter 4

THE INCIDENT had a sobering effect, as may be imagined. There was no more laughing or dawdling along the way, and after that no man left his post. I myself stood at the beginning of the stretch and hustled the column through those grizzly woods almost at a run, all the while my own scalp tingling and prickling and a spot between my shoulder blades burning as if a hot branding iron had been clapped to it.

But we were lucky. We got over the stretch without the loss of a man except the ancient with the wheelbarrow, who suffered a stroke at the sight, and dropped dead in his tracks. I breathed easier when, at last, we moved out onto the plain.

Apart from that one incident, however, that day was fairly typical of the first days, at least, of our flight. In mapping out our route I had been fully alive to the safety of the plains. Indeed, I had deliberately routed us considerably to the westward of the direct road just so that I might take advantage of them, and I was proud of having done so, for all but about eighty miles of our way lay across the rolling open. If I could I would have avoided those eighty miles, but there was no way that I could do it.

For the first five days we moved across about a hundred

248

miles of plains. Here and there mountain ridges and spurs ran across our path. But these could be avoided by swinging in a detour, and this I preferred to do rather than risk ambush in the hills. After that, however, the rugged bulk of the Big Hatchet Mountains barred the way, and there was nothing we could do but struggle over them, some fifty miles, through the steep-flanked cut of Big Hatchet Pass. It was here that our troubles began.

We began to climb into the foothills about midmorning, and at once I noticed the signal smokes rising ahead and behind. At once I passed the word to close up and go on guard, for I anticipated trouble, though not in the way it came. An hour before sundown I halted the column at the widest-open spot I could find and ordered the men to make camp in a circle with the women and animals in the center and armed men posted at intervals all around the outside. I waited impatiently for Flores and his rear-guard detachment to come in, which should have been within a matter of ten minutes. But when an hour passed and he did not come I began to suspect that something had happened to him and his men. When he did not arrive by dark I was certain of it. Undoubtedly they had been set upon silently, stealthily by creeping Indians and slaughtered to a man without a sound. That, at least, was what we had to believe, for we never saw any of them again!

That night Pepita insisted on sharing my blankets, even though I lay on the outer rim of the circle. But there was no billing and cooing. Nevertheless I was glad I had not insisted that she lie with the rest of the women, for I could feel her shiver as she lay within the circle of my arms, and I would not have her be alone then.

249

I routed them all out at dawn the next morning, hoping to get the train early on the road and perhaps get through the pass that day. But they were slow to respond, and it was almost an hour before we began to form in line of march. That was the instant when our savage enemy chose to attack. All at once the air was full of a shower of arrows and a ragged fusillade of shots that seemed to come from the boulder-strewn hillside on our left.

Instantly all was panic and confusion. Women screamed and children wailed and men ran in all directions, shouting and shooting. I managed, however, to turn a hundred or more rifles up the hill, and for about ten minutes we fired back, without so much as an answering shot. Apparently it was the Indians' tactic to fire one volley and then slip off among the rocks.

Gradually I managed to get the men to cease fire and preserve their ammunition and brought a little order out of the chaos. But a count of noses after it was done showed that the Apaches had managed to knock over some sixty of our number, which was a heavy toll for a single volley. To the intense anguish and distress of both Doña Luz and Don Urbano, both Doña Elena and Doña Beatriz were among those to fall at that opening fire, and I sympathized with them with all my heart, although later it occurred to me that they were probably lucky to go when they did, for by that they were spared much agony!

Needless to say, we did not get off to the early start I had hoped for, and when we did we struggled all day long through rugged, rocky mountain country, where the unseen enemy could hang upon our flanks, flitting along the ridges parallel with our line of march, and amuse himself and torment us by taking frequent pot shots into our midst. In this way, by nightfall, he accounted for thirty more of us, including poor old Don Emilio and ten more of our dwindling force of soldiers. For some reason I seemed to bear a charmed life, for never a bullet or an arrow ever seemed to come anywhere near me.

We camped that night on top of a knoll, some distance short of the pass, for I had no hankering to become benighted in the craggy defile, and I daresay because we were encamped on a hilltop, where they could not easily come at us, the savages did not attack us again the following dawn. The fact stirred a ray of hope in my breast that perhaps they had drawn off, though I should have known better. We were in the narrow gullet of the pass when they struck once more in whooping hordes, making no effort, this time, at concealment, and concentrating their attack, as I had feared, on the second division, in the center, where all our supplies as well as the women and children and old folk were concentrated.

I chanced to be riding at the fore, with the first division, when the first burst of yells and shots rang out behind us, and at once I turned our miners about and hurled them at the savage hordes upon the slope. At the same time Don Yancey flung his third division into the battle, and between us, after a hot skirmish that lasted more than an hour, we succeeded in driving the Indians off with considerable loss. As soon as the lull came I gathered the column together in a single unit, and almost literally swept them on through the pass. Nor did I dare stop to take stock of our losses until we had debouched upon the plain beyond. There I discovered, to my dismay, that two hundred and seventy-three of our number, men, women and children, had fallen, and this with the ninety we had already lost reduced the column to little more than two hundred — two hundred and twenty-seven, to be exact, out of six hundred who had marched from Santa Rita!

Apparently nothing short of complete extermination would satisfy our brutal foe!

It can be imagined, then, with what a feeling of relief I welcomed the respite of the next days. We were on the plain again now, and from the Big Hatchets all the way to Antelope Wells and beyond we would be safe from attack. Indeed, we had only thirty more miles of mountain travel, through a part of the Sierra Madres, before we came to Janos, and I allowed myself to dare to hope!

But there was another result of our battle, and this was the total loss of our spare livestock, which we had been forced to abandon, and the slaughter of more than half of our horses and pack mules. As a result many of us, including both Jode and Yancey, were afoot now, as was little Pepita. So far as she was concerned, at least, I solved the problem by taking her up on my horse behind me, for we were both so slight that her added weight made little difference, and to speak truly I think that she was secretly pleased at having lost her mount, for it meant that she must be with me at all times! The others, however, had to fall back on shank's mare.

But there was yet another, even more serious outcome of the fight. This was the loss of much of our carefully hoarded store of provisions. When I discovered it I foresaw hungry days ahead unless something were done, and that promptly. In consequence I came to a hasty decision. I made up my mind to slaughter the ox teams for meat, and to improvise harnesses from pack saddles and hitch several teams of mules to the remaining carretas. So long as the ox meat lasted we would eat beef. When that was gone we would have to fall back on the mules, which meat I knew from past experience was tough and stringy, but at least it would sustain life.

But it is true that it is an ill wind indeed that blows no good at all, and it was so in this case, for the shift to the more rapidly paced mules enabled us to go forward more swiftly. As a result we whisked across the plain in four days, instead of the five I had estimated, and at that we came to a halt about midafternoon of the fourth day, about ten miles southeastward of the Antelope Wells, and a mile or so before we entered the mountains, for our pace over the plains had encouraged me in the belief that we might be able to cover the remaining thirty miles that lay between us and Janos in a single long day's march. At any rate I proposed to try it, and I consulted with Don Urbano to that end. He was listless and apathetic, and it seemed to me that he had aged and shriveled since the death of his beloved wife. Still he gave his consent without hesitation, which was all I needed, and we started off at the crack of dawn, into the rugged mountain country. Indeed, but for the fact that we were using them to carry many of the children I would have left the carretas behind. As it was I jettisoned most of the packs and mounted many of the folk who had been left afoot on the mules that this released.

For the first half of that day's journey I believe that I held my breath more often than I sucked in air, and the pounding of my heart was loud in my ears. But when we passed midday, and soon after that the halfway mark, I felt easier. In fact I became almost confident that our journey's end was in sight. But that was a trap that I had myself never ceased to caution others about.

We made a brief halt in the early afternoon to refill our empty bellies, and then pressed on again. But I found that up there, in the deep canyons of the craggy Sierra, the sun set early, and the night came swiftly on its heels. By four in the afternoon the sun had dipped behind the spired ridge of the mountains; and by five, as we threaded our way through the last defile, with only eight more miles to go, the twilight was thickening. I, myself, rode a little distance in advance, with Pepita riding a-pillion behind me, a sort of dual advance guard on a single mount, trying to keep a sharp lookout ahead for skulking figures that would warn us of an ambush — though I must confess that with each advancing thud of my horse's hoofs my jubilation grew. Some twenty or thirty yards behind us Jode walked at the head of the little, compact column — all in one division now — and Doña Luz walked beside him leading her fine, white Arabian horse, for I had long since given up trying to keep them apart. Back, at the end of the line, strode Don Yancey, keeping faithfully to his post though I knew how it must have hurt him to see her walking with his former friend.

But, ay, por Dios, señores! That one for whom I felt the most was Don Urbano. It was as if the light of his life had been extinguished, and he walked and stumbled along the center flank of the little column, as old and bent and gaunt and gray as the sorriest peón that had started with us.

My heart went out to him, but what good was that? Madre mia, gentes! Who was to foresee the cruel, subtle

254

cunning of those savages? Beyond a doubt they had planned it deliberately, as a form of torment, to allow us to draw almost within shouting distance of safe haven — and then to attack. And, as they had before, they allowed the first part of the line to pass before they erupted from their hiding places among the rocks on either side and fell upon our center and rear with hideous whoops and yells and a very storm of shots and arrows.

I knew by the sound of their fury behind me that they did not intend that any of us should escape; that they meant to exterminate us down to the last living soul. Yet I dared to hope equally earnestly that at least one might get away. All in one movement I slid to the ground and boosted Pepita into the saddle I had just left. As I thrust the reins into her hand I jerked my rifle from its scabbard.

"Ride, chiquita!" I whispered hoarsely. "Ride swiftly, little Pepita. Hurry! And if you reach Janos safely send us back the soldados! Vaya con Dios, amada mia!"

And a cut on the rump with my quirt sent the horse rocketing off down the trail at a breakneck gallop that I was sure would not stop, short of a bullet or sheer exhaustion. Almost at once, before she had a chance to protest, they were swallowed up in the gathering dusk.

I turned then and ran back toward the sounds of battle, and saw that both Jode and Doña Luz were watching me with startled, almost shocked expressions. Clearly, I gathered, they had seen what I had done — and wondered.

"Now there's an idea!" I heard Jode remark, and he turned and plucked the reins of the white Arabian from the girl's grasp.

I thought — and plainly she did also — that he was merely

taking them to loop about the animal's neck prior to helping her into the saddle. But instead he swung up himself.

"Jode!" she cried out, and I could hear the shock and
surprise in her voice against the background of mounting
tumult, "Jodey — you — "

"Can't stop now, honey gal," he flung back over his
shoulder as he gathered up the reins and dug his heels into
the horse's flanks. "Time like this'n it's ever' man for himself."

He came flashing down past me, lashing the white horse
to a dead run, and I whirled and flung up my rifle. I hated
to do it to such a magnificent beast, but there was only one
way to stop him. I took quick aim and fired.

Gracias a Dios, señores, I have always been a good marks-
man! I squeezed the trigger and the white Arabian went
down on his knees and plowed the ground with his nose.
Jode went catapulting over his head, turned a complete
somersault, and came up, staggering, to his feet.

"Come back and fight like a man!" I bawled at him. And
then, without waiting to see what he did, I turned again and
ran toward the rising tumult of the fight, reloading as I
went.

Be assured, señores, that none of this took as long in the
happening as it does for me to tell it. No more than a minute
or two could have passed since I had slipped from the
saddle and sent Pepita hurtling off into the dusk. Yet as I
came up the battle was already in full bloom. As I had
taught them to do, the remaining men of the column had
turned to their nearest flank, on either side, thus placing the
women and children and the carretas as much as possible
between them, and I could see the bright orange stabs of

their defending gunfire, sharp in the twilight. But already the steep slopes on both sides and in the rear were swarming with Indians. In the half-light it seemed as though every bush and boulder were alive, and already many were bounding down for the kill, leaping and yelling, half naked and hideously grotesque with the horizontal white bars they had painted across their faces indicating that theirs was a war party.

Thinking back upon it afterward, and realizing the Apaches' actual war strength, I scarcely think they outnumbered us more than two to one, for I doubt they could muster more warriors without calling upon other tribes. Yet at that moment, in all the pandemonium and shouting and shooting, they seemed like a thousand! Up the hill, to my right, I caught sight of one squat, leather-faced, brightly painted young buck, racing downward toward us with upraised knife, scorning cover and screaming for blood. I rested my rifle on a sheltering boulder and sought to follow him in my sights. He was scarcely a score of paces away before I picked him up and centered the bead in the vee, just under his breastbone, and squeezed the trigger. Even in that light I could scarcely miss, and I had the satisfaction of seeing an expression of startled astonishment flood his face. His arms flew wide. His knees buckled beneath him, and he fell face forward and flopped over twice and then lay still in a crumpled lump, tangled in a clump of cactus.

I reloaded again and moved in closer to what was left of the embattled column. Already, I could see, more than half of our people were down. But the rest were fighting desperately. I found a rock that offered a small bit of protection on one side, at least, and dropped to my knees behind it, watching for a chance at another telling shot. As I did so her voice sounded at my elbow, indicating that she had been there close behind me all the time.

"Currito! My father — do you see him?"

"Madre de Dios, Doña Luz!" I cried, startled. "Por favor, get down! You will be killed!"

She crouched close to the rock, but there was no fear in her eyes as she looked at me.

"I think we will all be killed this time, Currito," she said simply. "But my father is there — somewhere, and I should be with him. I must find him!"

It was evident that she was quite serious about it — that she was fully determined. Nothing that I might say would stop her. I gave her a long, sober, searching look, wondering if there were not some way to send her back to the comparative safety of the brush and rocks below. But clearly there was none now. I waggled my hand at her, admonishing.

"Stay here then, Doña Luz — under cover. I will see if I can find him." And I stood up.

Señores, I assure you there was nothing of daring or bravado about that. There were buzzings and flutterings and whinings all around me that I could hear above the crackle of shots and the screams of the wounded, and I realize now that they were the sounds of bullets and arrows flying. But at that moment I was too much preoccupied with this problem of Doña Luz and her father to notice.

I searched with my eyes through the gloom toward the center — or where I judged the center ought to be, for it

258

was hard to tell in that surging melee — but I saw no sign of him.

"Wait!" I commanded, over my shoulder, and ran in that direction, never dreaming that she might not obey.

The distance was short, once I had started, and I was appalled to see the mortality our people had already suffered. Many that had seemed to me to be kneeling and firing over a bush or a rock were slumped against their breastwork in attitudes that were unmistakable while others writhed in agony on the ground. Not more than a handful seemed alive. Midway between the end and the beginning of the column I found him, crumpled in the shelter of a boulder, as if he were trying to shoot across it when he had been hit. I turned him over and laid him down gently, trying to make him as comfortable as I could on the stony ground, but it was clear that he was hurt beyond living. There was a gaping hole in his chest, from which the blood pumped in such force that it spattered me. And there was a clear cleft in his head that was matted with half-dried gore, suggesting an earlier wound. Yet even had we been able to give him medical aid I doubt if we would have been able to save him. The will to live was gone.

As I knelt beside him his daughter's voice sounded again from behind me.

"Papa!"

"Doña Luz!" I cried, starting up. "I told you to stay — "

"How could I?" she snapped over her shoulder, as she dropped to her knees beside him. "Can't you see I mus — "

Even as she spoke something hit against the rock beside my head with a loud span-n-n-ng. It seemed all at once that

259

the whole rock exploded, and I never did hear her finish what she was saying. Something caromed against the side of my skull, seeming to split it in two and snapping my head sharply to the side, and then I felt myself spinning, falling, lurching — down — down — down, into utter darkness.

## *Chapter 5*

$W$HEN I opened my eyes it was night dark. I had no way of knowing for a moment if I were alive or dead — or if I were alive, how long I had been unconscious. But if I was alive I was able to be surprised.

To be truthful, as I came slowly back to my senses and began to see where I was I began to wish that I was dead, for I was bound, spread-eagled, against the high wheel of a carreta, and directly before me, squatted about a small fire and a dark object on the ground, which I could not make out, hunkered some thirty Apache warriors, with the white bars painted across their cheeks and noses which indicated that they were on the warpath. My head ached vilely, as if it would burst like a ripe melon, and the whole side of my face was warm and wet and sticky — with blood I presumed.

Nevertheless I managed to twist my head slowly to one side and, to my dismay, saw that two other carretas had been drawn up in a sort of quarter circle at the edge of the firelight. To the wheel of the one closest to me, even as I was but in addition stripped to the skin, was bound the sandy-haired Yanqui, Yancey Cahoon. Beyond him, in the same condition and posture, was Jode Lassiter.

Here was enough to suck at my belly. Yet even as I saw

them I heard the sound of a half-stifled sob at the other side. I swung my head in that direction so quickly that it jangled my addled brain, and I almost cried out with the pain of it — as if the horror of what I saw were not enough. There, bound like the rest of us to the wheel of yet another carreta, her bright hair streaming down over her face, and her torn shirt hanging in ribbons from her waist, hung Doña Luz. Above the navel she was as naked as the day she was born, and I felt embarrassed for her, yet fascinated by the firm young breasts that thrust through the long strands of her hair like round, white moons glimpsed through scudding clouds.

Quickly, with a modesty that was something new to me, I averted my eyes and looked back at the Indians hunkered about the fire and wondered what they were doing. But even as I looked one of them reached out and plucked a burning brand from the tiny fire and dropped it on the bulk before them. A shrill scream of human agony arose, shattering the night, and the Indians clucked and chattered among themselves. Then they rose and moved back in a half circle, clearly to give us, tethered against the carreta wheels, an unobstructed view. To my horrified fascination I saw that the lump on the ground was a man, stark naked and tied spread-X-wise to stakes at wrist and ankle, face upward, and the flickering light of the fire revealed him to be the Capitán-Comandante, Don Tito Morales. I confess that I did not like the man, but I wished him no such fate as this, for the Indians were amusing themselves — or tormenting us, as the view might be — by slowly roasting him to death, a bit at a time.

I doubt, as a matter of fact, señores, that Don Tito lasted

much more than an hour before he died. But that hour was
enough, I think, for each of us onlookers to pardon him his
sins and offer a silent prayer for his soul. I know that my
brow was dripping the sweat of anguish as they heaped
the little coals about his testicles and he shrieked in agony.
I could see that Don Yancey's reaction was the same, while
Jode hung like a man crucified against his wheel. On the
other side of me Doña Luz drooped like a woman fainted,
and so I believed she had, until a low moan escaped her, and
I realized with a feeling of sickness at the pit of my stomach
that she had missed none of it.

When Don Tito's agonized soul had at last slipped from
his body and gone winging to whatever heaven or hell was
reserved for it; when he lay silent and rigid in the horror
of his death, an immense hulk of a savage rose from where
he had been squatting beyond the fire and came toward us.
I was surprised to recognize the huge Indian of the cathedral — Mangas Colorado — though I vaguely realized that
I should have known that it was he. Few Apaches were as
enormous as that.

He came directly across to me and peered into my face.
"A-ho!" he grunted. "You 'wake now?"

Señores, you will forgive me, I am sure, that I was yet
somewhat addled. Please to believe that I tried to keep up
with him, and to offer a properly defiant manner.

"Your playful friends roused me," I replied. "Lovable
little ones! Where are all the rest of your murdering devils?
Surely there were a lot more of you when I saw you last."

To tell the truth the faint hope in my heart was that we
had killed off all but those that we saw seated in the silent
ring beyond the fire. But he quickly disillusioned me.

"A-ho! Injum not murder," he growled. "White man murder. Injum take 'venge. All Santa Rita kill-dead, only you and copper hair woman and big white-eyes. Cuchillo Negro and warriors go back to Ojo Caliente to find other Pinda-lick-o-ye to kill. Mangas and few stay here to tend to prisoner. Soon we go back too."

That last was ominous. It seemed to me he as much as told us we were to suffer a similar fate to that of Don Tito. I could think of no quick answer, so I remained silent, while he squinted at me beadily.

"Where little squaw?" he demanded sharply.

"Unh?" I shook my head gingerly. "What?"

"Where pretty little squaw belong you?" he persisted. "Santa Rita woman — um?"

I became aware that he was asking about Pepita, and I struggled to keep my eyes open and glare at him. It occurred to me that I might learn, perhaps, whether or not she had escaped.

"She's dead," I growled surlily. "You bastards killed her — away back in the Big Hatchets."

He neither took offense at my insult nor flew into a rage at his followers.

"Mangas sorry," he said simply, and with surprising humility. "Mangas sorry for that. Mangas give order she no to be hurt. She belong you, and you save Injum life."

My heart thumped inside my ribs. He did not know then! Barring the hazards of the trail, she at least had escaped! I could almost feel Doña Luz's eyes staring at me, but I dared not look at her.

"My mistake!" I snarled sarcastically.

He shook his head.

264

"Not mistake," he retorted. "Save own life too. You good man. When Mangas finish here he set you free."

"Thanks!" I said dryly. "What about these others?"

"You watch!" he told me. "You see!"

He turned away and I called after him.

"Whatever you plan for them, give me too," I cried.

That was bravado, señores. I admit it. I was frightened, both for them and for myself. But how could I do otherwise? He did not seem to hear. At least he paid no attention. He waddled on his thick, stumpy legs to Doña Luz and lifted her luxuriant hair roughly in an enormous paw, running avid black spidery eyes over her creamy body.

"H-mm, a-ho!" he rumbled. "Copper-haired squaw be good wife for chief of copper mines Injum. I take — hmm'mph!"

He flung down her hair, slashing it across her breasts like so much hemp and turned away, facing Yancey and Jode.

"I take," he repeated. "But first Mangas meet big Pinda-lick-o-yes."

He glanced toward me, flinging out his bull chest and thumping his ribs; bragging in his own way, beyond doubt, and evidently pretending to do me a favor.

"These men friends to you," he rumbled. "Mangas not kill slow, Injum way. Mangas give them good chance. Mangas fight each one in turn — Apache fight — naked with knife — for copper-headed squaw. Winner take woman. Mangas win. You see!"

I was startled, but hardly surprised, for I had never seen one of these Indian duels but I had heard of them. At the same time I knew the Apaches to be inveterate gamblers, and to Mangas, I gathered, this seemed a sort of gambling. It seemed to me to be carrying games a little beyond their intent. Still, I was by no means sure of the outcome. Mangas was huge — at least a match for either of them and might well prove more powerful than both. He was as tall as Jode, but heavier; and thicker than Yancey, but as heavy. And it must be remembered that both Jode and Yancey had been hanging, spread-eagled, against their respective cart wheels for I knew not how long.

The Indian turned away from me and thrust out a stubby finger, as thick as an average man's thumb, pointing at Jode.

"Him first," he barked, and rapped out something in his own tongue at the half circle of his beady-eyed fellows.

Four of the savages rose and went over to where the dark, slender young giant hung like a naked Christ and cut him down, thrusting him roughly into the circle of firelight where Mangas Colorado stood waiting, knife in hand. One of them tossed in a knife that landed with a faint thud in the dust at Jode's feet, and Mangas signaled the tall Yanqui to pick it up.

I was astonished then at the swiftness with which things happened. Jode bent over and picked up the knife, and for a few seconds the Indian and the white man circled each other warily. Then Jode apparently thought he saw an opening and streaked in. But with agility that was amazing in such a hulk Mangas evaded him and caught at his knife arm with his own free hand, seizing the arm by the wrist and bending it up and back.

I stole a swift glance at Doña Luz, and saw that she was watching, staring in fascinated horror, yet so quickly did it all happen that even as I glanced at her I saw her eyes go wide with dismay and her lips form a round, silent O of protest.

I looked back quickly at what it was that so affected her. Between Mangas's brute strength and Jode's momentum, the outcome was brief and inevitable. Jode's arm bent almost double, until the knife in his hand almost touched his own back — and then it shattered. Where I hung tied I could hear the bone crack. Jode yelped — once, like a puppy kicked, and his knife clattered to the ground. Casually Mangas tossed his own weapon aside and caught Jode by the crotch and the back of the neck and lifted him above his head as easily as if he were no more than a baby. Then, as imperturbably as a man breaking a stick he brought the Yanqui down across his knee, back down.

Like a stick I heard Jode's back snap sharply. He screamed helplessly, and I heard Doña Luz and Don Yancey both cry out in protest. But Mangas paid no heed. Instead he bent casually and picked up his own knife and slashed it across the quivering throat. The scream died, trailing off into a hideous, gurgling, snoring sound that bubbled out of the voiceless throat for a long moment and then slowly died away.

So died Jode Lassiter! Mangas Colorado straightened as if he had done nothing more than slaughter a pig for fodder and pointed at Yancey.

"Now him!" he said.

Once again the same four savage assistants rose and, as they had with Jode, cut Yancey down and thrust him into the little ring of bright, black eyes. Yancey picked up the knife, still warm from Jode's sweating palm. But from that point on his tactics were different. He did not try to rush the gigantic Indian, but waited for Mangas to come to him, turning as the huge savage circled and never taking his eyes from Mangas's face.

I must say that I think I held my breath longer then than I have ever done before or since, and I am sure that Doña Luz did the same. I doubt their wary circling lasted more than a minute, yet it seemed hours to me. Then all at once it was Mangas who seemed to see the opening – or, perhaps, lost his patience – and rushed. And this time it was Yancey who slipped aside, with much the same astonishing agility that Mangas had shown previously. As the Indian rushed past, Yancey whipped up his knife and slashed, cutting a slice to the bone in Mangas's arm, and drawing first blood.

But the wound was like the infuriating jab of a picador to the Indian. He spun with the roar of a bull and rushed in again, and this time he caught Yancey before he could slip aside, catching the Yanqui's knife wrist in his free hand, and at the same time poising his own knife to strike.

"Yancey – oh Yancey, look out!" I heard Doña Luz cry to the side of me.

And I am sure that he heard it, too, for his eyes flickered momentarily in our direction, and at the same time he caught Mangas's knife wrist with his own free hand, so that they were locked, breast to breast, in a struggle of brute strength. Whichever could force the other's knife hand back, bend his opponent's arm and free his own, would win!

How can I say it, señores? In that long moment it almost seemed to me as though I were there and fighting myself. By the force of my will I tried to add my strength to that of Don Yancey, and I am sure that Doña Luz did also, though our mouths and throats were so dry that we could not cry out our encouragement.

But even Don Yancey could not stand forever against that inexorable might. For a moment that seemed endless as eternity they poised so, like a statue cast in bronze. Then slowly — slowly — the power of Mangas's barrel body began to assert itself. Slowly — slowly Yancey's knife hand bent back — and back — and back. His spine arched and his hand opened involuntarily, though I could see how he struggled against it. The knife fell into the dust behind him — and at that point I closed my eyes, for I could not bear to watch my friend die. Beside me I heard Doña Luz cry out.

"No — oh, no! No!"

Almost as if in answer there came a rumbling thunder, as of an earthquake — or the drumming of half a hundred hoofs rolling forward at a galloping charge. Startled, I opened my eyes involuntarily and shouted aloud for joy as I saw them sweep forward like a great, blue-crested wave looming out of the night — a full regiment of Mexican dragoons with a flushed and much disheveled Pepita riding at their head.

Perhaps, at this juncture, I should point out that it was an Apache policy of war to fight only from ambush or when odds were in their favor. "He who fights and runs away will live to fight another day" could have been their motto, and never did one fit more aptly. To them there was no sense in heroism, in standing out against overwhelming and inevitable odds when escape was possible. And here the odds were overwhelming — and escape was to be found.

For an instant Mangas's handful of henchmen seemed dumbfounded, and stood rooted where they were. Then a few flung scattered shots at the oncoming riders, and abruptly turned and flitted away like ghosts, into the darkness. Behind them the onsweeping cavalry broke into groups, pursuing this one or that of the Indian party. In the abandoned small circle of firelight Mangas Colorado stared for an instant in amazed disbelief at the sudden interruption. Then he caught sight of Pepita as she drove her horse straight across the fire toward me. The circle of light was small, but he was at the edge of it, and the distance was too great for him to snatch at her bridle. But the thoughts that flashed through his mind were as plain as day. He flung me a look that was accusing and hate-filled. For the moment he forgot Yancey and saw only that I had tricked him. He switched his knife, so that he held it by the tip, and drew back his arm to throw — and I was tied and quite unable to duck.

Señores, I heard the rustle of death's wings in that instant, I assure you. But even as it seemed to me that the end was near there came the rattle of hoofs halting abruptly, and the rustle of skirts, the patter of feet; and then soft arms went about my neck and a firm young body pressed hard against mine — a living shield.

"Pepita," I cried out in panic. "Look out!"

Had he loosed his knife in that moment he would have killed her, but not me.

But, as I have said, he evidently forgot Yancey, and it was the big Yanqui who caught at his knife wrist then, even as the Indian's arm swept forward to the throw, and wrenched it back with all his strength.

## CAMINO DEL MUERTE

The knife, poised for release, slipped from his grasp and went spinning crazily off into the darkness. Mangas Colorado stumbled and went down on one knee, then recovered himself and bounced back upright. For the space of a breath I thought he would fly at Yancey, but in that instant several of the blue-clad troopers bore down upon him, and it was clear now that there would not be time for him to kill the big Pinda-lick-o-ye with his bare hands. One of the troopers aimed a cut at him with his saber, and the enormous Indian displayed some of that same amazing agility that he had already shown in the duel in evading the slash. Then, before anyone could stop him, he turned and ran with what seemed the speed of light — one — two — three swift, bounding steps, to the horse Pepita had just left. So quickly that it seemed all one motion he vaulted into the saddle and drove his heels hard against the animal's flanks. There was a quick clatter of hoofs as the ring of soldiers closed in toward him, and then he was away, driving straight through them, lying low along his mount's neck, galloping away to disappear into the inky night.

# Chapter 6

*T*HAT, señores, I believe is about all there is to tell — gracias a Dios!

The soldados cut us down at once, and I am not ashamed to say that I gathered Pepita in my arms and wept unbashedly into her hair — and when I found the time to look I saw that over beyond the little fire Don Yancey and Doña Luz were doing the same, all unconcerned with their own nakedness, which somehow pleased me mightily.

Eh, cómo? Did I then marry my little Pepita, señores y señoras? Pues seguro! Of course! Had I not promised it? And am I a man to break his word? What is more I did not lie to say that I wished it! Indeed I married her the very next day in the little church at Janos, for I would wait no longer. In fact we made it a double ceremony, and only this Sunday last the señor Don Yancey and his señora Doña Luz and I with my little Pepita celebrated our thirtieth anniversary with a special mass at the Church of San Miguel, right here in Santa Fe. . . .

272

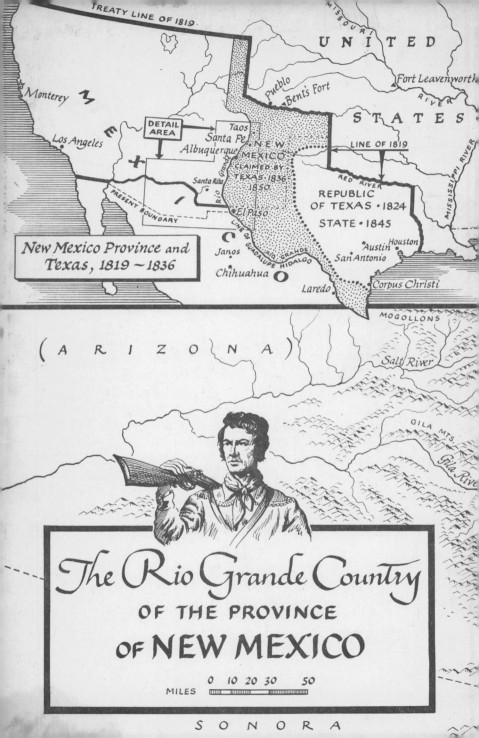

TREATY LINE OF 1819.

MISSOURI

UNITED

Fort Leavenworth

RIVER

Pueblo

Bent's Fort

STATES

Monterey

M E X I C O

Los Angeles

DETAIL
AREA

Taos
Santa Fe
Albuquerque

NEW
MEXICO

RIO GRANDE

PRESENT BOUNDARY

Santa Rita

CLAIMED BY
TEXAS.1836-
1850

LINE OF 1819

RED RIVER

MISSISSIPPI RIVER

El Paso

REPUBLIC
OF TEXAS · 1824
STATE · 1845

New Mexico Province and
Texas, 1819 ~ 1836

LINE OF GUADALUPE HIDALGO

Janos

Chihuahua

C

O

Austin

Houston

San Antonio

Laredo

Corpus Christi

MOGOLLONS

( A R I Z O N A )

Salt River

GILA MTS.

Gila River

The Rio Grande Country
OF THE PROVINCE
OF NEW MEXICO

MILES  0  10  20  30    50

S O N O R A